Letters To Cora

Blue Deco Publishing
www.bluedecopublishing.com

Letters To Cora

Cover by Colleen Nye
Editing by Genevieve Scholl
Formatting by Colleen Nye

Published by Blue Deco Publishing
PO BOX 1663 Royal Oak, MI 48068
BlueDecoPublishing@gmail.com

Printed in the United States of America

To love.

May you find those that have been lost in the wake of tragedy.

May you be a constant light in a world of darkness.

May you always persevere.

Sitting in my study, I had been surfing the web when I stumbled upon a home listing near the cliffs in England. My intention was to merely find a vacation spot. I didn't know what it was about the vast land, nor did I know what I would do with it or the brick house with the sunken roof and outbuildings. But there I was, placing a call at three in the morning to England to inquire on the listing and booking a flight simultaneously.

Taking on the daunting task of demolition on top of renovations for a house on the South-Eastern coast of England was probably foolish. Yes. I mean, what in the world was I thinking? My youngest kid had moved out and gone to college the autumn before. My townhouse in New York City had more space than I needed already. And my divorce had just been finalized. But as I saw it, I had just received my first six figure advance on a novel, and I needed a fresh ... well ... a fresh life.

Two months later, all of the paperwork was done and I owned a second home. It was four months later as I walked down the drive toward the edge of the property and toward the rock wall, a bucket of masonry grout and a trowel in my hands. I was wondering why my choosing of a new life needed to involve giving a new life to a rundown estate as well.

I stopped and looked back. The house was surely one of the area's former gems. It wasn't a castle, but it wasn't small by any means. It was three stories tall and several rooms wide. The brick was stark against the vast backdrop of woods and fields around it, as were what had become overgrown skeletons of what was obviously, formerly, a well sculpted and well-manicured landscaping on the immediate grounds.

The dirt drive was just about a half a mile long from the road and ended in a circle before the front door with a parking area off to one side. Two large, oak pieces marked the entryway, covered in ornate patterns with regal, metal handles. They were only a couple of what ended up being very few pieces in the house that were wood and not completely rotten.

I'd hired some local workers to help me on several bits of the project, but I was determined to have a hand in every aspect of the rebuilding of the home and its outbuildings in some way or another. In those four months, we'd stripped away all the old, rotting wood, replaced most of the windows aside from the custom ones we had needed to order, replaced all of the broken doors, refinishing the ones that could be salvaged and dug a well and septic for working plumbing—of which was next on the list. We also installed new roofs on the main house and the small buildings around the property to try to stop further damage, as well as refinishing the floors of the main house and started on the framing of the walls to re-establish rooms. The driveway was weeded and new pea gravel was laid, and we had started gutting the overgrowth in both the front and rear gardens. That day, I was determined to start on reinforcing the three foot high rock wall that ran along the South property line. It was going to be a daunting project, but it was one I felt that I needed to take on all on my own.

“We’re done for the day, ma’am,” Gerald announced, stopping his work truck before passing me by. “We will be back Monday morning. You going to work on that wall like we talked about earlier?”

“Yes. I am. Thank you for suggesting it, Gerald. See you Monday. Again, you can call me Nell,” I reminded him.

“See you Monday, Ms. Price.”

He nodded as he and his two brothers drove off.

I watched as the old truck putted its way down the freshly coated driveway, the tools bouncing around in the back. As much as I wanted him to call me by my first name, I didn’t shutter at the use of my last seeing as I had just taken it back after my divorce, wanting to return to my maiden name.

Gerald was a hard worker, even for being in his fifties. A lifetime handyman by trade, he and his brothers had started their business doing odd jobs for people in the nearby town that I had rented a flat in. So, when I asked the landlord if she knew of anyone that could help me, she didn’t hesitate to point me in the brothers’ direction.

Of course, I wasn’t capable of being in the middle of *all* of the projects. Some I had to be satisfied with helping gather tools or doing the cleanup, seeing that I wasn’t licensed nor trained. But helping was helping, so I did anything I could. Part of me figured that was why I took on the wall. It was something I could do all on my own. Something I would be able to look out on later, proud that it was one project I didn’t need help with.

Looking out over the land, I knew I’d felt drawn to the property. It was so much so that I hadn’t returned to my New York townhouse. I’d hired a company to go in and keep things cleaned and such, but it sat more or less abandoned since I left for England. I was perfectly content immersing myself in my new found project manor house. And when I wasn’t working on the manor and its lands, I was working on my next manuscript—of which I was struggling with due to a very frustrating bout of writer's block. But, aside from that, something about being there made being anywhere else in the world seem off ... maybe even wrong. So, I kept my head in the project and attempted to write between tasks.

I pondered that for a moment before feeling the handle of the mortar bucket in my hand again. Shrugging off my reverie, I finished my walk to the end of the stone wall and set down my tools. Nudging the stones to see which ones were loose, I started to pull them out of their spots, slather them in the grey paste, and place the stone back into its space. I continued that for a few hours until I noticed the sun was just about to slip under the horizon. It was a menial task, sure, but that was the beauty of it. It was a task where I could allow my thoughts to wander as I worked. And that was pretty much exactly what I figured I was looking for when I sought out the whole situation ... a way to get lost in something else for a while.

I tapped one last stone, acknowledged it as loose and pulled it out of its home. Dusting the old mortar off, I set the rock down next to me and reached into the vacant spot to clear away the old crumbled mortar. But instead of dust and pebbles, my fingers grazed the surface of what felt like paper. I carefully removed the aged letter and blew off the surface. *Cora, My Love* was written on its face. On the other was a wax seal.

Sitting back onto my heels, I looked at the paper for a moment before tucking it into my top and setting the stone back into the wall, leaving out the fresh mortar on purpose. I picked up my tools and the bucket, marked the spot where I left off with a piece of chalk and headed back up to the house.

It was going to be a clear night with fair temperatures, so I'd brought some camping supplies with me from the flat

I was renting. The roof and flooring hadn't been done long, so I hadn't had many chances to actually stay in the house. But I was excited. Sure, I'd bought it, but it hadn't felt like a home yet seeing as I was leaving every night to stay in a tiny, one room flat in a nearby town. Plus, I was hoping that the escape from the distractions of the internet and noises outside my flat's windows might help in some way with the fact that I hadn't written much of anything since before my new adventure started, despite spending a fair amount of time staring at the blinking cursor.

I tucked the bucket and tools into the foyer and made my way up the stairs to the room I'd picked out as my future bedroom. I unrolled my sleeping bag as my air mattress was filling, set my battery powered lantern up and pulled out my laptop. But instead of sitting down to write like planned, I caught a glimpse of the view outside of my balcony. I'd seen it in the daylight, which is why I'd picked that room. But the sight before me was something else entirely.

I stood again and walked over to the balcony doorway, pushing open the ornate french doors. A waft of salt water air rushed in over me. My eyes closed, and I breathed it in, holding for a moment before exhaling and stepping out into the night.

My breath caught as I saw the night sky. It seemed to go on forever with dots of light that appeared to punch through the various shades of dark blue backdrop. The moon was bright despite it being at only a quarter. And I could hear the waves crashing onto the rocks of the cliffs even though it was a decent walk from the house. The light radiating from the moon and stars lit up the landscape, making it unnecessary to turn on a light for a midnight stroll if one wanted to.

There was a point in my life when I would have thought it was too silent. Manhattan was *the* place to live for me. I flourished in the fast paced, constant atmosphere in some ways, or so I thought I had. There was always something to do, see, or hear. And I never had to be left alone with my thoughts. In some small way, possibly not so small, Manhattan was probably to blame for the deterioration of my marriage. I was involved in everything, which, no doubt, left my husband feeling ignored. And even though I was involved in groups and activities, I hid away emotionally. Not just from those people, but from my family, too.

So, it really shouldn't have been a surprise when he came home one day, after our youngest was gone away to college, and informed me that he was leaving me for a woman from the California office. He'd met her at a work party a year prior, and since had worked on several projects together.

I didn't want to know more than that. Nor did I allow myself to ask anything like how long had it been going on or how far things had gone. I told myself that I should have known. I should have noticed some signs or something. But I hadn't. And I could only attribute that to the possibility that I just wasn't in love with him anymore, and it was probably for the best. So, we parted on amicable terms, split everything fairly, and he moved out. It was that first night after he'd taken his last boxes and pieces of furniture that it hit me...

I was alone.

It took everything I had not to call up all of my three kids to check on them, and not call my ex-husband and beg him to come home. But I knew I shouldn't. I knew I had to face it; the reality that I was a single woman in my 40's. It was not the plan I'd intended for my life in the least. But it was what was happening.

My finger made its way to the ruby ring I'd only started wearing just before my move. It had been handed down to me; the story behind it being one over that spanned over many generations and was all but lost over the years. I hadn't asked much about it when it was given to me. I looked at the relic and tucked it away for many months until, one day, I was going through boxes in my closet and came across it. I didn't know what had changed, but instead of it being some tarnished, old ring I'd gotten that I would pass on to one of my daughters one day, I wanted to wear it. I had simply chalked it up to wanting to grasp as something from my past.

In that moment, I wondered if it had as rich of a history as the one behind the estate I was rebuilding. Histories, I figured, that were deeper and far more rich with scandal and intrigue than my own.

Having relived the previous year of my life while breathing in the cleansing night air, I went back inside to change out of my work clothes, use the handy wipes I'd gotten from the camping supplies store and pull on some sweats and a hoodie. As I lifted my shirt over my head, I heard the note from the rock wall tumble out and onto the floor in front of me.

I leaned down and picked it up, turning it over and over between my fingers to make sure that I hadn't damaged the antique paper and its seal. It was obviously very old, and I really wanted to crack the wax seal and see what was inside. But it was so perfect, and I didn't want to tear the paper by disturbing it. So, I walked across the room, blew off the dust from the fireplace mantle and set the letter down, touching it before walking away to finish cleaning up and changing.

Two hours later, I was more than frustrated with staring at the blank page on my screen. It seemed to be taunting me, teasing me that I had barely made it move the entire writing session. What little forward progress I'd had was hindered by an almost equal amount of backward movement as I deleted almost everything I'd written just as soon as I'd written it.

Huffing, I yanked a chocolate bar out of my bag and stomped over to the doorway to the balcony. Leaning against the frame, I sighed. "Some new life. I thought I wanted to get away from feeling alone. Not scare away even the characters in my own head."

I stood and worked on unwinding the new knot in my thoughts, trying to remind myself of why I was there. A fresh start. But something kept tugging at the edges of my mind. The more I tried to ignore it, the harder it pulled, until, finally, it just yanked. "Fine! I'll open the damned letter!"

My footfalls echoed through the empty room as I stomped my way back over to the fireplace. I picked up the folded page and sat down next to the lantern, flipping it on. I gently pinched the paper between my fingers and held it up, looking at the light shine through it. There was no doubt that this, whatever it was, was old, very old. A large part of me didn't want to break the wax seal, holding the words inside of their tomb, so I grabbed the lantern, went downstairs, pulled a clean putty knife out of the tool bag and went back up to the bedroom.

I sat back down and laid the letter onto the wooden floor, carefully slipping the metal under the hardened wax, lifting it away from the fragile paper. I wanted only to remove it from the page just enough to be able to unfold it rather than removing it entirely so that it would stay attached to the page just in case it was of some historical value.

My breath stopped on my last pass before it was freed. Once it was, I sat down the tool and gently unfolded the letter. It was stiff, so I made sure to move slow and to press down the folds as I opened them, doing my best not to push too hard and cause it to crack. Once it was opened, I paused, realizing that I was more curious than I thought I was about whatever message was written inside.

The letters were still a bold color, which surprised me. I expected the ink to have faded quite a lot more than it had. The writing was scrawled in an old fashioned cursive that I'd only seen in older documents or depictions of something from over a century ago. By modern times, the writing was feminine, but for the era it appeared to be from, it was decidedly masculine in penmanship.

16th of June, 1867
My Dearest Cora,

The past two days have been torture from not being able to see you. But, alas, by this time three days from now, we shall be united in wholly matrimony. I am truly sorry that our families can not be there for the blessed event and that they do not seem to support our love. But I assure you that we will build our own family, and we will have all the love and support we will ever need together.

I love you, Cora, more than words can express. I trust that you will receive this letter in the morning. So, in terms of the time frame in which you will be reading this, I will see you in just a few hours. The coach departs from the stop at half passed five. As planned, I will meet you there.

Do not fret, my love. Once we are married, your parents will come around. After all, they will not want to miss out on the joys of their future grandchildren once we start on that journey.

Yours Truly & Forever,
Joshua

I sat and looked at the letter, my heart swelling at the utter romance of the whole situation. My mind swirled with all of the possibilities that Joshua and Cora could have been going through and why there was an obvious disapproval from her parents about their marrying.

Was his family working class while hers was upper? Had he done something to disgrace his station in society? Was she already promised to someone else? Was there a true Shakespearean style feud between their families?

The possibilities were endless.

After reading over the letter another time, I folded it back up, propped it up on the fireplace mantle and settled in with my laptop. That night, I found myself inspired again, which was a welcome change from the writer's block I seemed to be treading water in for the previous weeks.

I had been tasked with starting a new story line by my publisher since my previous series had just wrapped up. Yet, the manuscript I'd been working on since right before the move had all but stalled. However, after reading Joshua's letter to Cora, something inside me ignited, and I was weeding through plot concept after plot concept. I scooted my sleeping back next to the balcony doors and propped myself up against a stack of left over flooring.

That night, I didn't switch back and forth between staring at the page and mentally beating myself up. I went back and forth between letting words flow out of my fingers and staring out at the clear sky full of stars.

Two

I woke the next morning and looked around the room. For a moment, I'd almost forgotten where I was. It was a difficult enough transition getting used to waking up in my tiny flat in town, but waking up to a large, empty room was something else altogether. Then, add in that I slept on a camping mattress, I wondered, for a moment, if I had reached my 90s and hadn't known it. It took a couple moments for me to process my location then a couple more minutes to get myself mobile.

I'd been working on the house and the grounds a lot, and I quickly discovered how out of shape I'd become, making most mornings a difficult transition of their own. All of the bending and kneeling the day before while working on the rock wall presented a whole new set of muscles that were ready to remind me that they hadn't been used in a very long time. I stretched, rubbed my aching legs and made a mental note to go into town and buy a better sleeping mat or air mattress if I was going to stay there again before my bed was moved in.

My laptop lay on the floor next to me, the battery dead. I picked up my phone and found the same for it. I searched through my overnight bag. "Damnit. Where is my backup battery?"

Finding the device and cords, I plugged both of the lifeless devices in and set them aside. I was rather proud of the progress I'd made on my storyline the night before. By the time I had fallen asleep, I had an outline of the main points of the plot and several characters and even rewrote a lot of the beginning, scrapping large portions of what I'd previously thrown at the page. I only needed the ending, but I knew it would come along in its own time.

Productive writing always seemed to bring with it a sense of accomplishment. Something about it made everything in my life feel more forward moving and ... well ... happy, I suppose. I would find some added confidence in my days as well as having something to look forward to do whenever I could. Creating new worlds, new loves and helping my characters, albeit fictional, to find their way, overcome obstacles and face their fears was something that made me feel good about myself; like maybe I was useful in a way I wasn't used to feeling outside of my writing.

The light on my laptop glowed, and I opened the lid, anxious to take a peek before starting my day of manual labor. I hit the power button and scrolled through the document, reviewing the previous night's progress.

Two people meet at a diner, neither having been there prior. They chat, instantly connecting. But at the end of the meal, they both pay and go their separate ways, realizing they were both late for work, forgetting to exchange contact information. Over the next few months, they both go back to the diner when their schedules allow, but they keep missing each other.

**Do they eventually find each other?*

**is one not from that time?*

**is one a ghost and doesn't know it and the one that isn't thinks back to their encounter and realizes that there are clues that the staff didn't really notice the other person?*

Especially once they start asking about them and none of the staff remember them?

**why the connection?*

More notes were written, and I skimmed through them, pretty happy with what I was reading. I closed the lid, set it aside to charge and decided against checking my cell phone for messages. Instead, I wanted to get out to the wall and keep working on the stones. As far as I'd gotten the day before, I knew it would take all that day and the next to knock it out. It was just good to be making progress again.

I grabbed my toiletries, went into the unfinished ensuite bathroom and freshened up, including using a jug of water for brushing my teeth and washing my face. I wandered to the East side of the level and stood at the window, taking in the sunrise across the land ... my land. The fiery reds, bold oranges and lemon yellows against the fading, watery blues up into the darker shades from the nightscape was absolutely gorgeous. Breathtaking. Coming from Manhattan, the sunrises and sunsets were very different. Not that they weren't beautiful in their own right. I absolutely loved sitting on the roof of one of the high-rises and watching either. But seeing them over the span of my own property without another building blocking a portion or the sound of horns honking and sirens blaring to distract from it was something completely different.

I breathed in the morning air a couple more times, pulled my hair up into a bun and headed down to the kitchen. The gas lines had been rerun to that portion of the house, and the propane tank had been installed. I'd made it a priority to have plumbing run to the kitchen along with a working stove, even if it was a temporary one. That way, our long days of working wouldn't be interrupted by the need to go into town for a hot meal.

With the window, I put a kettle on and sifted through the bin of various teas my realtor had gifted me when the closing happened on the property, welcoming me to England. "The land of tea drinkers," she'd exclaimed with a smile. Finding a strong one, I filled the diffuser, set it in a thermos and filled it with the hot water from the kettle.

Grabbing the mortar and tools on my way, I headed outside. It was early. There were birds chirping loudly in the trees throughout the grove out back. The sound of them reminded me that I was up far earlier than normal for me. However, I was feeling energized; ready to take on the world. Well, the wall anyway.

It was a new feeling. Before, I didn't sleep much, sure, but I normally spent most of my days dragging, feeling the effects of not sleeping. And when I did actually catch a few winks, it almost made me feel worse. I had been in a perpetual state of feeling like a zombie. So, I spent a lot of my time muddling through, just making it from one moment to the next, almost as if I'd lost my lust for life. I stayed active, but it was more like going through the motions than anything.

I made my way down the stone and mortar barrier until I found my chalk mark. I set the thermos and bucket down and began to stir up the paste. It had become thick overnight, so it took a little bit of effort to loosen it up. Satisfied that it was a good consistency, I tapped on the stones within reach along the top of the wall, removing the loose ones, cleaning out their homes, slathering in a new layer of mortar and resetting them into their spots. I continued down toward the ground, sweeping back and forth as far as I could reach from my position until I got back to the rock that I'd stopped on the night before; the rock that hid the love letter from Joshua to Cora.

I paused, unsure if I wanted to disturb it, but reason hit and I giggled at myself for being so sentimental. I pulled out the softball sized stone and reached in to clean out the hole again, wanting to make sure more mortar hadn't crumbled. A few pebble sized crumbles fell out, but, again, under the crumbled mortar, I felt a surface smoother than it was supposed to be.

Leaning down, I peered into the empty space. There sat another letter. "How did I miss that?"

I carefully plucked the antique paper from its hiding spot and looked back inside the mini cavern just to be sure I wasn't missing some sort of stack of them in there. Once I was satisfied that there was nothing more than aging mortar, I replaced the stone, again, leaving out the fresh layer of grey paste, marking the stone with a fresh "X".

This time, I didn't tuck it into my shirt for later; I left the bucket, tools and everything sitting there and bee-lined it into the main house, making my way back up to my bedroom and to the first letter. I compared the wax seals and the handwriting on the front of the folded sheets. They were identical, as I figured. I flipped them both over and compared the writing. Again, identical, except that this one was a little more crisp and not as dingy as the first. Thinking back to finding the first one, I couldn't believe that I had missed the second one lying just beneath it, but I chalked it up to having not inspected the hole further after my first discovery. It had taken me by surprise, and I was focused more on wondering what it was rather than if there was any others.

I smiled, reading the same inscription on the front: *Cora, My Love.*

This time, I was eager to open it and see what Joshua had to say to his beloved. I found the clean putty knife and loosened the wax seal enough to unfold the page and reveal its contents. Once again, I laid it out so I could press open the folds, being as gentle as I could.

17th of June, 1867
Dear Cora,

I waited at the stop, wanting to delay the carriage as long as possible, but you did not come, and they did not wait. My heart tells me that your reasoning is entwined with something your family has said, maybe even done. I cannot convince myself that you did not join me of your own volition.

I understand that this must be very difficult for you. It is not without conscious thought that we both have devised this plan, knowing that we will have to endure some strife. But people rarely find the kind of love that you and I have, so I know in my heart of hearts that we belong together. Once they see how happy their daughter is and what a beautiful family we will have, I cannot think that your parents will not eventually relinquish their anger and welcome us with open arms.

There is another carriage tomorrow night. I will wait for you again. In the meanwhile, I will send word to the pastor to inform him of our delay. As for tonight, I will be in town at The Golden Crown, having dinner. I hope that you can sneak away and join me. Please come. Even if it is to merely stop in and let me know that all is well, and our plans are still in motion.

I cannot wait to see you again and to start this new life together.

Yours Truly & Forever,
Joshua

I sighed, feeling the mixture of love and fear Joshua must have been experiencing. I wanted to know what happened to her. I wanted to know if she stood him up, or if her parents had stopped her. I wanted to find her and do what I could to help them be together any way I could. I also wanted to know why I suddenly became such a romantic; an emotion I'd spent my lifetime lacking in large.

I grabbed up my laptop, still attached to the backup battery, and carried it down to the table. Instead of going back outside to work on the rock wall, I ended up spending the day writing furiously. The story fell out of me as if I'd been planning it down to the tiniest of details. I was in the zone. Life around me ceased as I drowned inside my new world and its characters. Locations burst into my imagination. Dialogue flooded my mind. Words filled the page.

My focus shifted in my goal to one that was closer related to Joshua and Cora's story. Thoughts swirled as my questions grew. My fingers flurried across the keyboard and the beginning of the book practically fell out of my brain and onto the page. I then made an attempt to catalogue all of my thoughts about how I saw their situation playing out and to start outlining the people and events as I saw them in my head.

Joshua – Tall, dark haired, working class gentleman. Not averse to hard work but is a gentleman by society's standards.

Cora – Dark haired heiress to upper class family. Banking? Mining?

**Change their names?*

The couple meet at a ball. They spend time sneaking off to see each other as their love grows. Finally, he proposes. However, her father does not approve.

-Is he not upper class enough?

-Had he done something wrong?

-Had he accidentally insulted her father in some way?

-Maybe they were competitors in their field?

The two make plans to meet and run away, arranging an elopement in another village, but she doesn't show.

-Did her family stop her?

-Did she change her mind?

-Oooo... did something happen to one of them?

He waits for her...

I was inundated with more mental visualizations of the possibilities than I could keep up with. Often, I found myself daydreaming through a scenario and having to bring myself back to the task in front of me. I scoffed at myself and my newfound flood of writing material. *I could probably make ten books out of the different variations that I'm coming up with here.*

Before I knew it, the light was shining in through the windows on the West side of the house. Evening had descended, and I'd missed lunch. My stomach was growling. With the construction of the temporary kitchen being a new development, I hadn't brought but a few snacks aside from what I'd had for dinner the day before. Resolving to the need to head back into town, I saved my progress and closed my laptop. Upstairs, I tucked it into its bag, grabbed a few other items and cleaned up my scattered clothes.

Tossing my laptop bag into the back of my car, I drove into town. I figured I could shower and clean up, then leave my electronics, including the backup battery, in my flat to charge while I went for a walk downtown to scout out a restaurant. I grabbed a quick snack before hopping into the shower to tide me over.

As I was passing through the streets in the center of town, my jaw dropped. Right there across from where I was standing was The Golden Crown; the restaurant that Joshua went to, hoping that Cora would meet up with him. It still held an older feel about it. All of the downtown strip did actually. Despite the fact that windows, doors and signs had been updated, the updates were in the older architectural fashions that kept the area clinging to a time that made the automobiles look out of place.

Without hesitation, I went into the establishment and took a table in the back of the room. It was a clear view of the open floor plan as well as the front windows and door. I could imagine that, providing there hadn't been any major remodeling done in the meanwhile, this would have been the table that Joshua would have chosen. Along with the view, the table came with a certain amount of privacy being in the back corner. Of course, I giggled at myself for going to such an assumptive leap. But I was getting caught up in the romantic nature of their story that also contained an exciting mystery element. The wordsmith in me came alive while envisioning it all.

"May I get you something to drink?" The waitress was a small woman, slightly weathered by the years.

I broke from my daydream. "Yes, please. Can I have a water and a coffee?"

"Absolutely." She scribbled on her notepad. "American?"

I let out a humored breath, instantly knowing what she was asking and thinking she was not, by far, the only person to ask that very question. "Yes."

She tucked her notepad into her apron. "Here on holiday?"

I shook my head. "Actually, no. I just bought a project house nearby."

Realization lit up her eyes. "Oh! You must be Ms. Price. I heard an American woman had bought it and was fixing it up. It's about time someone paid some attention to that rundown old house. It's seen better days by far."

"You know the place?" I asked.

"Everybody knows that place. It used to belong to the Webb family; one of the area's most prestigious families. They were already from old money, but they made even more in the mining business through the eighteen hundreds." She became more poised as she spoke. "I'm sorry about rambling. Let me get you that coffee."

I held up the menu. "Can I also just have a burger and fries?"

"Absolutely," she replied, back in server mode.

"And then, can you come back and tell me more?" I requested.

She bowed her head. "I'd love to as long as we don't start filling up."

"I'm Nell by the way." I held my hand out.

She shook my hand. "Imogen." She hurried off to the kitchen.

Not long after she left, Imogen brought me my coffee, then my meal. Another couple had come in and sat at a nearby table. I glanced their way from time to time, thinking about the possibility of Joshua and Cora being similar to them, sitting there, enjoying a meal together, planning out a new life as a married couple. How they must have sat in that restaurant, chatting over a meal, just as those two were doing.

I'd barely touched my burger when Imogen stopped by my table. "Is there something wrong?"

I blinked, pausing before realizing what she was referring to. "Oh! No. Sorry. I'm just lost in thought I guess."

"Oh. Good. Is there anything more you need?" she asked.

"I think I'm good," I replied.

"Well, I should be off my shift here before long. If you'd like, I could join you to chat more." A small smile played on her lips.

I nodded my head. "I would love that. I don't think I've had any conversations with another person other than with the laborers since I arrived. Plus, it would be very cool to learn more about this house I seem to be a little obsessed with." My shoulders relaxed.

She set down my bill. "Then I will be back soon. Oh, and Iris will be able to help if you need anything else until I return. I'd like to hear more about this obsession."

"Haha! Okay. See you in a bit." I turned to my plate to try to finish my meal before she got back.

Just as Iris was clearing my dishes, Imogen came out and took a seat across the table from me. She'd let her hair down and put on a sweater, so it took me a moment before I recognized her.

She settled in. "So, how long have you been back on this side of the pond?"

"Just a few months. But the progress on the estate has been steady. So, that is good." I took the last sip of my coffee.

She motioned for Iris to come back with a pot. "So, tell me, why did you purchase the Webb estate?"

I really didn't know what to say. I'd made the purchase on a whim. But I couldn't deny that there was some sort of pull to the place. "I don't know, really."

"So you're connected to it?" She leaned forward, propping herself up on the table.

I blinked. "I guess you could say that. But I don't know anything about it, and I hadn't even thought to do any research. My family isn't one to really get sentimental about history, family or possessions."

"And yet you're an author?" Her eyebrows pulled in.

I sat up in my chair. "I guess word does get around here, huh?"

She leaned back again. "Yeah. You can say that. There's not a lot that goes on out here. England is a small country compared to some of your states as it is. However, you're staying in a village that is surrounded by historical estates and manor houses. Many of the families around here are ancient ones, as in hundreds of years of generations."

"Wow," my eyes widened. "So, the Webb family ... I don't believe that was the name on the deed when I signed everything. What happened?"

She thought for a moment, chewing on the inside of her cheek. "All I really know is that the family built it in the sixteen hundreds. They stayed there for a number of generations. But at some point, in the mid nineteen hundreds, the manor fell into disrepair. Eventually, they no longer were there. I am not sure if the decedents moved on, if they died off, if they sold it or if it was taken by the bank. But it has sat there continuing to rot as the years passed."

"That's interesting. I bet there's countless family homes that kind of fizzle out like that all over the world. You know, great families that eventually end up not so great as the times change?" I went off on a tangent.

She nodded in agreement. "It's a fairly common general history in England for these large estates, sadly."

I tapped my lips with the tip of my finger. "I bet I was simply drawn to the whole taking something else broken down and making it whole again."

She looked at me. "Something else?"

I took a sip of my water. "Yeah. I'm recently divorced."

"Oh dear. I'm so sorry." She reached out and patted my hand.

I waved her pity off. "Not at all. It wasn't a bad transition, and I really didn't take the news of him being in love with someone else as bad. I actually didn't feel much about anything. Not until I saw this house online."

"And you jumped on it, almost blindly?" She was leaning forward again.

"Exactly." I pursed my lips.

"Sounds like you're supposed to be here then," she exclaimed.

"Oh!" I pulled out the letters from my bag. "I found these in the rock wall along the South border of the property."

She took them and carefully looked them over without opening them. "These look very old. I bet they were a lot of fun to find."

"They've actually helped me to get over a stint of writer's block I've been dealing with." I slipped them back into my bag.

"Again, supposed to be here, dear." She patted my hand again. Reaching into her purse, she pulled out a business card and handed it to me. "Here. This is my cousin, Elijah Brown. He is a historian and works here in town. His specialty is this sort of thing. He would think it is brilliant to meet you and tell you all he knows. Maybe you can find some interesting information through him. Give him a ring tomorrow. He should be in the office most of the day."

I took the card. "Thank you. I will."

She gathered her things. "Well, I need to be off. I work the breakfast shift tomorrow. It was very nice to meet you, Ms. Price."

"Nell." I reached my hand out. "And it was very nice to meet you, too."

"Nell." She shook my hand and then took her leave.

I paid for my meal, stopped by my flat and drove back out to what I was happy to start referring to as Webb Manor. There was something in the name that felt fitting seeing that there had been quite a lot of spider webs when I'd first arrived.

I took my bags straight up to the bedroom and settled in for the night. This time, making an actual note to myself to be sure to pick up something a little more comfortable to sleep on the next day, pressing the sticky note to the outside of my wallet.

Thinking about a once very established family dispersing or possibly even losing everything fed my growing plotline on my new story even more that night. Could something about Joshua have affected the decline? Maybe Cora's father invested or risked a lot in order to keep them apart, and it was the catalyst for their fortune to deteriorate?

I was struggling more with trying to pick a direction on some of the aspects than trying to force something to come to mind. I couldn't honestly say it was a far better option, but at least there were options rather than a blank page with a taunting, blinking cursor. Regardless of the flow of options, I wrote plenty that night. Lots of notes formulated, as well as a continuation of where I had left off. By the time I fell asleep that night, I had written another twenty pages.

Needless to say, when I set my laptop down, I was completely, mentally worn out and slept extremely well that night, despite the lack of padding beneath me.

Three

The next morning, once again, I was feeling the effects of sleeping on a camping mat. I turned onto my side and peeked at my phone. It was eight in the morning, which was quite a bit later than I had been waking.

After a quick round of freshening up and a change of clothes, I headed downstairs. While the kettle was heating up, I riffled through the bag of food I brought the day before, which was getting pretty low. Picking some biscuits and a banana, I selected the same tea as I had the prior morning and filled my thermos.

I figured that as much as my imagination was running wild, maybe getting back to work would help things clear up and come together. Calling Imogen's cousin could wait until after lunch. So, once again, I gathered up the bucket and tools and made my way out to the wall. I found where I had left off, and I started tapping on the stones, purposefully ignoring the one that had concealed the letters. I had not made near as much progress as I had wanted to the day before, so I pushed all thoughts of Joshua and Cora out of my mind and focused on the project.

Yet, focusing wasn't in the cards. Granted, I made it a little over two hours, but the rock with the chalk "X" on it kept reaching out and nudging at my attention. I went back and forth between mortaring it and leaving it, thinking it would be fun to leave the one loose stone as a tribute to the found letters. But I couldn't concentrate. Nor could I decide. That loose stone kept creeping back into my thoughts, pushing me to think more about the unrequited love rather than the task I was working on.

I huffed and sat back onto the grass, the trowel in my hand, pointed up. I glared at the marked rock. It seemed to be staring back at me. "Fine!"

I stood and stomped my way over to the it and yanked the stone out of the wall. Being thorough, bordering on OCD, I reached in to make sure all of the loose pebbles were cleared out, I swiped my hand across the surface.

Then, I stopped; felt myself flush and straighten up. I pulled my hand back out slowly, disbelief rushed through me. Between my fingers was another folded letter with the same red, wax seal. And, just as with the others, on the front was *Cora, My Love.*

I didn't know if I should stand or duck down, but I was scared that someone might be watching. I was convinced then that someone must have been playing a joke on me or worse, trying to frighten me. As Imogen had said, most people knew most of the goings on as well as the people in the area. What if someone didn't take kindly to my purchasing of the estate and moving there? After all, I was American. Most countries don't exactly love it when someone from another country purchased land and moved in.

Staying low, I placed one hand on the top of the wall to brace myself and peered over. I scanned the perimeter, including my own land, trying to see if there was anyone watching me. My neck craned as I stretched to see around bushes, trees and other obstacles. But there was no sign of any lurkers.

Feeling foolish for my pitiful attempt at playing spy, I stood and tucked the letter into my jacket pocket. I took one last glance around, part of me hoping that someone would step out of the tree line and wave, laughing and telling me how it was all just a silly joke to greet the new neighbor. But no such person stepped forward. And there was still no sight of anyone around.

I gathered my things and speed walked back to the house. The bucket clanged loudly as I dropped it and the tools just inside the back door and locked it. Making a sweep around the floor, I checked every room for a possible intruder, locking every door and window along the way. Once I was satisfied that I was alone, I went back into the kitchen.

A set of dishes and silverware was still half packed in a box on the counter. I reached in, pulled out a butter knife and set the letter on the counter. As usual, I was careful as I pried the red wax away from the aged paper and slowly unfolded it.

18th of June, 1867
Dear Cora,

I missed you last night at The Golden Crown. Furthermore, I've missed you over the recent days since I have been unable to see you. However, it has not detoured me or my feelings. It has only served to make firm my knowledge that what we have is real.

The carriage departs from the stop this evening at seven. I will be there closer to half passed six just to be sure that everything is set.

I look forward to holding you once again, my love.

Yours Truly & Forever,
Joshua

My shoulders slumped. I honestly didn't know what to make of the letter. It was, by all appearances, made of the same ancient paper and closed with the same completely dried wax. However, I was quite certain that I had checked the spot the day before to be sure that there were no more letters stuffed into the wall. I was sure, without a shadow of a doubt, that the one from the day before was the last one. So, where did this one come from?

That question catapulted my mind into a flurry of other questions.

Are the letters actually old?

Was this all some prank?

What if they were real? Had I gotten the actual last letter out?

If they were real, and I keep getting the 'last one', why is someone putting them in the wall for me to find?

Frustrated, my fists hit the counter, sending a glass falling, shattering across the wood floor. I dropped my head into my hands and let out a growl. Mystery, action, drama: those were all concepts I had always left tucked neatly between book covers of my manuscripts. They were not things I had let into my personal life. I was more than happy to have the move and remodeling of some deteriorating home be the most of any sort of action in my life. But the possibilities that the letters brought with them was a little more than I had bargained for.

Yet, it seemed that was what I was facing. Clearly, I was literally holding some sort of mystery that you'd expect to find on the pages of some bestselling novel. Only, I had no clue as to what genre my little mystery was being written in.

Was it a murder case? Did I have a stalker? Was it a psychological thriller? Oooo ... maybe I was unwittingly participating in some paranormal plot line where I was actually receiving letters from another time period, intended for some long lost beloved.

I laughed at myself for how far I was allowing my imagination to run away with me. Glancing at the letter on the counter, I wrinkled my nose at the yellowed paper. I didn't like things I couldn't predict in my life. And this was a situation I had absolutely no idea what to make of.

My laptop bag was sitting on the table. I shoved the letters inside it, grabbed my purse, keys and overnight bag. I threw them into my car and stood, my hands on the frame and the door. Curiosity swelled in me, and I made my way back to the wall.

The rock was still sitting on the ground next to the wall. I pulled out my phone and knelt down. Turning the flashlight option on, I pointed it into the mini cavern. With my other hand, I scratched at the surface, flicking away any and all crumbling bits of rock and mortar. After a couple moments of inspection, I was satisfied that there was no sign of any lingering letters. I turned off the light from my phone and snapped a picture.

"There. That proves that I'm not crazy. I *have* doubled check thoroughly that there's no more. Today's letter should be the last. And now I'm talking to myself." I took in a deep breath and went back to the vehicle.

The drive into town was usually a nice one. The scenery was beautiful. The road was smooth. And up until that day, my thoughts were relaxed and happy. But on that drive, that day, I was in no mood to reflect on the beauty of the country. I was growing more curious about the letter situation.

I turned onto the main road through the village and parked the car in front of The Golden Crown. Remembering that Imogen had said she was working the day shift, I was hoping my newfound friend might be able to shed some light on the situation.

She greeted me at the door. "Nell! It's good to see you again so soon."

Something about seeing her helped calm my nerves. "Imogen. I'm very glad you're working."

"Oh?" She guided me to a booth near the server station. "You look dreadfully frazzled. What brings you in? I get the feeling it's not for a meal."

"Well, I actually could use a hot meal, but no, that's not my only reason for coming," I explained.

I pulled all three letters out of my laptop bag and placed them on the table. She looked down and slowly took the seat across from me. "So, you found another? Was it in the same place?"

"Yes." I tapped my finger on the table. "I was *sure* I had checked and there wasn't any more there yesterday. I'm starting to wonder if someone is messing with me."

She shook her head. "I don't know why anyone would."

"Maybe because I'm American? Maybe someone doesn't like that I bought the home and am going to be moving into it?" I speculated.

She shook her head again. "Despite what some would have you think, we don't actually dislike Americans. So, it doesn't make sense that someone would react to you like that."

"Then how else would you explain this?" I pointed at the folded pages.

She looked at them, turning them over on the table. "Maybe you simply overlooked it. It is possible you just missed it. Did you take a closer look today?"

"Yes." My reply was pointed. "I scratched at the mortar to be sure. But you're probably right. I probably didn't look very close." I relaxed a little.

She patted my hand. "I'm out shortly after the lunch rush. Eat something. Then, after, I will walk you to Elijah's office. It's just a few blocks away."

I had almost forgotten about her cousin, the historian. "That's probably a good idea. He can tell us if these are authentically old or just someone thinking they're funny."

"Exactly." She got up from the table. "I'll be back with a coffee and water. Our special today is a locally made sausage made into toad-in-a-hole. We also have a wonderful roast meat selection of beef, pork and lamb and the East London favorite, pie and mash. The chef is also featuring bubble and squeak."

I laughed. "I have no idea what you just offered me. How about I stick with pie and mash for today? I, at least, know what that is."

"Brilliant." She smiled as she jotted my order down.

I took my time eating, taking out my laptop and writing between bites. My frustration wasn't slowing me down on my manuscript in the least. Part of me wondered if it was possible that it was helping feed my imagination. But, nonetheless, I kept having to remind myself to take a bite every so often as I would get lost in the words. I barely even noticed when someone cleared my plate or refilled my coffee.

I wasn't sure how long I'd been there, but it was a while. Imogen returned to my table, her apron in hand and the same sweater draped across her shoulders. "Shall we?"

I looked up, my vision slightly blurry. "Oh! Yeah. Let me just save and put this away."

With my laptop bag and purse slung over my shoulder, we started up the street. She gave me a verbal tour of the area as we walked, sharing her knowledge of some of the town's history ... and even some of the gossip. Her voice was lively as she spoke, taking an even cheerier tone whenever I would ask questions.

We rounded a corner, and she stopped at the second door. She rang the bell, and we waited, still chatting away. After a minute, a man's voice came through the speaker on the wall. "Sorry, but we are closed on the weekend. Please come back Monday."

"You're never closed for family," Imogen sang into the intercom.

"Cousin?" he questioned.

She grinned. "The one and only."

"You're hardly my only cousin, but you're welcome to come on up," he retorted.

The buzzer signaled that he'd unlocked the door, and we made our way up the narrow stairway. Once there, we were greeted by a man in his fifties, short, wearing a threadbare suit jacket and slacks. His beard was unkempt, and his voice was husky. "Happy Saturday to you, ladies."

Imogen reached out and gave him a hug. "It is good to see you, Elijah."

He returned the sentiment. "Yes. We should make more time for lunches or something of the sort."

"Yes. We should." She squeezed his shoulder. "This is my new friend, Nell Price. She is from America, and she just purchased that run down Webb estate."

He held his hand out for me to shake it. "It is very nice to meet you, Nell. Is that short for anything?"

"Janelle. But it was my grandmother's name, and she is still alive. So, my family adopted calling me Nell instead." I peered around his office and the piles of clutter and stacks of paperwork that littered the space.

"Well, nice to meet you, Nell." He waved his arm, pushing the door the rest of the way open. "Do come in. How can I help you?"

"Thank you." I walked past him and took a seat as he removed stacks of newspapers off the chairs across from his desk, dusting them off and placing them in front of the nearest bookshelf. "Well, I'd love to learn more about the history of the area, especially the land I now own."

Imogen nudged me. "The letters, Nell. Show him the letters."

He sat in his regal, brown leather office chair that was showing wear from what must have been several years' worth of him working long days at that very desk. "Letters, you say? Did you find some in that old, deteriorating home that were left behind?"

"Not actually *in* the house. More like in the rock wall along the South perimeter," I explained.

He bobbed his head. "I see. How many?"

"Three." I fished them out of my bag.

I laid them on the desk and folded my hands in my lap. Elijah picked them up and examined the yellowed, stiff papers. He pulled out a magnifying glass and slipped each one under it, one by one. Finally, he pulled them open, again, one by one, and read their contents.

"All three of them were just stuffed behind a loose rock?" He was still looking over the letters.

"Well?" I paused.

He looked up. "Different rocks?"

I shrugged. "More like different days."

His expression became very puzzled.

I cleared my throat. "You see, I found the first one my first day working on the wall to stabilize each of the loose stones. But I hadn't checked for more. I was just a little surprised to find something in there. Then, when I went back out the second day, I found the second one. Honestly, I just figured I hadn't looked further once I pulled the first one from the spot. So, I looked a little closer to be sure there wasn't any more. But when I went back out to work on the wall today, I found the third letter."

"I see," he said.

"Of course, I made sure to look extra close just to be positive that there's no more in there." I sat up in my seat and folded my hands back into my lap.

"Well, the Webb family is an ancient name in the area. And the Webb estate was built by one of the brothers in the early sixteen hundreds, George Webb. He and his wife, Emma, were both from very old money and very high standing noble families. And for the next three hundreds years, the family prospered through various ventures; mining being one main one." Elijah was still looking over the pages.

He continued, "As for how it came to the disrepair it is in now is because of a very unfortunate series of events. Would you rather address that history first, or dive into these letters?"

My attention was peaked for both. "How about the history first since the letters will probably require some digging."

"Good idea." He bobbed his head again. "So, Carson Webb inherited the entire estate and all its fortunes during the first World War. At that point, money was flowing like water into the Webb bank accounts due to the need of the metals their mines were producing. But just as the second World War hit, the mines went dry. After over one hundred and fifty years of steady ore income, there was nothing more to be found. At first, he sunk quite a bit of money into better and newer ways to try to dig faster, sure that he would strike the needed metals again. But a few years in, it was obvious that just wasn't the case. He sold the mine and leaned heavily on the property they had invested in, raising the rates in an attempt to compensate for the income loss."

"But just as America did, we went through our own state of depression. Many of their business and living tenants could no longer afford the old rental rates, let alone the raised ones. Then, Carson fell ill. He never recovered, and the estate was left to his son, Tobias."

Elijah paused a moment, rereading the letters, his eyebrows furrowed and a mix of determination and confusion playing across his brow. "Tobias was a little less than responsible, to say the least. He didn't have the savvy business mind that his ancestors had, and the pressure of the failing ventures wasn't something he dealt with well. Soon, he found himself selling off some of the properties to make ends meet. Then, he fell into gambling and drinking to escape. And by the early nineteen sixties, things had become so destitute for Tobias that his wife divorced him, took the children and went home to her parents.

"The manor home hadn't been kept up since under Carson's ownership. So, by the time the bank took it from Tobias due to the delinquency of the loans he had from borrowing against its collateral, there were sections already unable to be used. The roof was failing. The plumbing to some parts of the house was leaking. Carson had extended the little bit of electricity that had been installed by his father, and Tobias attempted to do the same, but neither were able to wire the entire house, and some of it was shorting out. One short even caused a fire that shut down three of the rooms."

"I wondered if that area was fire damaged or not." I recalled a few rooms that the rotten wood left a black charcoal residue as we hauled it out of the structure.

"A gentleman with the last name of Wilkinson bought it back in the eighties, but he never did anything with it. And I believe he sold it back to the bank only five years later, taking quite the financial loss." He set the letters down in front of us.

Elijah chuckled at himself. "You know, I have a colleague that shares that same last name. I never have thought to ask if he is related to that bloke."

"A colleague?" I reiterated.

"Yes." Elijah tapped a finger on his chin. "He is a fellow historian. I know his office is just a few blocks away from here. He and I occasionally meet for lunch to chat about things we each are working on."

"That is probably handy from time to time," I exclaimed. "So, what do you make of the letters? I'm curious if they are authentic or if someone is trying to pull a prank on me."

"I find no reason to think that they are not authentic to the date that is written on them." He adjusted his glasses. "I will say, though, they are in fantastic condition. Especially the second and third letters." He looked up suddenly. "You know, that colleague of mine, Reid Wilkinson? He's brilliant with document authentication. And who knows. He may have more information on your estate. Let me ring him."

"Should we pester him on a weekend?" I felt bad for bothering one person with my inquiries, let alone two.

He waved me off, already punching the numbers on the keypad. "Ms. Price, we are single men and historians. We rarely do much other than work. Well, work and work over a pint." He chuckled.

"If you don't think he will mind," I attempted to interject.

It was too late. Reid must have already answered his phone. "Reid! How are you doing this weekend? Oh. Good, good. Well, I have Ms. Price sitting in my office. She is the new owner of the Webb estate. She has some very interesting letters here on my desk that she found, and I was curious if you might be..."

There was a pause.

"Yes ... She..."

Another pause.

"I will check." He pulled the phone away from his head and covered the microphone. "Ms. Price."

"Nell," I corrected him.

He grinned. "Nell, would you be adverse to accompanying me to The Golden Crown to meet up with

Mr. Wilkinson for a bite to eat and to dive a little further into the mystery of these letters?"

I shrugged and looked over at Imogen. "I don't see why not. Do you have time?"

"I actually need to be going home. But you are in more than capable hands here, if you feel secure enough for me to leave that is." She looked back and forth between us.

"Oh!" I didn't even think about the possibility that I might be holding her up form something. I felt completely rude. "I'm so sorry. No. I'm sure we will be just fine. Go. I've taken up enough of your time already."

"It is not a problem in the least, dear." She stood, handing me a piece of paper. "Do call if you need anything."

"I will. Thank you so much." I stood and gave her a hug.

She and Elijah also exchanged a hug, both expressing the longing to make time to get together some time in the near future, and she left.

I turned back and saw Elijah slipping each of the letters into a clear, plastic bag. He carefully folded over the flaps and placed them into an envelope. "For safe travels. I would hate for something to happen to them if they are, in fact, authentic, which I still believe they are. And since I'm dragging you all over town in order to clarify this, I just want to be sure they are safeguarded."

I took the envelope. "Thank you."

After he gathered a few items and cleared up his tea cup, we made our way back down the block. Part of our conversation centered on the fact that it was the restaurant that Joshua had requested that Cora meet him at in the second letter. And how I had stumbled upon it when I came into town that day. I told him that was where I had met his cousin, Imogen, which led me to him. It was a connect-the-dots trail of thought he seemed to appreciate.

We arrived at the restaurant, and he held the door open for me. "After you."

"Thank you." I bowed my head as I passed him.

Once inside, we both scanned the room. He stopped, a grin forming on his lips as he started across the room. "Reid! It is good to see you."

They exchanged a manly, back slapping hug. The other man, Reid, slightly disheveled in a zip up hoodie, *Flogging Molly* t-shirt and jeans. He was tall, a little over six foot, and his build was one of someone that didn't sit behind a desk all day. He was toned yet not bulky. And his brunette hair showed signs of being a bit sun-kissed. His boots showing obvious wear not just on the toes but the seams and soles as well. If I hadn't been told he was a historian, I would have mistaken him for a general laborer on the street. And if it wasn't for the slight wrinkling around his eyes, I would have thought he was in his twenties.

Elijah moved, allowing me to see Reid's face for the first time. "Reid, this is Nell, the woman I told you about."

Um..." I started to stammer. "Hello."

He grinned, which didn't help. "Hello, Nell. It is very nice to meet you. Please, have a seat. I'm famished. I've been working on a small home repair job all day." He pulled a chair out for me.

I followed his lead, setting my purse down on the floor and attempting to sit as gracefully as I could. "Thank you."

Reid waved down the waitress, who happened to be Iris. "Would either of you like to order something?"

"I could use a bite." Elijah raised a pointed finger. "An order of bangers and mash, please. And a tea."

She looked to me. "I'll just have a cup of the daily soup and a water, please."

Both men looked at me, Reid being the one to speak up. "Don't tell me this is one of those American women things where you're too shy to eat in front of men."

"No." I blushed, unsure why he was having such an effect on me. It wasn't like I hadn't been around plenty of good looking men. "I ate already."

"Oh. Well, if you are sure you don't need anything more." Elijah waited for me to respond.

I shook my head. "Nope. I'm good."

"Ok then." He returned to his menu. "I'll have the big breakfast and a coffee, please. Eggs sunny side up. A biscuit with jam and all bacon." He handed Iris our menus.

She took them and grinned. "I'll be right back with your beverages."

"So, tell me, Nell, what do you write?" Reid casually leaned back in his chair, across from me at the table.

"Oh, no. I didn't write the letters we called you about." I was concerned he was misunderstanding the situation.

He crossed his arms, obviously amused. "Not the letters Elijah called me about. We will get to that. I had heard that the person who bought the Webb estate was an author. I'm just curious about what it is that you write. Mystery? Romance? Poetry? Biographies?"

I fidgeted with my napkin. "Oh! I write fiction. Primarily paranormal, sci-fi and fantasy type stuff."

"Nice." A corner of his mouth rose in a smirk. "Not too many women write in those genres. At least, not that I've seen."

"Yeah. It's a growing phenomenon for us. But there's some great female authors in them now. Some women, in the States, have been getting some pretty high praise and recognition for their books, especially in the paranormal category. The rise in indie authors has really put a lot of writers on the map. Some are even up there with traditionally published ones like myself. Personally, I think it's great since there's some really great stories out now that were previously overlooked. Plus, the rise in small publishing houses. Granted, the industry is a little flooded now, but I don't think there's anything wrong at all with having a large selection of books. Honestly, I find it a good problem to have." I stopped myself, realizing I was rambling.

He just looked at me for a moment, the smirk still on his face, leaning back in his chair, arms still crossed. "I will have to take a look."

Iris came back with our drink orders and set them down. "Your meals should be up very soon."

Elijah acknowledged her. "Thank you."

Feeling myself blush again, I pulled out the envelope with the letters and laid it on the table. "Elijah was nice enough to package them to be transported."

"Yes." Elijah leaned forward, sliding the envelope in front of himself and opening it. "Honestly, all evidence points to them being completely authentic to the eighteen hundreds date written inside them. The wax even looks aged. But I know that you may have a bit more expertise than I do in these matters, so I figured you may want to take a look at them as well."

Reid took the clear packaged letters, his expression turning more serious.

Elijah slid the empty envelope back over to me. "You know, it dawned on me today that you may be related to the gentleman who purchased the Webb estate back in the nineteen eighties. You both share the same last name. I never connected it prior to today, but I'm curious now if you are. Related, that is."

"Yes. He was my grandfather; passed away a few years ago." Reid's attention was on the papers.

"Interesting." Elijah sipped on his tea.

I watched Reid's expression turn more and more serious. "So, what do you make of them?"

He flipped them over, and his eyes widened. He pulled one out from its new, plastic home and carefully unfolded it. Laying it out on the table after inspecting that the surface was dry and clean, I saw his breath catch. Hastily, he folded it back up, slipped it back into the plastic sleeve and stood. His posture was almost rigid. "I ... um... I'll be right back.

"Is everything alright?" Elijah stood.

Reid waved to our server as he was walking to the door, briskly. "Iris, I'll be back in a moment."

He left us sitting there, completely baffled.

Elijah shrugged. "Well, he must have thought of something in regards to the letters. Sometimes we academic types get in our own little world, as I'm sure you are familiar with."

I nodded, agreeing with what he said. "Yeah. I guess I can get pretty focused, especially when Im writing or researching."

He signaled for a refill on his tea. "He lives nearby, and his office is the on the floor below his flat. So, I doubt he will be long."

"Okay." I was puzzled over Reid's abrupt departure, worried I'd said or done something to offend him.

When Iris brought our orders, Elijah and I ate in silence. I sipped on my soup, glancing up at the door every time it opened and back down at the mysterious, folded pieces of paper, wrapped in plastic, lying on the table in front of me, almost like they were taunting me, trying to tell me something but unwilling to give me any clues that weren't riddles.

I was close to being done with my bowl and was pretty sure that Reid's meal was completely cold when he came bursting back through the door, a small, wooden box under his arm. He came straight for the table and sat down, mildly out of breath. He set the box onto the table, pushing his plate out of the way and rested his hands on top of it, not saying anything for a long moment.

Elijah finished chewing his bite. "What is this?"

Reid didn't take his eyes off the box. "I'm not positive yet."

He then picked one of my letters back up and turned the wax seal up. Then, he took a small key out of his pocket and opened the box. He reached in and pulled out another folded piece of paper, enclosed in a plastic envelope, that was very similar in coloring, a wax seal on top.

I sat up in my seat and leaned forward, trying to get a better look. My breath caught as I saw it. The seal. It was identical to the one on my letters. Not just the same color wax, but it was the same impression. You could even discern that the pressure into the wax must have been from the same hand since it was thicker on one side than the other in each of the seals, a detail I was very proud for catching..

I looked up just as he did, and we caught each other's eyes. I let out a gasp. "You have some of Joshua's letters, too?"

He ignored my question. "Where did you say you found these?"

"Behind a rock in the stone wall along the South property line." I was startled by his direct tone. I reached my hand out. "Yours. May I see one?"

He handed the letter from the case to me. "These have been bounced back and forth in my family for a few generations. Nobody really put much stock in them for importance, but, at the same time, nobody could bring themselves to toss them, either. I, being the kind of person that is fascinated by all things historical as well as being the sentimental type, have saved them, even examined them. And right now, my mind is all but blown seeing that there's more."

"You said examined them, but have you read them?" I asked.

His eyes were fixed on the box. "A couple. Three of them had already been opened. The wax seals were cracked. Someone showed a lot less care in getting to their contents then you have appeared to. Thank you for that."

"I almost didn't break the seals. I'm so sorry. I kind of feel like I've invaded something very personal." I started tearing tiny pieces off my napkin, feeling fidgety. Something about his distance made me feel uncomfortable.

Elijah patted my hand, a gesture his cousin was also prone to doing. "I don't think anyone else would see it that way, Nell."

"What?" Reid looked up, shaking his head to clear his thoughts. "Invade? No. Not at all. You did a a great job at preserving the wax as well as the page. And had I been in your shoes? I probably would have been curious enough to read them as well."

I glanced into the box, seeing a stack of them in there. "Then why not read all of those?"

He chuckled. "That is a very good question. I guess I didn't see any mystery behind them. My great-great-great-great-great-grandfather was in love with someone who's family didn't approve of their love. I didn't really see much into it. Seemed like a typical Shakespearean style love story. And, if I'm honest, I'm rarely into that sort of thing."

I threw my hands in the air. "But what about getting to know your ancestor? Didn't you wonder if the letters told you more? Maybe, on a historian aspect, it might have allowed you to delve into the ways of the people of the time in a way you don't just get from a book."

He laughed loudly. "Yup. You're quite the author. Nonetheless, you are not incorrect. I just never really saw it that way."

"So, do you know who Cora is? Did they end up together?" I couldn't help but ask. I was dying to know.

He thought for a moment. "I actually don't know for sure, but I don't think so. Thinking over what little genealogy I've had the chance to do, I don't believe that was the name of his wife, and I do not believe he remarried."

"You've done some research on your ancestry?" I asked, hoping maybe he would have some notes in his office that could shed some light on things.

Reid started flipping through the letters in the box. He took a bite of his meal and chewed thoughtfully for a moment, finally swallowing before he spoke again. "I should have some time tomorrow, maybe about eleven? If you can spare a couple hours, why don't you come to my office? I can pull out my genealogy files, and we can sort through. Plus, maybe we can take a look at town records and try to figure out who this Cora was. That is, if your curiosity is that strong."

My eyes grew wide. "You sure? I mean, this is your family. Not mine. I'm just some silly woman that's curious because of the romantic aspects of it all. I really don't mean to intrude."

He smiled. "Nell, you brought these letters to show me. They are yours. And you have every right to delve into their story. And its not like you're going to come and read my personal mail or go through my underwear drawer. Besides, I could use a break from the tedious research I've been trudging through."

His words, *underwear drawer*, rang through my mind, turning my face about sixteen shades of red. I coughed when my words caught in my throat. "Okay. Yeah. I'd love to help you research this. These letters have shaken me out of my writer's block that I've been battling with for weeks. Not only am I deeply curious about the two of them. Who knows. Maybe it'll keep giving me the inspiration to write more."

"Well then, we can't take that away from you then, now can we? Not if it is a help to your work." He leaned back, tossing an arm over the back of his chair casually.

Elijah took a moment away from his dish. "Besides, having a fresh set of eyes in our line of work can be a real blessing. Sometimes, it is easy to drown yourself in all of the information and miss a few key points."

"That's a very good point," agreed Reid.

The two men exchanged a look that told me it was an *It's a historian thing* sort of thing. I just laughed softly, pretended to get it and took the opportunity to actually take another spoonful of my cold soup.

"So, eleven works for you then?" Reid eyed me, hopeful.

"Yes. Eleven sounds great!" Embarrassed by the sound of my eager response.

"Elijah? Are you going to be joining us?" Reid finished his meal and pushed the plate aside.

Elijah glanced between us. "No. I, sadly, have plenty to keep me busy in my own practice. But if it isn't too much trouble, would you keep me informed? I would love to know what you both come up with."

"Absolutely." Reid tipped his imaginary hat. "As for you, Ms. Price, may I hang on to those letters? You will get them back, I promise. But I would love to sit and read them if you do not mind. Maybe look a little closer at them? Chalk it up to family sentimentality, I suppose."

I was surprised he would ask. "Of course I don't mind. Actually, I kind of feel like they are yours. I simply found them in a wall. Other than the excitement of the unanswered questions, I don't really have much reason to hold on to them. They belong in your collection. I'm just grateful you'll allow me to help you."

He picked them up and put them inside the box, locking it and returning the key to his pocket. He scribbled his address and a phone number onto a piece of paper and slid it across the table to me. “Thank you, Nell. So, Elijah, tell us about this project you’re working on.”

Four

That night, I chose to sleep in my flat. I hadn't taken the time to buy something more comfortable to sleep on. I just figured it would have to be my afternoon stop after going to see Reid. When I woke early that morning, I was more than ready to head back to the estate, get some work done on the wall and make sure the laborers were all set before I left again.

The drive back there was beautiful and peaceful again after a good night's sleep. It was a warm morning, and I kept the windows rolled down, feeling the air whip through my hair, caressing my cheeks. Thoughts of Reid kept sweeping through my mind as I drove along. A smile would creep its way across my lips as thoughts of spending time as just the two of us played out in various ways against the backdrop of the landscape.

About half way there, I turned on the radio and sang along with the music to distract myself. Outside of writing, singing has always been a release for me. I just rarely ever did it in front of people, despite being complimented on my voice. But whenever I needed to work through something, it was a perfect way to clear my head and sort it all out. For that drive, I just wanted to stop fascinating about Reid, especially before I was to go be alone with him. Last thing I needed was to have my attraction for him be spelled out all across my face.

I was sure he had no shortage of attention from women. He was extremely attractive. And he had a charisma that was both alluring and captivating. He was definitely not the kind of guy I expected to meet when I was told I'd be meeting another historian. Yet, finding unexpected things was starting to be the norm around there.

Back at the Webb Estate, which I was starting to affectionately call Webb Manor in my head, Gerald and his brothers were already there. "Hello, Ms. Price! We are early, so we went ahead and cleared out the rear gardens on the East end of the property."

"I'm so sorry I wasn't here." I waved to the others, who were leaning against the truck. "So, where are we?"

Gerald used a handkerchief to wipe off his brow. "I believe the plumbers are coming throughout this week, as are the electricians. I gave them your instructions about starting on opposite sides of the house and moving around to avoid each other. I agree. I can't imagine working with electrical and water in the same room. Kind of seems like a recipe for disaster." He chuckled.

I pulled my purse and a bag of waters and snacks out of the back seat. "Right? We don't need any major setbacks. That's for sure. Are we sure we're ready for plumbing and electrical to be ran?"

"Yes." He nodded with confidence. "The walls are all in place, and it's best to do them now before drywall is installed. This way, it's just the bones of the house they have to work around."

I glanced over at the brick manor house. "How long do they say it will take to finish it all?"

He pursed his lips. "They say it should take them a couple weeks. Both of them. Of course, that is baring that there's no major setbacks. I'm hoping all goes smooth and they'll be done sooner than that. They're just running everything brand new. They do not have to disassemble or fix anything. Hopefully, that will speed up the process."

"Good." My mind was starting to wander again.

"Ms. Price?" He leaned into my line of sight.

"Nell." I gave him a weak smile.

"Nell," he repeated. "Are you sure you wouldn't want to hire one of those big contractors from the city?"

I looked at him, puzzled. "Do you think you can't handle this? Do you need more money?"

"No, no." He waved his hands. "I can, but I'm just advertised as a handyman. Granted, I have thirty years of experience, but I don't have a degree, and I am not a part of some big business that is designed for this sort of thing."

"That's why I like you for the job." I crossed my arms. "You will do the house right. Not by some dollar amount you think you can get from me."

His lips turned up, the smile almost closing his eyes. "Thank you, Nell. That is quite a compliment."

"That is exactly how I meant it." I adjusted the bag on my arm and started walking toward the front door, Gerald falling in step next to me. "Well, I didn't get as much work done this weekend as I had wanted. Oh! Wait! Do you know much about the history of this house or the area?"

"No. Sadly, I don't. Well, nothing of much interest, anyway. I'm not into things like that much. I know what I know, and I tend to stay out of things unless needed," he replied. "Why?"

I shook the idea out of my head. "I found a couple letters in the rock wall as I was stabilizing the loose rocks. I'm just looking for someone to maybe shed some light on who the people in the letters were.

"Letters, huh?" He smirked. "Sounds like an interesting mystery for one of your books."

"Yeah; it does, doesn't it?" I trailed to thoughts about my notes for my story.

"There's a man in town. Reid Wilkinson. He does something with researching older relics and documents. I bet he might be able to help," Gerald suggested.

"Actually, I met him last night. I'm going there..." I glanced at my watch. "...in four hours, actually. Turns out, the man who wrote the letters was an ancestor of his. There's others, and I will get to take a look at them."

Gerald nudged my arm with his elbow. "Sounds like kismet, Nell."

I blushed. thinking of Reid thinking about me like that for even a second, feeling like a girl again with how giggly he was making me feel. "Kismet? Maybe just fate bringing me here to help him with his family history, I'm sure, if anything. I doubt he would want anything to do with a divorcee American woman."

"Don't be so American, Nell." Gerald stopped and looked at me. "You have your own very appealing qualities. Many of the workers have been more than happy to work a little longer and a lot harder than on other jobs just because you're their boss. If he hasn't noticed something in you, then he's blind or ignorant. And I have a feeling he is neither."

My blush deepened. "Thank you, Gerald."

"I aim to speak the truth." He gave a slight bow. "But now, I need to gather up my brothers from their break and get inside to finish cleaning up before the crews get here in an hour."

I straightened my stand. "I'm going to spend a little more time on the wall before I get back into town."

Gerald jogged off, and I went around to the kitchen, setting the bag down onto the dusty counter and grabbing the mortar and tools. His words had added a new spring in my step. It was then that I realized that my self confidence was a bit dented. I'd always been a confident woman, almost intimidatingly so. But I hadn't realized how I'd let my insecurities slip out over the years.

It felt good to be coming back around. My only concern was that my attraction for him would allow some teenage insecurities to surface and make me look like a fool. It was a territory I had long walked away from before my marriage. It felt like having to go through that portion of puberty all over again. Only, this time, I had a divorce and a crumbled love life to nudge the edges of my confidence with it.

I stopped, took a deep breath, composed myself and reminded the adult me that I was, in fact, in my forties. I needed to get a grip, focus on the estate and enjoy the added bonus of the romantic mystery between Joshua and Cora.

Once out at the wall, I looked around for my stopping point chalk mark. There had been a light rain in the night, so I figured it would be faint. I scanned for a couple minutes, ignoring the "X" on the stone where I'd found the letters as much as possible. Finding the spot, I started tapping on the stones and slathering in the fresh mortar for the loose ones. However, the process was a bit slower as I took an extra moment to check each hole thoroughly for any hiding letters.

Just as before, I kept looking back at the stone with the "X" on it. I knew I had made sure there was nothing else in there, but the fiction writer in me wanted to know with certainty. I stood, shoving the trowel down into the wet mortar, and made my way down the wall. Kneeling in front of the marked stone, I placed my hand on it.

I paused.

A moment later, I was feeling completely foolish. I used the wall for leverage as I stood, but as I rose, something caught my attention. Slipping out under the bottom of the rock was something yellowed and pointed, triangular in shape.

This time, I shot up and froze.

I stared at the foreign object as if it was a threatening being, an ominous presence, willing it to go away. Then, my heart started racing, and I looked around me, trying to see if there was someone else nearby.

But nobody else was there. Just Gerald and his brothers. And they hadn't been there all weekend. But nobody had been there all night. There wasn't fences or security; anyone could wander onto the property day or night. And Gerald had said they had been there for a while that morning.

I yanked the rock out of its home and glared at the new letter sitting there, wax seal facing up. There was no way I had missed it being there the day before. I had even scratched at the stone. The shading of the paper wasn't even the same coloring as the aged mortar, let alone the rocks. That letter had been placed there between my last visit to the wall and then.

The entire situation sent chills up my spine.

Again, I looked around. This time, gripping the stone in my hand tightly, waiting to have to strike. I felt something touch my shoulder, and I whipped around, my hand coming up to start swinging.

"Nell!" Gerald shouted.

I dropped it and exhaled. "Gerald! I'm so sorry!"

"Are you alright?" He looked me over. "You look like you just saw a ghost."

I turned to the side and pointed. "There's another letter."

"Another one?" He stepped forward and pulled the paper from the wall. "It looks very old. Are you sure it is the same place as you found the others?"

I picked up the rock and turned it over, revealing the mark. "Either someone is messing with me by leaving the letters, or they're messing with me by moving my marks and loosening stones in the areas I've already worked."

He scratched his head. "Maybe you should set up some cameras, just to be sure."

For a moment, I entertained that idea. Then, I let the calm side of me take over. "I'll take this in and let Mr. Wilkinson take a look at it. Maybe he will have an idea where they're coming from."

"Brilliant. I can handle the crews when they get here." He put his hand on my shoulder. "Maybe take the evening to do something fun. You may be overworking yourself."

"You're probably right." I took the letter as he held it out and replaced the stone in the wall. "I'll pop back in later today."

"See you then." He walked back toward the house.

I looked down at the letter, sitting in my hand. I was torn between wanting to drop it to the ground and never go back to the wall, or opening it as fast as possible to see what it said. I opted for swinging through the house, grabbing my keys and purse and driving into town and straight to Reid's office. I forced myself not to open the letter or let my thoughts wander to ideas of stalkers or even pranks by nearby residents to scare me away. Instead, I kept my focus on the road and trying to find the address he had scribbled on the scrap paper. But no matter how hard I tried, I couldn't shake the slight panic rising in me completely.

By the time I found the door to his business, my restraint against the swirling thoughts was growing weak. I could feel my imagination creeping in and very strong. My heart rate was up. My palms were sweaty. And I was breathing fast.

I banged on the door harder than I'd intended.

The door sprang open. "Nell? Is everything okay?"

I looked at Reid. It was like he was in a picture where everything around him was blurry, and he was the only thing in focus. His right hand was on the door, the left on the frame. And I was still attempting to slow my breathing.

"Nell?" He started to reach out.

I took a step back. "I'm so sorry. I'm very early. It's just that..."

I suddenly felt stupid. I was letting my imagination get the best of me. And I chocked on my words before I started rambling about the various suspicions I had along my drive into town. Instead, I pulled out the letter I'd found that morning. "This was in the wall this morning, in the same place as the others. I was sure that there were no more. I have no clue where this one came from." My hands were trembling as I held it out in front of him.

His eyes traveled from my face down to my hand. He reached out and slipped the letter from my grip with one hand and took my hand with his other one, gently pulling me inside. "Come in, Nell. Come in."

He walked me up a flight of stairs, taking a sweater from the coat rack just inside the door and tossing it around my shoulders. He guided me into the living room and to the couch, excusing himself to get me some water.

"Here. Drink." He passed me a glass and sat in the chair across from me. "You found this one this morning? In the same spot?"

"Mmhmm."

He examined the letter. "And you haven't opened it?"

I swallowed hard. "No. I didn't stay on the property last night. I stayed in my flat here in the village. It was there when I went out to do some work before our appointment this morning."

He flipped the letter over a couple times, trying to work out the situation. "What is it that you think is going on?"

"I..." My words caught in my throat once again. I stood and started for the door. "I'm so sorry. I'm being ridiculous. And I shouldn't have barged in like this."

He had followed me and put a hand on my arm. "You are welcome here, and there is nothing to be sorry for. I completely understand your fears and concerns. This is a strange situation for sure. But come back in. I'll pour us some tea, and we will look at what it says together. How does that sound?"

I looked up at him through freshly wet eyelashes. "Yes. Thank you." I gathered my composure. "Do you have some coffee? I rather miss a nice cup of coffee."

"I think I can find us some, yes." He left the room and went down the stairs.

It wasn't long before he came back up, started the percolator and filled the french press. He brought it to the table with two mugs, quickly followed by some milk and sugar. We made our own adjustments to our coffees, mixing in our own preference of additives.

Taking his first sip, he set down the mug and picked up a butter knife. "Shall we?"

I nodded from behind my coffee.

He slid the letter in front of him, slipped the edge of the blunt knife under the wax seal and wiggled it ever so slightly until it was free of all but the single flap. His eyes moved to me for a moment as if he was checking my expression before continuing. Satisfied that I was okay, he unfolded the letter.

He read the contents, his eyes moving back and forth across the scrawled lines. Then, he let the page go, sat back and crossed his arms. "Hmmm..."

"Hmmm?" I wasn't expecting that reaction.

He bit his lip. "Yep. Hmmm..."

"Hmmm what?" I sat up.

"It's peculiar. These seem to be in line with each other, where he's trying to stick to their plan, but she seems to have gone missing." He reached forward and flattened the page.

"Missing?" I pulled the letter over to me and read it.

19th of June, 1867
Dear Cora,

I waited for you again last night. The carriage came and went, but you did not show. With a heavy heart, I departed the stop and returned home.

I have always understood that doing this was a risk. Not just for me, but for us both. We have discussed what it meant for you when it came to your family. However, I was under the understanding that it was not something that would detour you from our course.

But, alas, it is just that which seems to be the case.

As I sit here, writing this letter, I still cannot bring myself to be angry with you. Yes. I am afeared that something has happened to you. Even if you have no intentions of continuing our life together, I would request that you please send word that you are safe.

In the meanwhile, I will work diligently on closing off my feelings for you and moving on. That way, if we are to cross paths, which is inevitable in our society, I will be able to see you without emotional complication.

Just know, no matter how much I work on that, I will always love you. That, I feel, is not something I will get past.

Yours Truly & Forever,
Joshua

My eyes were filled with tears as I read the last line. Cora hadn't shown again, and I could only imagine how heartbroken Joshua must have been. Yes. It would have hurt for her to have told him she was ending things, but she didn't even do that. She just left him to wonder.

"I can't believe her." I sniffed.

Reid handed me a box of tissues. "Bloody harsh."

"Yeah," I agreed. "She could have at least told him she wasn't going to go through with it."

"That would have been the respectable thing to do."

I slowed my breathing. "That is, unless something happened to her."

"Like?" He tilted his head slightly.

"I don't know." I thought for a moment. "Maybe her parents locked her up? Maybe they took her somewhere else? Maybe..." I trailed off, thinking about all kinds of scenarios that could have happened.

"Maybe." He seemed to be drifting off in thought as well.

Then, I shot up. "But it's still strange that this one showed up even after my thorough inspection of that spot in the wall. I *know* there wasn't anything more there. I *know* it. I mean, sure, logic says that there's a possibility that I'd missed it, but I really don't think so."

"So who put it there?" Reid's eyebrows furrowed in.

I shrugged. "I don't know. Could be someone trying to spook me away."

"You really think someone would do that?" He paused, looking at the expression on my face. "Oh yeah. That's right. American. I suppose wherever you're from it might not be a stretch."

"Come on. Don't tell me you don't have crazies here." I was almost offended by his comment.

He took a sip of his coffee, glancing at mine for refill necessity. "Yes; we do. Yet, not near as many as you do over there."

I dismissed his comparison. "That's only because your entire country is the size of one of our states."

"Fair enough." He laughed. "But knowing the people in this area, nobody comes to mind that would do such a thing.

I'm honestly at a loss as to an answer other than you must have overlooked it."

"I'm not ruling that out. But what do you say to a drive out to the estate? You can inspect the wall yourself. Then, if any more show up, at least you won't look at me like I'm insane." I got up from the table.

He didn't hesitate before joining me. "That is a very good plan, Nell. Plus, then I can see where these letters were left."

The drive out to the property seemed to go fast. Reid filled me in on a little more of the area's history, pointing out various manor homes and their ancestral inhabitants. He was even able to show me a few places where homes used to stand that were no longer there and why. Some of the stories were filled with tragedy.

As we approached the house, coming up the long drive, the parking area was full with work trucks and equipment. I could see a lot of activity going on in the house, which made me smile.

Reid motioned toward the front door. "You've certainly accomplished a lot. And it seems that the work is not slowing one bit."

"No." I smiled. "Aside from my regular workers, there's electricians and plumbers here this week, too."

I watched the buzzing going on through the windows before realizing he was waiting on me. "Sorry. It's this way."

We crossed the grass and walked to the wall. It wasn't a short walk, so I took the opportunity to tell him about some of the improvements we had made on the grounds. So much of it had been so overgrown that it took a team of landscapers almost a week to uncover some portions, including our destination. The rock wall had been covered in vines and thorn-covered rose bushes that I hadn't even known that the wall was even there. It simply looked like a dying hedge.

I stumbled, almost falling as my foot caught on something in the grass. Reid reached out and caught me, pulling me up to him before I went toppling over and onto the ground.

"Did you see that?" He gripped me harder and pointed toward the tree line.

I was completely embarrassed by my sudden lack of grace. However, I struggled less with hiding that than hiding the way I flushed at the feel of his arm around me and my body against his. "What? I didn't see anything beyond the ground hurdling up at me."

He looked down, realizing how tight his arm was around me, holding me against his side. "Oh. Wow. I'm so sorry, Nell. Are you alright?"

"Yes." I straightened my clothes as he loosened his hold on me. "Thank you. I don't have a clue what I tripped on."

We glanced at the ground around us, neither of us coming up with anything in sight that could have caused my stumble. I then looked back to the tree line. "What did you see?"

He nodded. "I am pretty sure it was a man. Some sort of shadowy figure."

I searched the shadows to see if it was still there. "That's why I'm scared of some creep being the one putting these here."

"I completely understand now." He pulled out his phone. "I'm going to call the police."

I held my hands up. "I really don't want this to be a huge ordeal. I'm sure I just overlooked the letter. And whatever you saw ... maybe just a deer or something."

He was already dialing. "Let them at least make a sweep and ask the workers if they know anything. That way, maybe, if someone is doing this, they will see that you're being looked after."

Reluctantly, I saw his point of view. "You're probably right."

Reid turned toward the house, his hand protecting the microphone from the wind. "Hello?" Pause. "Yes. This is Reid Wilkinson." Pause. "Yes. I am doing very well. Thank you. I'm actually calling to request for an officer to come out to the old Webb Estate and take a look around for an unwelcome guest." Pause. "I am aware that there's a new owner. She is standing next to me. There's just been some suspicious behavior, and I believe I just saw someone lurking out in the tree line at the rear of the property." Pause. "Thank you. Yes; I'll wait here with her."

He hung up and tucked the phone back into his pocket. "They will be here straight away."

My anxiety was stating to soar despite trying to stay calm. I tried to distract myself. "Do you want to see the wall before they arrive?"

"Point the way." He fanned his arm out for me to go ahead. "Just watch your step."

"Ha. Ha." I mock laughed.

We closed the gap to the wall, and I searched for the "X". It was easy to find, and I knelt down in front of it. I tapped the stone and looked up at him. "This one."

""X" marks the spot?" he joked.

"It was the first thing that came to mind when I wanted to put something there to remind myself which one it was," I explained.

He pulled a flashlight and small paint brush out of his pocket. "No. It makes sense."

I watched as he gently pulled the stone out, examined it and set it on the ground. He turned the flashlight on and aimed it into the tiny cavern, looking in before starting on the deteriorating mortar with the brush. He worked diligently for a couple of minutes, discerning the contents of that hole, ensuring not to destroy it as well as testing a few nearby spots, making sure I hadn't been confusing them and just finding letters in more than one place.

Once satisfied, he stood and shoved the tools back in his pocket. "Well? I'm just as puzzled as you are. But, it looks like that was the final letter."

"You know, I'm kind of torn about that," I admitted.

"Torn? Why?"

I lifted a shoulder. "I'm actually enjoying the romance of the letters themselves. I want to know what led up to this point and what happened to them. But, not feeling a bit creeped out over it all would be nice, too."

"I can see that. But as far as their history, don't forget; I may be able to help with that." He placed a hand on my arm.

I'd almost forgotten about the other letters in my panic. Relieved that there might be some answers still, a distraction at the least, I relaxed a little. "Would you like to go inside while we wait for the police? We can brew some tea. My realtor, Marion, gave me a really nice basket when we closed on the sale. Maybe you can tell me what some of them are."

His hand went from my arm to my lower back. "That is a brilliant idea."

Inside, I made my rounds through the house, checking on the progress of the work while Reid sorted through the teas and started a pot of water. I spoke with the lead electrician and plumber to find out a timeline as well as find out their thoughts on the project. Both said it would take a few weeks to do everything, but they were impressed with how ready we were. Gerald and his team were assisting in any way needed. When they couldn't, they were working on various smaller jobs, biding their time until they could start hanging drywall and installing fixtures in each of the rooms.

When I got back to the kitchen, Reid had poured us both mugs of tea. "It is a low caffeine green tea mix. I figured you could use something calming rather than a jolt."

I slumped into one of the chairs. "Thank you. I guess I am probably a bit wound up."

He took the seat next to mine, turning his chair to face me. "You think? I have wanted to make you sit and rub your shoulders all day. You're making *me* tense."

I tilted my head back. "Oh lord. That would be amazing."

"I'm no pro, but I'm told I'm not bad." He stood and walked around to the back of my chair.

"Wait." I sat up. "No. You really don't have to..."

It was too late. His hands were kneading out the knots and tension that were seemingly pulling my shoulders right into my ears. At least, that was how it felt with how tense I'd been.

I closed my eyes and felt myself relax. "Mmmm..."

He slowed. "Feel good?"

My words came out slowly. "You have no idea."

I had gotten lost in the massage and had completely lost track of how much time was passing by when I heard a knock on the doorframe. "Ms. Price? Mr. Wilkinson?"

I shot up and spun around, almost as if I had gotten caught with my hand in the cookie jar. "Yes?" My voice was eager. "I'm Ms. Price."

"Hello. I'm Officer Hughes. I understand that there has been a sighting of someone on the property? Is it alright if Officer Bernhart and I take a look around?" He was very formal.

I took a sip of my tea, cringing at it being cold. "Yes. Whatever you need. There's work crews in the house, but I don't have anyone working in the smaller buildings or on the landscaping today."

He tipped his hat to me. "We will be back to report our findings."

"Thank you." I bowed my head.

"Officer." Reid nodded.

Officer Hughes tipped his hat again. "Reid."

After both of the officers exited the house, I took my mug over to the sink and poured it out, refilling it with hot water and the same tea Reid had used. He did the same, stopping next to me at the counter as I dumped two tablespoons of sugar into the mixture.

"Not an avid tea drinker, are you?" He smirked at me.

I stirred my drink. "Not at all. I'm trying to get used to it. It's not that it's bad. I just prefer my coffee or a great hot chocolate. Hot chocolate is actually my preference. I'm not one for a lot of caffeine unless I need to meet a deadline or something. But Marion gave these to me, and I feel bad letting them go to waste."

"Hot chocolate?" He quirked an eyebrow.

I sipped my tea, fighting another cringe. "Yes. With whipped cream, please."

He reached passed me, slightly brushing my hip as he did, pulled the bin from Marion toward him, riffled around through it, under the teas, and pulled out two packets. Taking my mug and his, he dumped them into the sink, rinsed them out, refilled them with the rest of the hot water and emptied the packets into them. Instantly, I smelled the beverage and took it in.

He stirred each and handed me my mug back. "There's no whipped cream, but this will do for now."

"Were those in there this whole time?" I glanced down, seeing the bottom of the basket was lined with several more packets.

"Must have been." He grinned. "This is *much* better."

I looked up from my mug and saw he was looking back at me. As if on cue, I inhaled sharply just as I tried to take a drink. It went in the wrong way, and I started coughing, thus spilling my hot chocolate down the front of me.

Reid grabbed the roll of paper towels, handed me a bundle and took my cup, setting it on the counter. "Are you alright?"

"Yes." I was more embarrassed than I'd ever remembered being. "I honestly don't know what's gotten into me."

"Here, let me help." He ripped off another paper towel and took a step closer. With gentle motions, he wiped off what must have been some lingering liquid from my cheek. I swallowed hard, unable to look away from his eyes. Thankfully, he was looking at the paper towel.

In my head, I was fighting the old battle of 'does he like me or doesn't he' against the backdrop of remembering I wasn't a teenager. I hadn't been in the dating world for over twenty years. And I certainly hadn't even thought about getting out there since the divorce. At least, not as far as seeing someone went. Getting out there as far as buying property in other countries? Sure. But attempting to connect with someone? No.

He lingered at my chin a moment longer than necessary, his eyes still following the paper towel. "Nell?"

I reached up and took the damp paper towel from him. His hand stayed in the air, and I wasn't sure which way he would move ... let it drop to his side, or reach out and touch me. "Yes?"

"Excuse me." Officer Hughes cleared his throat from the doorway. "I don't mean to interrupt, but we didn't find anything on the property. I asked a couple of the workers, but nobody has seen anything."

I wanted to yell at him for interrupting, but at the same time, I was glad he barged in. I was certain I would have made a complete spectacle of myself. More than I had already. "Nothing at all?"

He stepped forward and handed me a business card. "No, ma'am. But do not hesitate to ring us if you see anything more. And please, do not stay out here alone until the project is finished. Either way, be sure you lock the doors and windows."

I tucked the card in my pocket. "Thank you, Officer." I walked them out the front door, shaking their hands as they left.

When I returned to the kitchen, Reid was washing his mug out. His posture had changed. He wasn't giving off his usual, casual charm. Instead, he was a little rigid. When I entered the room, he wouldn't look at me.

I tested the change. "Did you want to head into your office and take a look at those other letters?"

He dried off his hands. "Actually, I have some work I need to finish up that I didn't get to this morning. How about I do that today and work on the seals? Maybe we can dive into them tomorrow?"

I stepped into his line of sight. "Did I make that much of a fool of myself?"

"No. Not at all." He took a step back. "I just ... I mean ... Will tomorrow work for you?"

"Sure." I tossed my hot chocolate into the sink, unsure why I was so affected by this guy. "Tomorrow will work fine. That will give me time to do some stuff around here."

His footsteps toward the door were abrupt and loud. "I'll, um, see you tomorrow. Eleven should work again."

"I'll try not to show up early again." I attempted to laugh it off.

He didn't react. He just left. And I stood there, completely dumbfounded as to what had just happened. Maybe he had picked up on my painfully obvious attraction, and it made him uncomfortable. I'd been in those situations. You know, where someone can't help but show you how they feel, but you don't feel the same for them? You just want to flee the situation ... fast.

I literally facepalmed myself, realizing that scenario was distinctly possible.

Five

Later that evening, after the crews had left, I picked up my phone and dialed Reid's number. I couldn't get his abrupt exit out of my head and the ensuing embarrassment that followed it. I wasn't sure I really wanted to face him the next day, even if it was to see what I could find about the whole Joshua and Cora romance. Instead, I figured it best to pretend I had something come up. That way, maybe I wouldn't look like I was eager to see him again. I just hoped it would allow for another day when things would be less awkward.

"Hello?" His voice was hoarse.

"Hello. Sorry to interrupt," I replied.

He cleared his throat. "You're not. I was just working. Probably good something pulled me out of it so I could remember to drink some water."

I was relieved he didn't seem as distant as he had earlier. "About tomorrow."

"About today," he interrupted me. "I'm sorry for my rude behavior."

"Rude?" I tried to play coy.

"Yes. When I left suddenly," he reminded me. "I felt a little like I was overstaying my welcome. I didn't mean to over step any boundaries."

I didn't know what to say. None of the scenarios that I ran through ever involved him feeling like he was on that end of things. "You didn't."

"Are you sure? I don't know why I thought it was okay to be so casual. It just felt..."

I finished his sentence. "Comfortable?"

"Exactly."

I stifled a giggle. "Reid, I was happy to have you here. It was I that made a complete fool of myself. You were a gentleman. Aside from me stumbling all over myself, it was a very pleasant visit ... as far as visits that start because one person is panicking over something ridiculous go."

There was a silence.

"Nell?" He sounded hesitant.

"Yes?"

"How would you like to get dinner with me?"

I couldn't fight the smile on my face. "Sure. Just let me know when you have time."

"I meant tonight."

"I, uh, I..." I was struggling to not blurt out my reply.

"If you're busy, that's fine. I don't want to intrude." He offered me a way out.

Realizing I probably sounded disinterested with my stammering, I responded, "Yes. I mean, no. I mean, I would love to meet you for dinner. I just need to finish up here before I can go back to my flat and shower."

"Are the crews still there?" he asked.

"No. They all left a little bit ago. I've just been cleaning up after them a little." I bent over and picked up a chunk of wood, carrying it over to the pile and tossing it on top.

"You're there alone?" He sounded concerned.

I had forgotten about that in the chaos of the day. "I am. And now that you bring it up, I should probably work a little faster."

"How about I just come out there?" he suggested.

I looked down at my dingy outfit. "I really need to shower."

"I'd rather you be safe than squeaky clean." His words were pointed. "How much more do you have to do? If you'd rather, just leave it and head into town before the sun sets here soon. I can join you tomorrow morning to finish before we come here to look over the letters."

I scanned the room, easily persuaded, feeling a bit nervous about being there by myself as the sun was starting to sink below the horizon. Aside from general cleanup, I had finished the bulk of my tasks. I grabbed my keys and purse and headed for my car.

"I'm leaving now." I got in and turned on the engine.

"Are you okay? Did something happen?" He sounded worried. "I thought you had more to do."

I felt silly. "Yeah. I know. But you reminding me about this morning, I got a little spooked."

"I said I could come out there."

I drove down the driveway and onto the road. "I know, but it would take you just as long to get here than it would for me to get finished. I'll just have to hold you to coming out with me in the morning."

"Promise." His tone lightened. "Would you like me to pick you up at your flat?"

"Where are we going? I don't want to put you out." I mentally inventoried what I had for clothes that didn't need to be washed.

"How about I surprise you? I'll be at your flat in an hour."

I sped up a little. "See you then."

Once there, I threw my keys and purse onto the couch and ran into the bathroom. The water wasn't even lukewarm before I jumped in, figuring it would be less uncomfortable than having him get there and me still be in a towel or without makeup.

I washed, dried, threw on an outfit and primped in record time. As I started to relax, seeing I had a few more minutes, I noticed that my apartment looked more like a bachelor pad than the flat of a responsible, mature woman. So, my adrenaline kicked back in as I rushed around to clean up.

I heard a knock on the door, and I stopped in my tracks. He didn't specifically say it was a date. So, I worked at not jumping to any conclusions. But, regardless, I still wanted to look nice, even if it was just a friends' outing. I smoothed out my clothes, checked the mirror that my eyeshadow was still in place and went to the door.

I opened it. "Hello."

"Hello." He grinned. "Ready?"

"Just let me get my purse." I left the door open.

He peeked in and looked around. "This is quite a difference from that large home out in the country."

I agreed, "Yeah. I wish I could buy this place as well and have both. The options are nice. If I want quiet and nature, I can go out there. If I want a little bit of city life and a little less to take care of, this place is nice." I followed him out the door, locking it behind me.

He opened the car door for me. "I never asked. The Webb estate is such a huge place. I take it you're not moving into it alone?"

I hadn't actually taken that into consideration; the fact that it was going to be just me in that place once it was done. Part of me felt a little guilty about it. Part of me flashed back to that moment in Manhattan that spurred my new adventure, when I sat in my townhouse feeling a loneliness that I had never felt before then.

"Nope. Just me." I resisted a shudder.

His expression revealed his shock. "That's right. I'm sorry. I heard about your divorce. But why come here and buy such an estate? Why not just get the flat? Then again, why make such a move?"

"I can't really answer that, Reid." I looked out the car window. "I had pretty much gotten myself into a rut. In Manhattan, it's easy to do and not realize since there's so much to do there. To most other places, the Manhattan life is full and active. But to someone living there, it's.."

"Strange, yet easy to have your life be active and full yet still slightly stagnant and routine?" He finished my sentence.

I looked back to him. "Exactly."

"I used to live in London. That is pretty much why I started my own business and moved out here." The street was crowded, but he found a space and put the car in park.

The storefront was elegant; a combination of old world charm with a splash of contemporary feel to it. I liked it ... a lot. Its walls and silver accents were inspiring for my plans for finishing the manor house.

The host took us to a table and handed us menus. Reid took mine and smiled. "I will order, if that is alright with you."

I placed my hands in my lap. "Certainly. I'm curious."

"Nothing strange. Sometimes, I just like to have a selection of toppas rather than an entire meal. Plus, it makes for a more interactive meal." He told the server our order, including a hot chocolate for each of us.

My cheeks flushed. "Hot chocolate, huh? I thought you wanted a drink."

"But you don't. So, I figured something far more tasty would be in order." He handed the menus to the server.

The server excused himself, and I leaned forward, resting my arms on the table. "I appreciate the gesture, but you don't have to go to such lengths to apologize."

"This isn't an apology. I did that over the phone." He looked humored.

"Then why all this?" I asked.

He shrugged. "Because I wanted to see you again."

I wasn't sure how to respond. Thankfully, the server returned with our beverages. "Your food will be out shortly."

"Thank you." I adjusted in my seat.

Reid's eyes were on me as I fidgeted with my silverware. "So, what do you plan to do with all that space and the smaller outbuildings once it is finished? Other than live in it, I suppose."

"I don't really know. I actually couldn't tell you why I bought it in the first place. I was looking for a vacation destination. You know, some place to get away for a little while. But I stumbled upon the sale listing. It was three in the morning, and I just picked up my phone and dialed the realtor." I snickered at myself.

He shook his head, like he was trying to wrap his head around the concept. "You mean to say that you just purchased a giant estate on a whim?"

I thought for a moment. "Yup. That's pretty much what I'm saying. I flew over that day, looked at it in person and signed papers. Two months later, it was mine. I've been working on it ever since."

"But why?" His eyebrows were pulled in, showing genuine confusion.

I shrugged. "I don't know. I just felt I needed to."

"You don't know?" He let out a laugh. "You bought a broken down old estate in another country, across an ocean, and you don't know why?"

I chewed my lower lip. "Pretty much."

He roared with laughter. "You are certainly one of a kind, Nell."

I crossed my arms. "Is that a good thing?"

"Yes." He quieted his laugh. "In my opinion? Yes it is. But tell me, are you telling the truth when you say you don't know what you're going to do with so much space and land?"

"Nope." I lifted my shoulder. "I have three kids, but they're all grown. I thought of designing three of the bedrooms in each of their styles so they would have a place to stay when they come visit. One room can be a workout room. One can be an extra spare bedroom. One can be ... I'm not sure. I guess maybe a crafting room?"

"Crafting, huh?" He set his napkin in his lap as the server set down our plates.

"Is there anything more you need?"

Reid inspected the dishes. "No. Thank you. We appear to be set."

"Do not hesitate to let me know if you do." The young man bowed his head and retreated to the kitchen.

Reid returned his attention to me as he dished some of each of the appetizers onto my plate. "I suppose it won't be too difficult to fill the rooms with things. But what about the land and the other buildings?"

"As far as the buildings near the main house, one is going to be storage. One of the smaller ones will be for landscaping and gardening supplies. Then, I've considered taking the cluster of smaller buildings on the far North side of the property and updating them. If I understand right from what Marion said, they were tenants' homes a couple hundred years ago. People who worked the land and in the mines lived in them?"

"Yes. I do believe that's correct," he said, taking a bite.

I finished chewing mine. "I believe there's six of them in decent shape. I was considering doing a writing program and renting them out after I remodel them."

"Rent them out?" He seemed shocked.

I kind of tossed my hands up a little. "Why not? I was thinking about creating a writers' retreat kind of rental space. Somewhere people from all over can come and spend some time in England, or a part they're not from, and do some writing. The countryside is absolutely gorgeous, and the atmosphere is truly inspiring."

"That it is." His eyes were wide.

I continued, "I thought I could do some short term residences for various things. But also offer rental options, when space permits, for those that want to come on their own dime but make it affordable."

He was looking at me with a smile that spoke of pride and awe. "That is a fantastic idea."

"Thank you." I grinned shyly. "Oh! You said you wanted to see me again. Did you forget something or think of some questions about the letters?"

He looked set back by my question. "No. I just wanted to see you again."

My brain was having trouble accepting what he was hinting at. I just sat, not saying anything, as he reached forward and touched my hand. I almost pulled back, but I held still, wanting so much to be able to accept that he might have similar affections toward me as I did him.

He ran his fingers over the back of my hand before lacing his fingers with mine. "I'm glad you came."

"Me, too." I stifled a squeal, repeating the mantra *you're an adult* over and over in my head.

The rest of the evening, we chatted about how he got into being a historian, by direction of his father, and why I became a writer. I told him about my kids, and he told me about his parents, of which, his mother had died when he was a boy. I didn't talk much about mine since my relationship with my mother was very strained. It wasn't a topic I was fond of, and he didn't pry.

Conversation flowed easily from topic to topic. We weaved in and out of serious subject matter to laughing over the smallest of thing. After four hours, he drove me back to my flat.

We got out of the car, and he walked me to my door. "Again, thank you for coming out tonight, Nell. Are we still on for the morning? I can pick you up at eight. Unless you think we will need more than a couple hours to wrap up what needs to be done out there before going into my office to start reviewing the letters."

My mind calculated the fact that I would probably not get much sleep that night, knowing I would just lay in bed thinking about him. Thinking about the fact that it had been so long since I felt anything like how I was feeling. Either way, eight was probably the safest bet. "Yeah. Eight. Eight sounds good."

"If you're up earlier, give me a ring. I'm usually up and at my desk by six," he said.

I grinned and pulled out my keys. "Will do."

He went back one step. "Until then?"

"Until then," I repeated.

We lingered, looking at each other for a long moment. Finally, he gave a slight wave. "Goodnight." He turned to walk away.

I stood and watched as he took a few steps down the path. Then, he turned and retraced his steps, faster than he'd left, this time, his strides having purpose. He climbed the two steps up to where I was standing, placed a hand on the back of my neck and looked at me just long enough for my breath to catch before placing a gentle kiss on my cheek.

He dropped his arms, turned and left, only looking back as he got into his car. I just stood, in awe, confused.

On the cheek? What was that? I had no idea. His hand on my neck and the look in his eyes spoke of one thing. But a kiss on the cheek said another. And I was at a loss as to how to interpret the combination of the two.

His car disappeared down the road amongst the slightly winding pavement, cars lining it and buildings that were connected one after another. A light breeze came up from the path he'd disappeared down, sending a slight chill down my arms. Speckled in goosebumps, I ran my hands over my skin and went inside.

Just as I'd figured, I didn't sleep much that night.

***

I rolled over and squeezed my eyes shut as I rolled into a beam of sunlight coming in through the window. Consciousness poked its holes through my sleep fog, and I realized it was morning. I reached over and snagged my phone off the side table.

7:45am

I jumped up and raced to the shower, texting him on the way. **I overslept. Getting in the shower now. The door is unlocked. Feel free to let yourself in. I won't be long.**

After turning on the faucet, I raced to the front door, unlocked it, started the coffee maker and bolted back to the bathroom. The concept that I so comfortably invited him into my home as I showered dawned on me, but it was done. I ignored the thought and focused on getting ready.

Twenty minutes later, I stepped out of the bathroom, my makeup done but drying my hair with a towel still. I hadn't gotten a response from Reid, so I figured I had time to grab a quick cup of coffee before finishing up.

"Good morning, cutie." Reid was sitting on the couch, flipping through the book of Yousuf Karsh photography that had been resting on my coffee table.

"Good morning." I tried to stay cool. "I see you got my text."

"Yes. Thank you. And don't worry. This book is rather fascinating. It's kept my attention quite well while waiting." He tipped the book up.

"He's one of my favorites." The pot was full. I poured us both a mug and brought out the cream and sugar. Holding one mug up toward him, I said, "Coffee? I'll only be a couple more minutes. Need to dry this mop before it starts to poof like a cotton ball."

He set the book down and joined me in the tiny kitchen. "Yes. Thank you very much. Did you sleep well?"

My breath caught as he pushed a strand of hair out of my eyes. "What little I slept? Yes."

"Are you up to being productive today?" The corner of his mouth turned up.

I yawned. "Yup. Sure am." No matter how little I had slept, something about being near him sent a surge through me that could probably keep me going for days.

He chuckled and nudged me in the side with his elbow. "Sure you are."

I headed back into the bathroom and ran the blow dryer over my hair long enough to be sure the frizz was contained, threw it up into a bun and checked my makeup. I cleaned up my things a little in case he asked to use the restroom before we left.

He called from the other room. "Do you have any thermoses so we can take these with us?"

"Under the microwave on the stand," I called back.

I heard him rustling around. He reached an arm in the door, keeping it shut so he couldn't see anything in case I wasn't decent. "Hand me yours?"

I did as he requested. "Thanks."

A few minutes later, we were on the road.

Conversation stayed light, and neither of us broached the subject of any sort of emotions. The weather, the beautiful morning sky, the history of the town, the fact that I hadn't ventured away from the estate and the village since I'd arrived (which he felt was something that needed to be remedied) ... those were the topics of the morning, well into getting started on everything for cleanup.

About ten, the crews were all focused on their work. We'd created more than a dent in the cleanup, and I was enjoying washing my hands in one of the newly installed bathrooms on the main floor. The drywall was still to be hung, and the floor still needed to be laid, but the sink, toilet and tub were all in place. I'd pulled a towel, soap and one décor item out of one of the boxes I'd already moved in for days like that, happy to give them a home in the half-completed bathroom.

Reid came in to wash his hands as well, nudging me softly with his hip as he slipped his hands under the water with mine. "Would you like to take a walk?"

"You sure we have time?" I asked.

He dried his hands and handed me the towel. "Yes. And I'd very much like to if you'd join me."

I placed the towel back on the side of the sink. "Sure. A walk sounds nice."

We checked in on Gerald to be sure that everything was set before we stepped outside. Exiting the door out the back of the kitchen, Reid slipped his hand in mine as we started for the garden behind the house.

He breathed in the warm, summer air. "Have you any regrets about moving across an ocean and taking on such a huge project?"

It wasn't a question I expected. "No." The reply came without me even having to think about it. "I think I needed to do this."

"Oh?" He let me pass first as we walked between a set of border hedges.

"No," I repeated. "Really. I actually asked myself, not long ago, why I felt that I needed to take on something like this at the same time as such major changes were going on in my life."

He looked over at me, curiosity obvious in his eyes. "Did you have an answer for yourself?"

"I think so?" I chewed the inside of my lip.

He laughed. "You think so, huh?"

"Yeah," I replied distractedly. Shaking my head, I explained, "For a few years, I've kind of distanced myself from everyone without really noticing I was doing it. My kids and I are still close. I actually talk to at least one of them every day."

"It must be fantastic to have a close relationship with them after not having one with your own mother. How many kids did you say you have?" he asked.

I smiled. "Three. You?"

"None. I spent too much time with my nose down in my work that I never even married." He guided me over a large root.

I went on. "Well, I was married. Last year, just after our youngest moved away for college, he came home and said he was in love with someone else."

"Ouch." He cringed.

"Actually," I stopped walking, "I didn't feel anything."

He looked puzzled. "Nothing?"

I pointed to a nearby path that led out of the garden, and we headed there. "Not *nothing*. But I wasn't heartbroken. I wasn't even scared of the change. It was then that I realized that, obviously, the marriage *must* be over. And in the following months, neither of us second guessed it. We simply split up our property, money and investments."

"So, everything went smoothly?" He guided me toward the back of the rock wall.

I took a seat on top of it, allowing my legs to dangle. "Actually, yes. We're still friends. His new relationship seems very fitting for him. It wasn't that we were bad for each other or anything. We actually worked really well around each other. But that's the thing, we were functioning around each other. Not with each other. We were more like the perfect roommates. Not husband and wife."

He gave an approving nod. "Sounds like you both made the right choice to allow yourselves to find something more."

"Exactly." I shrugged.

"But what about all this? How did this come about?" He motioned toward the house. "Certainly, it wasn't as simple as a mid-night, spontaneous decision."

"Ah. Yes. *This*." I thought back to the night my ex carried out the last of his belongings. "The day Sam finished moving his things out of our townhouse in Manhattan, I sat down at the kitchen table. Suddenly, I felt alone. Mind you, I'd been distancing myself from most people for a few years. Feeling alone when you've got people around is one thing. But looking around your own home after you had kids and a husband all living there with you, and you suddenly realize they've all gone and moved out to carry on their lives elsewhere and with other people? There's a sense of loneliness that buries its way down into your soul."

I kicked my feet, feeling a bit over dramatic. "Well, anyway, that night, like I said before, I thought maybe I'd take a vacation over here somewhere. But instead of finding a vacation destination, I stumbled on to the listing of this place. It was about three in the morning, and I simply picked up my phone, dialed Marion, organized a meeting to see it and booked a flight within twenty minutes."

He blinked. "So, you did just jump on a plane and flew over? Just like that?"

"Yup." I knew how foolish it sounded. I'd had that thought myself. "I honestly don't know why, but I felt compelled to do it. I felt pulled."

"Pulled, huh?" He eyed me, trying to figure me out.

"So, yeah," I went on. "I think something about giving this estate a new life is representative of giving myself one. You know? Like it's my chance to wake back up to the world and feel whole and beautiful and of some use again. I think I lost sight of all of that within myself over the last few years."

He stepped in front of me, my knees on either side of his waist. "Nell, you do not lack in the being beautiful department, inside or out."

I pleasantly shivered as he put his hands on my hips. "Thank you." My voice came out soft and quiet.

"But I understand what you mean. And I think it's brilliant." He rested his forehead against mine and closed his eyes. "I understand the feeling of being pulled."

"You do?" My words caught in my throat.

"Yes." He stepped back, leaving me almost falling forward. "You. I can't help but feel drawn to you in a way I've never felt before. It takes everything I have not to let myself fall into it. And we've only just met." He started walking away along the wall.

I let myself down and followed him. "Is that why you keep getting so close then pulling away so abruptly?"

He didn't reply. He just kept walking.

"Hey!" I shouted after him, falling behind slightly since his strides were much longer than my own. "Why are you so afraid of me?"

He stopped and looked down. “I’m not afraid of *you*.”

I caught up and put a hand on his shoulder. “Then what?”

He turned, worry pulling at his expression. “Remember how I told you that my mother died when I was young?”

“Yes.” I pulled my hand back, giving him room to speak.

He closed his eyes for a moment before replying. “I watched my father struggle with her loss. He still does. As much as love is supposed to be this fantastic and brilliant thing, all I know is that losing it is the most painful thing. Whether it be the death of someone you love or the split of a relationship you weren’t ready to have end. It doesn't matter. I’ve seen friends get divorced, cheated on, left for various reasons. My father’s fight against despair without my mother was scary. And the idea of letting someone that close to affect me that much? I’ve never been able to let myself. I simply don't know if I want to chance my ability to make it through such pain. No. I don’t know what it feels like. But after seeing people I care about go through it, I don’t ever want to. But you. You make me question that. You make me want to take that risk.”

I was completely set back by his response. And I couldn’t fault him for the way he saw it. Not at all. While I was busy spending my life not feeling enough, he spent his days feeling so much more.

We both stood there, thoughts racing, looking at each other. Neither of us knowing what to say next. Then, he took a step forward, closing the gap between us, placed both hands on the sides of my face, pressed himself against the length of my body and kissed me. It wasn’t on the cheek. And it wasn’t soft. His lips met mine revealing a level of passion that had been locked up behind an iron gate inside him, fiercely wanting to get out.

I placed my hands on his back and pulled myself into him. He slid his hands down my sides, lifted me up and set me on top of the wall, his lips never parting from mine. My legs wrapped around him, pulling him in closer. His lips made their way down over my jawline, eagerly kissing my neck to my collarbone as his hands glided up my back. I tilted my head, allowing him more of my neck, opening my eyes slightly while trying to contain the feeling that I was going to burst.

Then I saw it - a shadowy figure along the tree line on the back of the property. I sat up, almost pushing him away.

I didn't see the startled look that must have covered his face, but I heard it in his voice. "I'm sorry. I didn't..."

"No." I was still searching the trees. "He was there."

"Who?"

I tuned back, realizing I must have been confusing him. "Oh lord. I'm so sorry. No. Back there." I pointed. "I swear I saw someone."

He looked back. "Like a person without features? More like a shadow? But it was too quick to know for sure if you saw something?"

"Yes. I mean, no." I paused to gather myself. "Yes, like a shadowy figure. But no; he lingered. He was there. I saw him there long enough to *know*. I couldn't see his face, but I swear he was looking at us."

He broke physical contact with me. "I should go look."

I grabbed his arm, hopping off the wall. "Wait."

Something hit the back of my leg, and I jumped. We both looked down and saw a stone had fallen out of the wall. It was marked with an "X". Then, we both saw the corner of a letter that was lying in the space that the rock had just fallen out of.

Reid went rigid as he touched my arm. "Stay right here."

I watched as he ran for the tree line. A minute later, Gerald came running out of the house. "You okay, ma'am? I saw Mr. Wilkinson take off for the woods."

I just stood and scanned the property line.

"Nell?" Gerald was in front of me. When I didn't respond, he touched my arm in the same place Reid just had. "Nell! What is going on?"

It was as if when Reid touched me, it put me on pause; Gerald pressed play. I turned and pulled the letter out of the wall and held it out.

"It looks very old," he observed. "What do they say?"

I made eye contact. "That's the strangest part. There's been one every day since Friday, and they're written by some guy in the eighteen hundreds to a woman he was in love with. They were supposed to run away together against her parents' wishes, but she apparently never showed."

"I would have to agree. That is strange," he said.

The winds picked up, and I pulled the letter into me. "But that's the thing. That's not even the strangest part. First: I've checked after the last couple letters to be sure that there was nothing more in there. But every day, there has been. Second: there's been a couple times we have seen a shadowy figure just outside the trees. Reid saw it yesterday, and I just saw it today. That's what he's looking for. Third: Reid is a direct descendent of this Joshua guy. Plus, he has other letters his family has kind of passed on through the generations, but nobody has looked through, really. We were going to be going into his office here shortly to start reading through them to see if we could piece together more about Joshua and Cora - the woman he's writing to. But the fact that the letters keep coming is making things a little more than strange."

"Okay. I can see how you're a little less than gathered over this. I think I should go help him look around a bit." Gerald started walking away.

But Reid was on his way back.

I asked. "Have you seen anyone around out this way?"

He thought for a moment. "To be honest, I've not kept a diligent watch or anything. But thinking about it, I can't say that I have. Everyone, aside from my brothers and I, have worked inside. And I know your neighbors. To the South, Mr. Crandall is in town living in a nursing home. His house is going through the courts for which of his children are going to get it.

"To the North, there's a couple miles past your smaller village homes before the Pearl family estate. That has been in their family for several generations. They're in their thirties with three young children. I can't imagine any of them would being doing this.

"To the East? There's the wooded area that is part of your land. It goes back for a few acres. But then, on the other side is the back end of the Adams estate. They have quite the substantial amount of land there they use to farm various crops. He is married, and they have two teenage children. But their house is quite a distance across an open field."

I finished the area's verbal tour. "And to the West, there's the small bit of land owned by the government then the cliffs and the ocean."

"More or less." He held his hand out to Reid as he approached. "Mr. Wilkinson. I'm Gerald, lead of Ms. Price's general work crew her at the estate."

Reid shook his hand. "Nice to meet you. Has she been filling you in on what's going on here?"

"Yes. She has. I was just going over who her neighbors are. I can't honestly think of anyone nearby that would be doing this. Nor have I seen any of the crews here coming outside. Not near the rock wall, anyway. It is, indeed, a very peculiar situation," Gerald explained.

"I see." Reid saw what was in my hand, reaching out to take the letter and looking it over. "I think it best for us to head back in to my office and take a look."

Gerald excused himself as Reid bent down to inspect the hole in the wall. Standing, he replaced the rock. I reached out and took the letter back, glancing back to the trees as we started walking.

As we came near the house, Gerald called out from the back door, "I should get back in and make sure everyone is on task. I will let you know if I see anyone lurking around."

"Thank you, Gerald." I waved.

Neither Reid or I spoke much on the drive back. I pulled my legs up and wrapped my arms around my knees, staring out the window. Part of me was scared, yes. There was someone leaving letters in my wall that appeared to have been written about a hundred and fifty years prior. Why? What possibly could be their motive? But, on the other hand, I couldn't explain what else I was feeling about it all. It was a mystery. It was romance. It was sucking me in, and I had no idea why I was so determined to find out more.

Reid walked to the kitchen. "What would you like to drink?"

"Just a water, please. I definitely do *not* need anything with caffeine," I called back.

He came back into the dining room a moment later with a bottle of water and a mug of coffee. He handed me the water and sat down next to me. "So, do we open today's letter first, or do we start organizing the others in order to read them?"

I bee-lined it to the newest letter. "Oh. We need to see what this one says for sure."

We sat at the table, and he pulled his chair over next to mine. Carefully, just as we had with the others, he removed the wax seal just enough to open the folds. Slowly, he pressed flat the page, and we leaned in.

20th of June, 1867
Dear Cora,

Yesterday, I saw a woman at the wall as I passed by it. I hoped with all my might that it would have been you to leave me a message. Alas, when I returned to it later on to check, there was no letter.

I know that I said I would work on letting you go. But until I know that you are safe, I cannot.

Please, just tell me that you are safe. I need to know.

I love you.

Yours Truly & Forever,
Joshua

My eyes were filled with tears again as I finished the short plea, and my heart broke for him. "What could make someone do such a callous thing like leave their lover worried half to death about you?"

I could see he was a little caught up in the emotion of it. He leaned back in his chair and took a long, deep breath. "Well, it still could be anything. For all we know, her family may have whisked her away to break them apart."

"You're right." I gathered my composure.

He slid the box of letters over in front of us. "Shall we start going through these and see if they say anything? I don't know if they're all from him or a mix; if they're all to her or others. It has been a number of years since I have gone through them, and my father didn't seem to act like he found them of any importance."

I reached in and grabbed a couple. "I say we take a look! Let's go through them and sort out the ones that do not pertain to this situation. Then, we can put them in chronological order."

"Sounds like a plan." He took a small stack out and placed it in front of himself.

We spent the next forty-five minutes sorting and stacking each of the letters. The aged papers mirrored those of the ones I'd been finding. Most were from Joshua. However, we found a few from Cora, one from who we assumed might be Cora's father, Bernard Webb, and a couple from a man named Clive Brown. As far as those from

Joshua, I noticed that, yes, most were to Cora. But one was for Clive.

After arranging them in order by date, we tucked in the additional letters from other people into the timeline, turning them sideways. I reached into the box to be sure we hadn't missed anything. Satisfied that we had retrieved them all, I set the box back, out of the way.

"Are you ready?" He grinned.

Anxiety was creeping in. "Very. I need to know more."

"Alright then." He picked up the first one. "Let's get started.

He read it out loud as I followed along on the page.

10th of February, 1867
Dear Miss Cora Webb,

Hello,

I write this as the sun is rising, and my thoughts are still lingering on memories of the ball just hours ago. Meeting you last night, as I rarely do social engagements such as those, was a blessing. I had a rather enjoyable time and was disappointed when I had to relinquish your attentions for you to leave.

I would like to invite you to my home for dinner in one week. I will be having a gathering of sorts for friends and family. It would make me very happy to not only see you again but have the honor of calling you my companion for the evening, as well as have the chance to get to know you more.

I look forward to receiving your reply and hope you share the same sentiment.

Sincerely,
Mr. Joshua Wilkinson

He set the letter down, and we both sat, letting our eyes wander over the page, rereading bits again. Finally, I spoke. "That was a lot more formal."

"It's sweet," he added.

"Yes."

"They met only a few months prior, it seems, according to the date on this letter and the ones you found." He pointed to the top of the page. "They met in February that year and were running away to be married in June."

I compared the two dates in my mine. "Four months. That is fast."

"Can't help who or how you fall in love, no?" He was already reaching for the next letter.

12th of February, 1867
Dear Miss Cora Webb,

Good day,

I received your response to my invitation and am elated that you will be able to make it. I look forward to seeing your beautiful eyes and hearing your angelic voice once again.

Until Then,
Mr. Joshua Wilkinson

Again, we sat, contemplating the contents of the second letter.

He picked up the next one. Only, it wasn't from Joshua. It was from Cora. Her handwriting was very elegant. Her penmanship along with the way she worded things showed evidence that she was from very good breeding. I figured she must have been educated in both academic fields as well as etiquette. A picture of this young woman started to form in my mind.

This time, I read the letter aloud as he followed along.

18th of February, 1867
My Dear Joshua,

Good day my kind sir,

I awoke this morning with a smile. At the risk of being too bold, I have to admit, the sun was brighter. The birds were happier. The grass was greener. Or, quite possibly, I simply was seeing things in a brighter light having spent the previous evening with you.

To be formal, thank you for the invitation and your hospitality to your little gathering in your home. It was delightful and rather enjoyable. You are a wonderful host.

To be bold once again, I very much enjoyed seeing you, and it was an honour to be your companion for your dinner gathering. I am not sure which was more pleasurable. The delicious foods you served or your company.

As to what you asked of me before I departed, yes. I would be honoured to accompany you Saturday. I very much enjoy the library. I understand that Mr. Lewis Carroll is in town, making some rounds, reading some of his works. It would be just lovely if he were to be there that day.

Until Then,
Miss Cora Webb

One corner of my mouth lifted as I set the letter onto the table.

Reid tilted his head to see my expression. "What is on your mind?"

"You can tell she comes from money," I replied.

He pursed his lips. "How so?"

I pointed to the spot in the letter about her wishful thinking in regards to seeing Lewis Carroll. "There. She is hoping to get something more out of his invitation than the pleasure of his company, which is, incidentally, what he is hoping she would be focusing on. Instead, she's expressing her eagerness to see someone else."

"I don't think she meant it in that regard," he countered.

Realizing how that sounded, I waved my hand. "No. I didn't mean to imply she wanted to see him *because* he's another man. I just meant that she took the focus off him. It's just ... well ... it was a little insensitive."

He squinted at the page. "Okay. I can see that."

"I'm not saying she's shallow. I just felt that was rude."

He smirked. "Fair enough. I think I see your point."

"So, want to read the next one?" I lifted it from the pile.

"No," I blurted out.

His eyes grew wide. "No?"

"No. I don't think so."

"Did you want me to read it?" he asked.

"No."

"Why not?" He pushed the stack of letters back.

I turned in my chair to face him. "I don't get it."

"Don't get what?"

I picked up the most recent letter and scanned it. "This. The fact that letters are showing up daily. I don't understand. And it really has me unsettled."

He put a hand on my knee. "You're right. I have been more wrapped up in the content of the letters than seeing how their coming daily is, in fact, very strange, indeed."

"Part of me has, too. It's been exciting getting to delve into this romantic mystery. Especially knowing they were real people, and you're related to one of them. But why do they keep coming? Who keeps putting them there? And what was it I saw out there today; that you saw yesterday?"

I felt myself rambling. "I'm sorry. I'll stop. I am just unnerved about it … or, at least, I feel like I should be."

"Like you should be?" He started running his hands up and down the tops of my thighs comfortingly.

"Yes. Someone is putting them there. You saw it was empty, but there was another one today. I don't know how to explain that."

He stopped his hands at my knees. "But you said that you don't feel like you're as concerned as you should be. What do you mean?"

I wasn't sure how to put it exactly, so I just let words flow. "I should be in a panic, shouldn't I? I mean, someone is putting letters from a man in the eighteen hundreds in the wall on my property. I don't know how. Hell. I don't even know why. Meanwhile, we've both seen this shadowy figure back by the trees. It was one thing when it was possibly a random person doing this. That was confusing and worrisome enough, but it kept everything bundled into one big irritating yet tolerable issue. But then, I saw it. I *saw* it, Reid. It didn't have human features; just a human shape. And I can't make sense of it all."

"I want to say that we will figure this out. I want to tell you that there's nothing to worry about. But the truth is, I don't have a clue." His shoulders slumped. "I am just as puzzled as you are about all of this."

"Nothing adds up." I leaned forward and laid my head on his shoulder.

He moved his chair over closer to mine and wrapped his arms around me. "I can say this: I don't think this is some neighbor or random person trying to scare you."

"Why? What makes you rule that out so easily?" I asked.

He tilted my chin up and looked into my eyes. "Nell, I'm not usually very into spiritual things. I probably more lean toward science and things I can see proof of that are tangible. But that's the thing with this situation. The proof points toward something less than *normal*."

He shuffled some of the letters around. "How is it that you came across these? I don't know. I don't know who is putting them there. But, it's strange to think that you stumbled upon the rock that the letter was behind; that you wanted to work on that wall when there was so much more to do. Then, how you were directed to me out of all of the places you could have sought out to find information. Plus, this shadowy figure? It all seems rather coincidental. It is actually bordering on spooky."

"I agree. And, yes, I've considered that there's something more going on here. But what?" I was getting frustrated with speculating but still coming up empty handed as far as answers.

"I do not know." He ran his hand over my hair.

"And what now?" I feared the answer to my question.

The sun had made its way across the sky and was starting to come through his window. "We wait. No matter if it is someone trying to scare you or something a bit more paranormal, it won't be over, right? There'll be something more I would think. So, we wait to see what comes next."

I sat up. "That feels like we're not doing anything."

"Yes. But, obviously, there's not a lot we can do. There's nothing really to be done." He stacked the letters we'd read into a second pile and pushed them back.

"You're right." I squeezed my eyes shut. "I just feel like we're missing something. Or that we're supposed to be seeing something or know something. *Something*!"

A scraping sound pulled me back as he turned his chair across the wooden floor. "But we are not seeing it, or we do not know whatever it is. But I can feel that whatever it is, it will come to us."

"Right." I sounded defeated.

"Nell?" He took my hands. "I know this is bothering you. But whatever is going on, I'm glad it is."

"You are?" I looked up at him.

The tension of the conversation left his face, and a grin started to form. "Yes. Because of all of this, I met you."

I felt like a complete jerk. I had been so busy trying to damn the events in my mind and fearing that it was something ominous, but he was obviously seeing all of it as something fortuitous or even serendipitous. He saw it as a blessing, and by the look on his face, he wished I did as well.

"Will you promise me something?" I did my best to shirk off my tense stance.

He picked up his mug. "I'd consider it."

"Promise me that you will help me figure this out?" I grabbed my empty bottle and followed him into the kitchen.

He handed me a full water before emptying the pot into his mug. "Of course."

"So ... what now?" We walked back to the table. His hand brushed my lower back as I sat, sending shivers through me.

"I suppose we can work on going through these and seeing why their love was so forbidden."

I nodded, almost giggling at myself. I felt more than a little over dramatic. "That makes sense." Switching my brain over from the mystery of where the letters were coming from to the mystery of their love story was a welcome change.

We spent the next couple of hours unfolding and reading. Joshua and Cora had written virtually every single day. Some were longer. Some were shorter. And after they started proclaiming their love of one another, Cora would sometimes send a simple, *I Love You*.

To which, Joshua would send a reply letter to each of hers that simply stated, *With All My Heart*.

At the very least, she would add her *I Love You*, and he would add his *With All My Heart* to their signature lines. And those few, tiny words would put such meaning behind their correspondences to each other. A depth.

With all my heart ... a line that probably would hit me hard for the rest of my life. This man, in a time when *men were men*, and it was commonplace to be a physical disciplinarian of your loved ones, was so tender and so romantic. It wasn't difficult to see that he meant it ... *with all his heart*.

Sometimes, as I read, I would catch Reid watching me, his eyes gentle and a slight smile on his lips. I would do my best to not allow my excitement to flood my face. But, sometimes, I couldn't help it.

Eventually, Joshua and Cora's conversations turned to a more serious matter. Marriage. A part of me wished that their proposal would have happened on the page, but that was just wishful thinking. I mean, of course he did it in person, and we only got a glimpse of it in writing.

27th of May, 1867
My Dear Joshua,

I have been up all night. The sheer excitement of the future has me slightly more than elated. Soon, to have the honour of being called Mrs. Joshua Wilkinson. It has a ring to it that makes my heart sing.

You have made me believe in true love, and I cannot wait to start this life together with you.

Tomorrow, we can tell my parents. I know my father has always strove to ensure I have been happy. I have no doubt that he will give us his blessing. I will tell them at breakfast of your calling. Do not fret their cold nature that you've been subjected to. That is simply their way. Once they see the joy you've brought me, I cannot think anything other than their open-arm nature will be extended to you.

Until Then,
I Love You,
Cora

I quickly reached over and started on the next letter. It was from Joshua.

28th of May, 1867
Cora, My Love,

I sincerely apologize for how things painfully transverse from the original plans during our meeting with your parents. Making him as clearly upset as he was, was not my intention. I, just as you, truly believed they would give us their blessing.

Sadly, this is not the case.

At this time, I am unsure what to do. I do not understand why they refuse. On the same lines, I do not want to do anything to tarnish your reputation. I simply want to make you happy.

So, please, as difficult as it may be, if you need to let me go, do. I, in no way, want to cause you or your family strife. But if there is a way to convince your father to change his mind, I will do it.

Please, Cora, just tell me what to do to make this right.

Yours Truly & Forever,
With All My heart,
Joshua

I was frustrated. Not only because I was angry that Cora's father was so cruel as to not allow them to be together, but the letter from Joshua didn't reveal anything in regards to the reason.

I almost speed read through the next several correspondences. It seemed they were writing two to three times a day for the next few days. Mostly, they were just expressing their love for each other and that no matter how she begged, Bernard refused to be swayed. But I saw nothing of what happened to make her father's decisions so absolute.

Reid started rubbing my back after returning with a fresh bottle of water. "Nell, maybe you need a break?"

"I *need* to know." I picked up the next letter.

Staring at the words, my eyes were blurry, and I tried to rub them back into focus. My shoulders dropped, and I set the paper on the table.

He sat down, picked it up and read it aloud.

2nd of June, 1867
Cora, My Love,

Your father's unwavering refusal to allow us to marry has come with a heavy weight. In the midst of it all, I hadn't even thought to wonder why other than a simple dislike of my character. To be honest, that is not a far reach for conclusion. He and I are very different creatures, and I am convinced that if it were not for you in our lives, we would never have been cordial acquaintances.

Yet, my good friend, Clive, has come to me with information. He has come to learn that your father has been extending the knowledge of our love and our longing to be married to others in town. Not only that. He has been loose of lip in telling some that his reasons are not only because he does not care for me. He also states that I do not have enough fortune to tempt him into letting you go.

What is worse, he talks about my late wife and how her death has left me with a son to raise on my own. And, according to Clive, his words reveal a contempt for my situation. I do believe that he feels that you mustn't marry me, if for no other reason than that any wealth our children may be in line to inherent through either myself or your family estate would go to my first son, and he cannot stand for this.

In light of now knowing why he refuses to give us his blessing, I cannot bring myself to care about his feelings any longer. However, if his unhappiness is of great consequence to you, I will respect that. For you. Not for him. My only concern at this point is for you. And I propose we leave town and get married elsewhere. Then, once it is done, we can return to my home and hope they learn to accept us.

I anxiously await your response.

Yours Truly & Forever,
With All My heart,
Joshua

"That bastard!" I blurted.

Reid set the letter aside and crossed his arms. He didn't say anything. He just sat there.

"How can he do that? How can he deny them a happy life together for such frivolous reasons?" I was furious.

"But they were not frivolous reasons back then, Nell." Reid's jaw was set.

I was stunned by his response. "So, you side with Bernard?"

"No!" He almost hissed the word. "That bastard looked down upon my ancestor simply because of circumstance. Not because of character. That simply is bollucks!"

I rested my head in my hands. "Okay. So Joshua had a son, and he wasn't as wealthy as the Webbs were."

"Right," he agreed.

"Well? We might as well read the rest." I picked up the next on the diminishing stack.

"Are you sure you don't need to rest?" He leaned back in his chair, half amused.

I picked up the next letter and looked at him, determination set in my eyes. "There's only a few more."

Just as I suspected, Cora was unsure about eloping. The several letters that followed were the two of them going back and forth until they both came to rest on the decision to do it. They were going to run off and get married. We read along as they planned it all out and started to get very excited.

Then, Reid picked up the next one on top and looked at it curiously.

I touched his arm. "What is that?"

"It's the letter from Clive to Joshua." He just sat with it in his hand.

I pressed my fingers into his forearm, squeezing it slightly to try to get his attention. "Are you going to read it?"

"Huh?" He blinked. "Oh. Yes."

12th of June, 1867
Joshua,

Joshua, you have always been my best friend. Ever since we were seven years old, and you pulled me back away from the edge of the cliffs when I was trying too hard to see over, probably saving me from my own curiosity and possible death. I vowed right then to always be there for you whenever you need me.

I find it brilliant that you have found love again. I knew how it nearly ruined you when you lost Katherine. However, running off with the Webb daughter, their only heir, just may be a dangerous decision. I know that Mr. Webb is a stubborn man that is used to getting his way in all things he pleases. I wouldn't want to see to what lengths he may go to get things to go his way in this regard.

I know you well enough to know that you will do as you will do. However, I implore you to be sure you are prepared to reap whatever your decisions sow. By all means, be sure this woman is worth everything you are risking.

You still have a son to bear in mind. He is counting on you. Not to provide a mother but to provide a home, clothing, food and love. Do not risk that lightly.

Yet, if you decide to go through with this, yes, I would be honoured to go with you both on your venture and stand by you on your wedding day.

Your Friend
Clive Brown

I finally let out my breath. "Do you think..."

"...that Bernard had something to do with Cora not showing? Absolutely. Have we not speculated that all along?" His eyes were searching the document.

"Right. True. That jerk must have taken pretty extreme measures to convince Cora not to go with Joshua." I stomped off to the kitchen to throw away my empty bottle, making a quick stop by the bathroom.

When I returned, Reid was standing at the window, looking out, arms back to being crossed. I walked up behind him and set my hands on his back. He was tense, almost rigid.

I leaned my cheek on his shoulder. "You okay?"

"I just do not understand." His fingers tightened on his biceps. "If it isn't the people in love messing it up, there always seems to be someone on the outside that's standing ready, ticket in hand."

"That's not true," I countered. "Not every couple gets spoiled. Some make it happily."

"Rarely." He stayed firm.

I couldn't argue. It seemed like that was the case. More so in modern days than ever before. At least, back in their time, when two people got married, they honored the 'til death do us part concept. Not anymore, though. Divorces seemed more frequent than falling leaves on a windy autumn day in a forest. It was something I could attest to personally after all.

"I wish I could say something to ease your mind, but I do know some make it. Even for those that don't, many of us would never trade in the good times to avoid the bad ones." I tugged on his arm until he gave in and sat back down. I continued, "Yes. My marriage is over. And, no, not every day was a beautiful experience. But I would never give up what we had to not have to go through the rest. I wouldn't wish to not have my kids. And I certainly wouldn't want to risk being where I am today just to not have to go through it all ... to not be here with you."

I could see that a crack had formed in his steel wall, but he was doing his best to patch it up, with no luck. It was spidering, and I was getting through to him. However, knowing the concept of overloading a person, I chose to back off for a bit. I didn't want to push too hard to try to get him to let me in and end up on the other side of a second layer instead.

I passed him his mug. "Here. Let's go through the last few."

He took a sip. "Sounds good."

The remaining correspondences consisted of them planning out their escape and who would be involved in making it all happen. Of course, Cora wavered slightly a couple of times, wanting so badly to figure out how to get her parents to come around, but no matter what she tried, it seemed her replies to Joshua were filled with failed attempts.

Finally, we were back to where we started - with the first letter I had found only a few days before. That, and it was dark out. We had spent the day reading them all. But we finally had our answers. Not that we felt better about the situation or anything.

Seven

Despite Reid's continued attempts at holding me as far away from his emotions as possible, that night, I stayed at his place with him, by his request. I didn't allow things to go too far, but we both were more than happy to be in each other's arms that night.

Both of us were obviously fighting the very scary step of letting the other in. However, we both were, even more obviously, struggling with keeping the other out as well. It was a tug of war. And the part I know I feared most? That was the fact that no matter what I was battling at any point, he was finding his way to my heart regardless. Lying there that night, I could feel that his struggle mirrored mine.

The next morning, he had a meeting to attend at the local university about some relics that had come in for display. I made my way back out to the manor to check on the progress.

So much had been done. As I looked around, I started feeling like I was neglecting doing my part. I picked up a trash bag and started cleaning up whatever trash I could find, which wasn't much. Things had been taken care of for the most part.

On the second level, I found Gerald doing the same. "Hey! This is amazing, Gerald. These crews really know what they're doing! Thank you."

He tied his bag shut and pulled an empty one out of his pocket. "I'm glad you approve. They're great to work with as well. Clean, respectful and well worth what they charge."

"Yes," I agreed. "Thank you for recommending them."

"Absolutely no problem, Nell."

I smiled that he used my first name without prompting. "You know, I don't know how I could have possibly gotten this far without you. You've been a godsend."

He picked up the full bag and patted my shoulder. "That is why I am here. We all have our purpose in life."

I nodded as he passed me and headed down the stairs. Something about the way he said such a simple statement stuck with me.

We all have our purpose in life.

I suppose, in our own ways, yes, we do. But that wasn't what glued itself to the inside of my thoughts. It was something about the way it seemed to pertain to him. And not just him in general, but his presence in my life.

Gerald was one of the first people I met when I arrived in England. I went right from the airport to the estate to meet up with the realtor. We were to meet in town at Red Shield petrol station. I was going to follow her out there. However, she had been delayed.

Feeling slightly peckish, I had gone inside and purchased a couple snacks and a bottle of water, taking a seat in the grass next to the station. I'd been reading a book for about twenty minutes, well long enough to be lost in its world of far away lands and struggling love, that I was startled when a man walked up and placed a hand on my shoulder.

I nearly dropped my book. "Hello?"

"Are you alright, miss?" he inquired. "I called out to you, but you were not responding."

I looked around me. "Yes. I am fine. Thank you."

I tried to go back to reading in an attempt to signal to the stranger that I wasn't interested in conversing any longer. It was, after all, a very New York kind of thing to do. Well, American, really. But he was a little more concerned about my safety than I had realized.

"Is your vehicle broke down? Maybe it is something I can help with?" He stood upright and took a step back.

Admittedly, I was a little taken back by his offer. "No. It's fine. It's actually a rental. I'm supposed to be meeting with a realtor to go out and see about an estate a few miles out of town."

He smiled. "Miles, huh? Well, you wouldn't happen to be coming to look at that broken down, old manor house and property just outside of town, would you?"

He was right, but it must have been a little obvious. It wasn't like the nearest town was a very large one. "Yes. That I am."

He let out a chuckle and handed me a business card. "My name is Gerald Brown. I, and my brothers, do various maintenance jobs as well as landscaping. Marion - I presume that is who you are waiting to meet with - has used us regularly to do small jobs around there. I tell her that there's no use with as bad as that property is at the moment."

"That bad?" I started imagining the worst and wondering if I had just wasted my time by flying all the way there so spontaneously.

"It is not pretty, my dear." He thought for a moment. "But with the right person, it could be fantastic once again."

I felt a little defeated. "Well, thank you," I glanced at the card. "Gerald."

He tipped his hat and started walking away. Before getting into his truck, he called out, "Marion is usually an average of forty-five minutes late for every appointment, just so you are aware."

"Thank you!" I called back.

As he pulled away, he tipped his hat once again and gave me a warm smile. I picked my book back up and settled in. If he was correct, I had another twenty minutes to wait.

Sure enough, just about forty-five minutes after the time we had set up, Marion drove into the petrol station parking lot. She apologized profusely as she ushered me into her car, explaining that because of her tardiness, she didn't feel I should have to spend the funds on petrol for the drive.

As we pulled up the long driveway and the house came into view, I was instantly in love. I didn't see a sunken roof or the deteriorating layers of brick mortar. I saw a magnificent home that would light up the area and bring a sense of awe to the eyes of its viewers.

"I'll take it. How fast can we push the paperwork through?" I handed her the signed document to start the process before she could even inquire.

"Ummm ..." She stumbled over her words. "I'll see what I can do."

"Gerald." I pulled out the man's business card. "Gerald Brown. Is he someone I can trust to not only do a good job but also a safe person to be around?"

"Oh yes," she replied as if she was shocked I'd even ask.

"And his brothers?"

"The entire family is well respected in the area. You can trust them. And he will not charge you through the roof." She cringed at the slip of tongue as she considered the major roof replacement project I was going to have to tackle.

We laughed at the comparison and headed back to town. She recommended a place to stay until I found a more permanent residence as well as the governmental offices to start the process of being allowed to stay longer than my visitor visa would allow. Then, after we parted ways, I called Gerald and told him that I would be needing his services within the following few months. He was more than happy to reserve the time.

As he walked down the hall, away from me, the walls starting to go up in some of the rooms, the crews busily working away and he, with his brothers, pushing it all along, I knew that he was supposed to be there.

Then, it dawned on me. "Gerald?"

"Yes?" He looked back.

"Brown. You wouldn't happen to be related to Imogen and Elijah, would you?"

A corner of his mouth upturned. "I am. We are cousins."

With that, he turned back and disappeared around the next corner. He didn't ask why I wanted to know. He didn't say anything more about them. He just gave a knowing smirk and confirmed their relationship.

We all have our purpose in life.

"Yes, Gerald. We certainly do."

I went downstairs and out back to take a walk. There was so much going on, and I was feeling myself piece things together. Yet, part of me wanted to just walk and clear my head.

However, clearing my head wasn't in the cards. I got outside and started along to the back of the property, but before I got too far, something caught my eye. By the tree line, there, again, stood the figure Reid and I had seen. This time, I swore it had some features. Nothing concrete. Then, just as before, it disappeared before I could be certain.

But it wasn't the tree line I was pulled to. Nor was I concerned with my safety. Instead, I felt an overwhelming urge to check the wall.

I bee-lined it to the marked stone and yanked it from its spot. My heart didn't skip a beat. My breath didn't catch. My eyes didn't widen. But I did find myself staring right at another letter. The crisp, aged paper folded perfectly and sealed shut with a red, wax seal. On the front, the usual greeting:

Cora, My Love

I glanced back at the trees to be sure the figure had not reappeared and shoved the rock back into the wall, turned on my heels and went straight for my car. Sending Gerald a quick text to tell him I needed to run into town, I sped out of the driveway.

I hit redial on Reid's number and tapped my thumb on my steering wheel, going well over the speed limit down the long and empty street. It rang five times before going to voicemail.

I dialed again. But, again, it went to voice mail.

"Damnit, Reid! Answer your phone!" I tossed the phone into the passenger seat.

It landed next to the letter, which I'd set down there to keep from wrinkling in my pocket. My mind trailed momentarily as I stared at it, and I forgot, for just a moment, that I was still behind the wheel.

I shook myself from my daze and looked back in front of me. I was barreling down on the curve that turned the road from South East to East, toward town. In that moment, my heart stopped, my breathing froze and time seemed to slow down to an agonizing crawl.

I pressed my foot on the brake pedal as hard as I could. My knuckles turned white as I gripped the steering wheel as if the tightness of my hands on it may somehow have aided in slowing down the couple ton, out of control death machine.

The tires squealed, and I remember thinking that they must have been leaving those black skid marks on the pavement with the noise they were making. Then, I thought it was odd that *that* was what was running through my mind in that moment.

Things came back into focus just as quickly as they'd wandered. I turned the wheel to the right in a vain attempt to try to make it around the curve. I wasn't sure why since I knew, as far as physics had taught me, I was going far too fast. The inertion of the metal I was encased in was on a path that I could do nothing about. The result of the sudden change in direction of the tires caused the car to turn sideways and threw me into a stronger panic as I saw the tree in the bend of the road was getting closer at a speed that was surely deadly.

I closed my eyes, and everything went black. They tell you to try to stay calm and not to tense. They say that the reason drunk people generally don't get hurt as much in accidents is because they stay loose and don't react, thus not giving a taught set of muscles and ligaments to pull at your bones, causing more breaks upon impact. But when you're sliding across the pavement, unable to gain control of your vehicle, and you're sure, beyond a shadow of a doubt, that you're about to careen into a solid object, there's something that kicks in to try to shield you that automatically takes all your soft tissue and tries to make it rock hard.

Then, everything stopped.

I didn't open my eyes. I was numb. And for a very long moment, I was comfortable inside my little world of blackness. That is, until my eyes started to hurt from how tight I was squeezing them shut. I relaxed my eyelids, took a breath for what seemed like the first time and tried to bring myself back into my body. Mentally scanning, I tried to assess any broken bones or wounds.

I didn't believe I was hurt, but I knew I needed to take a better look. Some people don't think they have been wounded when they're in shock. Tilting my head down, I braved a glance at my legs. They appeared to be fine. There wasn't any glass on the floorboard, and from what I could tell, I was still upright.

I moved my hands and arms and felt around my head. No blood. No searing pain. From what I could tell, I was fine. And so was the car.

I slammed the car into park and looked around me and saw that no windows were broken. All tires seemed to still be inflated. The letter was even still in the passenger seat.

But I wasn't on the road any longer. I was parked. And what was more, that tree that I was skidding toward was between me and the pavement, still standing proudly, in one piece. There was no way I didn't hit it. I couldn't have swung around the trunk. Not from the angle I was coming from.

I climbed out of the vehicle, not taking my eyes off the ancient tree and stumbled over the rough terrain toward it. It stood tall, lording over the patch of grass it called home that served as a cushion between the curve of the road and the field that was producing a crop of grain. I stopped about six feet from it and stood, not believing that it could possibly be solid and I somehow missed it.

Leaning in, I pressed my palms flat against the bark and gave a slight shove. It didn't move. Not that I expected it to. But, with one hand still on the trunk, I walked around it and checked for marks. Again, I came up empty. Then, I whipped around and looked at the car. My door was open and the engine was still on, and it was making a repetitive dinging noise to remind me that I'd forgotten something. I sprinted back to it, circling all four sides, my hands grazing its surface as I inspected it for damage.

But there was none.

I had no explanation.

In one moment, I was headed straight for the tree, sideways, with no option of saving myself. The next, I was safely deposited in the grass on the other side of it. Not a scratch was on me, the tree or the car. But my mind? It was completely rattled.

"Are you alright?" a man called out from the road.

I was leaning against the hood of the car.

"Nell?" he called out again.

I waved a hand, still looking down trying to catch my breath. "I'm fine. Thank you."

"What happened?" the voice was closer.

I felt hands on my shoulders.

"I'm fine, really." I shot up. Seeing Reid's face, my words caught in my throat. "Reid?"

"How did... What... Are you okay?" He looked me over.

I glanced around to make sure I hadn't been imagining it all. "I lost control. I was speeding back into town, and I looked away for just a minute. I didn't realize I was so close to the curve, and I was going too fast. I slammed on the brakes, but it was too late. But when I opened my eyes, I was here. I should have hit the tree. I shouldn't be fine. I don't understand."

"You were coming from the house into town?" He pointed up the street. "From that direction?"

"Yes."

His eyes scanned the scene. "And you're sure you didn't hit it?"

"I'm sure. I don't understand, but I'm sure." I did a little spin to show him I wasn't lying.

He placed his hands on the sides of my head and started physically examining me. "You obviously have someone looking out for you. But why were you speeding into town? I didn't think we were getting together until later."

I walked over and reached into the passenger seat, grabbing the new letter. "This."

He just looked at me. "Did you take it with you?"

"Nope."

“Did you forget to bring it with the others?” His tone was cautious.

“Nope.”

Hesitantly, he reached out. “Did you find this one in the wall today?”

“Yep.”

“Jesus, Nell.” He flipped it over. “I don’t understand.”

I threw my hands in the air. “Me either!” I started breathing faster in response to my heart rate speeding up. “What were you doing out here?”

“I was taking a lunch break and thought you’d enjoy some warm food instead of those packaged snacks you have stored out there.” His eyes didn’t leave the letter. “You didn’t read it yet?”

“Of course not.” I took the letter back. “But that’s not all.”

He looked up, a hint of fear pulling his eyes into a squint. “No?”

“That figure? The one we’ve both seen by the woods?” I swallowed. “I think I saw features today.”

“Features? Like a face?” he asked.

I bit my lip. “Not exactly. Just as if it was starting to come into focus a little.”

“Color?”

“A little.”

“Are you sure?”

I nodded. “Yes.”

He took a deep breath and took my arm. “Can you drive?”

“I think so.” I pinched the bridge of my nose. “I’m just shaken up.”

“I would be, too.” He led me to the driver’s side of my vehicle, nervously looking around. “I’ll follow you back to my place.”

The car drove out of the grassy patch easily, and we turned for town. I parked and sat to finish composing myself. My nerves were frayed, and I still couldn't find any explanation that could explain either the figure by the trees or how I managed to come to a stop without being in the hospital.

He tapped on the window of my door before opening it, holding his hand out. "Let me help."

I took his hand and got out. "I didn't get hurt."

"Maybe not physically, but you seem a little more than rattled, my dear." He took my purse and held my arm as we walked to the front door.

I set the letter down on the table next to all the others that were still here. "Will you do it?"

"Of course." He pulled my chair out, got me a glass of water and sat down to unseal the latest correspondence.

21st of June, 1867
Dear Cora,

Today, I am leaving one last letter to attempt to reach you. I do this with a heavy heart. Neigh, I do this with a hole in my heart at the thought of spending the rest of my life without you in it.

Please know that I will never resolve the feelings I have for you. I will always look for word of your safety. But I will no longer seek you out unless I receive a sign to do so. But that is all I will need. You say the word, my love, and I will come for you.

Yours Truly & Forever,
With all my heart,
Joshua

He lowered the page onto the table and pulled out a notebook from his desk. "Here. Write to him."

"What?" I stared at the blank page.

"Write to him. Ask why the letters are coming now. Ask who he is. Or she for that matter. We need to try to get some answers. I can't think of any other direct way to get them. Write back to whoever is putting them in the wall." He pushed the tablet toward me.

My fingers pressed down onto the paper a little harder than I intended as I slid the notebook toward myself. I had no idea what to write. *Do I reply as Cora? Do I reply as if the person putting the letters into the wall is also the author? Do I address some unknown person that's leaving the letters there for me to find for some unknown reason?*

I eyed Reid.

He seemed to be able to read my mind. "What does your gut tell you?"

The ball point of my pen wavered over the lined paper. Part of me expected to see a drop of ink fall down and make a minute splash. "The aggravated part of me wants to write to a person that might be trying to freak me out. You know, that blank, logical portion of my brain that refuses to acknowledge any other option. But there's this entire inner layer to my mind that seems to be pushing me to have a conversation with a man that's probably been dead for well over one hundred years." A wave of guilt washed over me at the insensitivity of my words. "Sorry. I know he's your relative. I didn't mean to be so callous about how I said that."

"It isn't as if I knew the bloke." Reid gave me a sympathetic smile.

I nodded. "Thanks."

The pen didn't move, despite my wishing that it would just take over and write on its own, saving me from having to make the choice. But it stayed lying in my hands, propped up between my fingers, useless without my own share of the effort.

"Damned pen," I muttered under my breath.

"What was that?" He chuckled.

I blushed at my own behavior. "Nothing. I'm just fighting an inner argument over here and wishing a silly inanimate object would settle the issue."

"I see." His head bobbed in amused understanding.

I took a breath and set the pen to the page.

Dear Mystery Person,

Today, I found another letter stuck behind one of the stones in the rock wall on the property I purchased a few months ago. And while finding the first letter or two was a unique experience and even a welcome one since I love antiques, the ensuing experiences of finding more on the following days has me a little concerned as to their origin.

If you have more letters, I would appreciate you possibly finding the time to come to the property while I am there with the work crews, understanding that this single letter per day thing has become a little creepy. I am very curious as to what more you have. I also am working with a historian on learning more about Joshua and Cora, who happens to be Joshua's descendant. He would love to hear what you know about this unrequited couple.

I would be a crazy person to pretend that these letters are actually coming from a Mr. Joshua Wilkinson from back is 1867; considering that it is now the year 2017 and all, 150 years later exactly.

If there are no more, please come to the estate and let me know. We would still love to meet you and pick your brain about the origins of these correspondences that you have been leaving for me to find.

Looking forward to hearing from you,
Nell

I set the pen down. “One hundred and fifty years exactly.”

“Pardon me?” Reid looked confused.

“Its 2017. The letters from Joshua are from 1867. That's one hundred and fifty years exactly,” I explained.

He thought for a moment. “You’re right. How peculiar.”

It *was* peculiar. The whole thing was. If it was someone leaving the letters, that was creepy. If they were originating from the one hundred and fifty year old author, manifesting in modern day? That was simply crazy. And I was starting to consider finding a local therapist for even considering it.

I folded the newly drafted letter and looked around the room. Reid was, once again, one step ahead of me, handing me an envelope. I slid it into the sleeve, sealed it and wrote on the front.

“About Joshua”

With the letter and the pen lying on the table in front of me, I leaned back, taking a mental note that the pen had completed a half roll after I set it down, coming to rest against its hook. The act made the object look as if the act of writing the letter was a strain, and it had rolled over, exhausted, once relinquished from its duties. Something I was fully aware was simply me transferring my own experience of drafting the letter.

"I'll drive you out there if you would like me to." He set down a fresh glass of water.

I hadn't even noticed that he'd gotten up from the table. "Yes. Please."

He hadn't sat down. Instead, he rerouted himself, picking up my purse, tucking the addressed envelope into it and holding his hand out. "Shall we?"

"Now?"

He shrugged. "We don't know when the letters are delivered. So we might as well get it there as soon as we can, do you not think?"

Again, I agreed with him. "Okay. Right. But I want to see it happen. Would you be willing to stay there with me today and maybe tonight to watch? If possible, I want to catch them at the wall."

"But do you really think they'll brave going to the wall with us there?" he asked.

I thought back to my first overnight at Webb Manor. "They have before."

"True," he said.

"If you don't want to, or can't, I completely understand. You've done so much for me already. I don't want to inconvenience you any more than I already have."

His response came quick. "You're not inconveniencing me in the least. On top of my burning curiosity for what is actually going on here, I am finding that I rather enjoy your company."

My cheeks turned red. "So, you'll come?"

He nodded. "Yes. But let me pack a few camping items since we may need them."

He kissed my cheek and rushed out of the room. A few minutes later, he returned with a duffle bag packed. Once again, he picked up my purse and held a hand out to me. "Okay. *Now* are we ready?"

"One more favor?" I asked, shyly.

He rolled his eyes and exhaled loudly, obviously stifling a smile. "Oh dear lord. What now?"

I pushed his shoulder. "Funny. Don't. I already feel like I'm taking advantage of your kindness."

"Nell, I am only teasing you." He put a hand on my cheek and kissed me softly. "Would you like me to take you to your flat to grab a few things?"

I relaxed, thankful he still seemed to be inside my head. "Yes. I won't be long. I just want to grab a couple things."

"Not a problem what so ever, dear." He waved toward the door. "Shall we?"

Just as I'd said, I didn't take long packing my bag, and we were out to the estate before I knew it. Reid took our bags up to my room, and I dropped off a paper sack of a few groceries I'd grabbed so I could make us a couple meals while we were camping out.

He joined me in the kitchen with a couple camping chairs and a blanket tucked under his arm. "I had these in my trunk. I thought maybe we could use them to sit outside later on and watch the stars."

I took the blanket and handed him a bottle of water. "That sounds perfect."

I made my rounds, checking on the progress of the crews. Gerald was thorough in explaining where everyone was at and was more than willing to take me around and show me what stage each room was at. Admittedly, I was more than pleased with how fast they were getting it all done. He explained that the fact that we'd taken everything down to the studs, even rebuilding many of them, in fact, was a huge contributor to why it was going to be a fast job for both the electrical and plumbing.

His brothers were well into the task of hanging drywall in the couple of rooms where pipes and wires had been run so that the workers could go back through easily and attach mounts and fixtures. I loved seeing some of the rooms looking so close to being done.

"Your room." Gerald opened the door. "I asked Mr. Wilkinson to refrain from giving you an update so I could show you myself."

I crossed the threshold, and my breath caught in my chest. "Wow."

"I asked the men to work on it this morning for a surprise. Well, honestly, we had started it yesterday. The adjoining bathroom as well. Now you just need to have the flooring installed and final touches on the walls done." He looked so proud as he spoke.

The chandelier hung in the center of the room, perfectly enhancing the light switch covers I'd picked out and even the trim work. "How did you get this all here already?"

"I have a connection or two around here." He smirked.

I hugged him. "Thank you, Gerald. And tell everyone that I appreciate it more than I can say."

"Well, you need to get out there and put that letter in the wall." He held the door open, motioning for me to exit first.

"How did you..."

He patted my shoulder gently. "Connections, my dear."

Reid. I thought, shaking my head as I headed downstairs, leaving Gerald to rejoin his brothers.

"Let's get this out there before we forget." Reid was leaning on the railing at the bottom of the stairs, the letter in his outstretched hand.

I took it from him. "You told Gerald about this?"

"Not that I recall," he replied.

"Mmmhmmm." I quirked an eyebrow.

"Why?" He followed me out the back door. "Did he say something like he knew about it?"

"Yes. He told me to get it out to the wall."

"He told you to get the letter out to the wall? That specific?"

I paused, looking Reid over to gauge if he was seriously confused or playing along. Seeing his questioning was genuine, I replied, "Yes. That's what he said virtually verbatim."

Reid glanced back at the house. "Strange." He followed me out the door.

"Do you think he's involved?" I asked.

"I couldn't tell you," he replied. "But chances are, he's probably just seen you out there a couple times. Maybe he's amused."

"Maybe..." I pushed it aside and went back to my task.

At the wall, I knelt down and removed the rock. Glancing around, I checked the tree line to see if the figure was back there again. Reid was doing the same as I slipped the envelope into the open space and wedged the rock in on top of it, wiggling it slightly to be sure that it wasn't going to drop back out.

I stood and chewed on my lip.

He took my hand. "Let's go in. We will keep watch from inside."

I spun and followed him back in. "You hungry? My stomach is growling. I don't know if it is nerves or the fact that I haven't eaten, but either way..."

"I could eat a bite. Did you want me to go into town and grab something?" he asked.

I pulled out some chicken from the fridge. "No. I brought enough food to make a couple meals."

"Good call." He took a seat on one of the stools at the breakfast bar. "So, what are you going to make?"

"You'll see." I smirked.

We spent the day keeping busy back and forth between helping with work on the house and checking on the wall. I kept telling him that he didn't need to work, and he could be doing some of his actual job work that he wasn't getting to because of my little mystery, but he said he was more than happy to get his hands dirty for a change, also citing that it was his ancestor's love that bound him to the estate, and he felt a little pull of sentimentality because of it. I didn't argue once he posed that part of it since, after all, I didn't have any connection to it all. But I seemed to be pulled to the estate all the way from another country. So, what could I actually say? No matter how much I wanted to cling to it being someone trying to prank me, I knew he was beginning to believe it was something more paranormal.

The crews filtered out, and we shared a quiet dinner out in the rear garden, taking his blanket and outdoor chairs with us. After our meal, we sat out in an open part of the yard where we could keep an eye out and yet kick back and, as he had wanted to do, watch the stars.

The day had passed, and neither of us had any sightings of anyone out near the wall, alive, shadowy, or otherwise. That is, unless you count the deer that wandered in from the field at dusk nibbling on a nearby patch of shrubbery.

My eyes were drooping, and, occasionally, my head bobbed as I dozed off for a split second. I had been holding Reid's hand on my lap, but in my exhaustion, my grip had loosened. We'd been having a conversation about the differences in vehicles in America verses in England, but both of us had gone quiet and were relaxing in the cool, summer night air.

He squeezed my fingers. "Would you like to go in and get some sleep?"

"What time is it?" My voice was hoarse with sleepiness.

He glanced at his phone. "It is after two in the morning."

I stretched and yawned. "Sleep sounds fantastic."

I barely remember going upstairs or him laying out the air mattress. But that night's rest was peaceful and exactly what I needed. He wrapped his arms around me, leaving the balcony doors open as we slept. I woke the next morning, happy to see him curled up next to me, his arm draped across my hip and nose almost touching my shoulder.

I slipped out from under the covers and into the bathroom, carefully, trying not to wake him. Taking a moment to freshen up before heading down to the kitchen to brew a pot of coffee.

Standing at the window, I stared out at the wall. Everything looked like it pointed to it being a typical morning. The sun was shining, which was nice since it had been cloudy off and on for a couple of days. I heard birds out back playing in the feeder that I'd hung my first day there. It had been tucked away in one of the small out buildings along with a shepherd's hook I had found while cleaning.

Reid came up behind me, wrapping his arms around my waist, and nuzzled into my neck. "Good morning, beautiful. See anything interesting out there?"

Absently, I replied, "No ... Coffee?"

He took the mug I'd set out for him on the counter and filled it. "You seem focused. Is everything okay?"

"Yeah." I felt distant. "It's just..."

I trailed off, feeling something gnawing at me.

"Nell?" He tried to get my attention.

I set my mug down and went out the back door without warning. Storming to the wall, I ripped the rock out and tossed it aside. The letter was sitting there. But as I looked closer, I realized it wasn't the one I left. It was a different one. One of the same parchment and wax seal as I'd been finding. Not one from a modern author.

I yanked it out and looked it over. There was no writing on the outside.

I was half way back to the house when Reid met up with me. "What is it?"

I held it up without a word.

His eyes opened wide as he saw what I was holding. "Is that a new one?'

I nodded and went straight for the back door.

Inside, I tossed it onto the counter, went around and pulled out a knife and stood there, glaring at it for a moment before breaking the seal and almost hastily unfolding the creases. "We didn't see anyone. Neither of us did. I mean, we didn't watch it the entire time, and there was time in the middle of the night. But you'd think we would have seen someone lurking, and we didn't!" I was practically yelling.

He took my hand. "Let's see what it says. Maybe this will tell us everything we need to know."

I took a couple breaths to calm myself. "Maybe."

We both read it silently.

1867
Dear Nell,

I would like to start by sending my sincerest apologies for giving you any sort of fright. That has not been my intentions in the least. Honestly, I couldn't have imagined anyone other than my beloved Cora retrieving my letters.

You said that you purchased this estate a few months ago. However, that leaves me puzzled since the Webb family has owned it since its construction, and I have not heard word about them selling. Yet, this does not concern me as much as the date you claim to be writing from, 2017. I beg you not to play jokes on me. But, considering the strangeness of the paper, its containment sleeve, as well as the neatness of the ink you scribed in? I have to question each of these.

I suppose we have a bit of a confusion here.

To start, I know not of any Nell in the area. You say you are new, so I may not have heard of your arrival as of yet. I know that I have spotted a woman I thought was possibly my Cora, but she has not written back recently. Maybe you are a relative that has acquired the property and home, and I have not been informed of some unfortunate happening? This concerns me greatly for, as I stated, I have not heard from Cora as of late.

You also say that you are in contact with a descendent of mine. I'm curious by which branch of my family tree they claim to be from.

I think that if we were to correspond and work out a few details, we may be able to get to the bottom of this. I will look for your next letter.

Until Then,
Joshua Wilkinson

"That's it!" I shouted. "Reid, can you take me into town and to a store that has electrical equipment? I'm buying a flipping camera. This has *got* to stop."

He sat, completely puzzled, rereading the letter. "I don't exactly know how to respond. If this is a person that is messing with you, how did they get the ink, wax and paper to age so authentically? And why would they go to such lengths? I don't know anyone in the area that would be so utterly cruel to another person, no matter who they are. At least not without provocation."

"I don't know anymore. This is way over the top." I paced the room.

"Yes. It is," he agreed. Flipping the page over, pausing to inspect each side more than once, he questioned it all, "But how is it so authentic?"

I slammed my hands down onto the table. "Well, whoever this psycho is, I'm going to catch them on camera."

"But what if it truly is him?" His eyes didn't leave the page.

I walked to the back door, crossing my arms. "I can't even imagine allowing myself to entertain that concept."

"Why not?" He was crossing the room.

I went rigid.

"Does that thought really bother you *that* much?" He put his hands on my shoulders.

I didn't respond. I was staring right at the figure along the tree line. And this time, I could make out even more features. But no matter how hard I tried, they were still blurry to me. "I just can't."

I was refusing to acknowledge that option fully. It was too far away from how I believed the world worked. That, and I was scared to let my guard down on it being some psycho neighbor. It didn't matter how much the evidence stacked up toward what Reid was beginning to believe. I wanted to completely rule out the possibility of some prankster neighbor before moving on to something that could get me institutionalized ... even if by my own volition.

He sighed. "Fine. I will respect that. At least until we get more evidence one way or the other. How about I go into town to get that camera system and you stay to write another letter. When I come back, I will ask Gerald to see if he would kindly assist in installing it."

"Thank you." I tightened my arms around myself as the figure vanished.

I didn't know why I didn't tell Reid about seeing the shadow figure or that it was coming into focus more and more each day. Maybe it was because I was feeling like I was losing my mind, and I didn't want him to think I was, too? Sure, he was trying to get me to acknowledge the possibility of the situation being one of a more paranormal nature. But what if? What if I started to come around to the idea and he freaked out once actually faced with it being a reality?

Back in Manhattan, I had created my own little bubble. One where things didn't change much. I kept everything and everyone for that matter, about arm's length. The change and excitement that happened in my life was well contained and manageable, nice and neat and completely within my control ... on the page.

Before kids, I was a little wild. I'd take off on adventures whenever they were possible. I would try new things, eat new foods and loved to meet new people. But settling down with a husband and children seemed to not only domesticate me, but I seemed to almost petrify.

But then, my kids were all out on their own, my husband left me for someone new, and I moved across an ocean. Granted, I knew that, one day, my kids would move out. And I wasn't even that affected with my husband's moving on. I mean, we were still friends, and after he broke the news of someone new, I knew that was all we had been for quite some time.

And then there was the move.

I had been so busy keeping my head down and working hard on the project that I really hadn't allowed myself time to look up and acknowledge what I had done ... or what I had gotten myself into. I was simply diving into the muck of it and splashing around.

So when Reid would touch on the option of our situation being one involving a time traveling round of correspondences with a man from one hundred and fifty years priors? Yeah, no. That wasn't something I was prepared to wrap my head around.

Sure, I had experiences like so many others that were unexplained but probably debunked rather easily if any half trained ghost hunting team had been there. Ghosts, spirits, energies, etc? Those were things I'd never really entertained in either direction as real or fiction. I had never a reason to. My opinion of them simply was not solid in either direction.

That day, the sighting of whatever it was out along the tree line and the fact that it was slowly coming into view for me was not something I was prepared to talk about. I wasn't even prepared to process it fully in my own mind. And that was what I needed to do - process it. I needed to write another letter, see if I got a response and go from there.

I turned around and wrapped my arms around his waist. Allowing my tension to slide off my shoulders, I put on a playful smile. "Think about anything you may want me to say in the letter. I'll get started while you're gone."

"Will do." He kissed me and headed out the front door.

I turned back around and resumed my stance at the back of the house, arms around myself. Reid had this way about him that seemed to take everything in stride. Maybe even a little light hearted. And I was seeing just how stoic and dramatized I had become. I didn't like it. Having to take so many steps in order to grasp something that, back in the day, I would have ran with it. My hesitation was not settling with me any more than the situation itself. Which, of course, was adding to the drama going on in my head.

Reid seemed like a good man, and I was certainly enjoying our time together. Plus, I was seeing that he was also becoming a good influence on me. I needed to return to the old me that I missed so much. The one that was invited to everything instead of the me that turned down what few invitations I would receive. The woman that bought a house in another country on a whim. She was still in me, not only crying to come back out but breaking free on her own. I just needed to figure out how to stop stifling her.

Write. I inhaled a deep, slow breath.

Writing always helped clear my mind. I wasn't sure where to start on the letter for the wall yet. So many thoughts were swimming around in a tiny fishbowl inside my mind. I needed to let the waters calm. So, I pulled out my laptop, sat at the table and opened the manuscript I'd started.

Almost as soon as I found my place on the page, the words started flowing. And they didn't stop. I felt myself center as everything dropped away around me. My fingers flew across the keyboard as I weaved more of the story line for my characters.

Cora became Caroline. Joshua became Aidan. The couple met at a ball in the mid eighteen hundreds and fell in love at first sight. And, just as Joshua had dealt with, Aidan had lost a wife and was saddled with a child to raise on his own; not an easy feat for someone in any time, let alone back then.

I'd picked up where I'd left off, the two of them running off together for lunches, dinners, horseback rides through the neighboring landscapes, and even the occasional walk through the fields. And, just as Cora and Joshua apparently went through, Caroline's father did not approve of their love. Aidan pleaded with the man, begging him to reconsider and even had an inner dialogue with himself about challenging him to a duel considering the implications that the patriarch of his love's household implied about his character. Coming to the conclusion that it would only taint the love she had for him, he refrained.

I bounced around between a few different scenes that were strong in my mind about things that Cora and Joshua had gone through by their letters, embellishing as needed to give sustenance to the page, which, honestly, wasn't much considering how full their story was on its own.

"Nell?" Reid called out from the front door.

I looked up from the keyboard, my eyes slightly blurry. "In the kitchen."

"Sorry I took so long. I figured out something that we could put in the letter, but I had to stop by my office to grab some documents." His voice grew louder as he entered the room.

"What is that?" I inquired.

He held up a folder, stuffed with pages. "My lineage."

"Your lineage?" I was confused. "Why? I mean, what would that solve?"

"I don't know for sure, but I know that if we simply ask who the son was to connect the dots on our end, if this is someone else writing these letters, they could easily know this information. But if we tell him the lineage, maybe he will say something that will help us go in one direction or the other." He set the folder down on the table and glanced at the screen. "Did you get it written?"

"Well?" I giggled. "I got stuff written. But not the letter. I was actually working on the manuscript."

He sat down, obviously curious. "That's good! Feeling inspired is always good."

"Yes. And my inspiration is them. Cora and Joshua; their story. I want to write it." I looked at him to see his reaction, hoping that it would be something he approved of.

He put a hand on my knee. "Nell, if nothing else, that just may be why you're here; to write their story."

I mulled that over for a moment, shaking my head. "That's possible."

He stood. "Well, it is good to see you in better spirits. The first page in that folder has my family tree for you to add to the letter. I'll go seek out Gerald and get this camera system installed."

"Sounds good." I returned to my computer.

I smiled at the words on my screen, happy with the amount of progress I'd made and the direction it was going in. Then, I opened a blank document and started to type.

2017
Dear "Joshua",

Yes. I agree. we seem to have a misunderstanding. You seem to think you're writing from 1867. I seem to think I'm writing from 2017. That's one hundred and fifty years between us. And that's an impossibility.

I suppose if I am to give a few details, maybe they can spark something to help clarify. Now, if you are someone modern day that is simply pulling a prank? It's not funny. Please stop this madness.

Okay. Where to start?

Well? Your friend, Clive Brown? He's the ancestor of our friends Elijah and Imogen, or so I believe. Their last name is Brown as well. My land worker is Gerald Brown. He has been a huge help and seems to be connected to the area. But my friend Reid Wilkinson? You should recognize the last name since he's the one I mentioned is a descendant of yours.

Your son, Clive, is the great-grandfather, three times removed, of my friend, Reid. That makes you his four times removed great-grandfather. The lineage goes like this:

You (Joshua Wilkinson) - 1842 - 1867
Clive (I assume after your friend) Wilkinson - 1863 – 1894
Edward Wilkinson – 1885 – 1951
Lawrence Wilkinson – 1907 – 1978
Samuel Wilkinson – 1933 – 2001
Stanley Wilkinson – 1956 – 1998
Reid Wilkinson – 1978 – Present

When I acquired this estate, I lived in Manhattan, New York, United States. The place was empty and in ruins, and the roof was caved in. We are currently working on fixing things, but there was extensive damage and rotting due to the fact that it has sat, vacant, for a few decades after the last of the area Webb family members let it go.

I am really not sure what to say from here to help work this out. But, if you are, by chance, wandering the woods, sometimes coming to the edge to look out? Maybe you're confused and lost? Maybe injured? Come up to the house. We will be more than happy to get you some help.

Sincerely,
Nell Price

I folded the letter after printing it and ran out of the room, searching for Reid. Finding him out by the wall, I paused before I could speak, completely out of breath. While taking a moment to compose myself, I thrust the page at him. "Here," I panted. "Tell me what you think."

His eyes scrolled the page. He folded it back up, looking pleased. "Yeah. Looks great. I can't think of anything else to add in."

"Are you sure? I'm still completely lost as to how to trip this guy up into giving us proof this is all a hoax. Maybe I should give some false information from back then to trip him up." I scanned the document for a good place to insert my suggestion.

He put a hand on mine. "Nell, it is just fine as it is. Let's see how or even if they respond. Save that for next time if there ends up being one."

I fidgeted with the letter. "You're probably right. I'll go put it in the wall."

He kissed my forehead. "Your neurotic reaction to this is adorable."

"Neurotic?" I glared at him, my lips pursed. "Get back to work, mister. I'll handle my *neurotic* mess."

He laughed. "Adorable."

Eight

I placed the letter in its new home after doing a quick and thorough inspection of the empty space behind the rock. I didn't know what I expected to see there. Probably nothing. But the uncertainty of the entire situation had me double guessing a lot.

The sun was out, and I stopped as I was crossing the yard heading back to the house. With my head tilted back and my eyes closed, I allowed myself a moment to feel the breeze on my face and the rays from the sun to warm my cheeks. For the first time since I'd found the first letter, I allowed myself to slow down and just be.

I felt arms snake their way around my waist and clasp in front of me as his body pressed against mine from behind. Reid quietly wrapped around me and kissed my shoulder. "It is good to see you so calm, even if it is a fleeting moment."

I didn't open my eyes. Instead, I soaked in the air, the sun, and the feeling of his body against me. "I miss this feeling."

"What? The feel of a man wrapped around you?" He kissed my neck.

"Mmmm..." I placed my hands on his forearms. "That's nice for sure. But no. I meant the whole being calm thing. More specifically, allowing myself moments like this one where I let everything roll off my shoulders and clear my head."

"You need to do it more often." He turned me to face him. "It isn't healthy to stay so tense or to let things get to you so much. Don't get me wrong. I understand what it is about this whole thing that has you a bit tousled. But, as we have said, we don't know enough yet to presume either way. So we simply have to let it play out a tad more before we can act."

"I know." I leaned my forehead on his chest. "You're right. I know you are. And the me from twenty years ago would be right there with you in that calm, chill demeanor. But, apparently, along with distancing myself from everyone, I have grown a little ... easily shaken? I don't do as well outside of my comfort zone as I once did. And even *that* bugs me!"

He chuckled. "Nell, you are truly adorable."

"Thanks." I huffed.

"Give this a little more time. I understand that you want to solve the mystery right now, but we can't. We are doing everything we can, including the cameras."

I trailed back to the many questions I had about the situation. "I had a thought. I mean, I doubt it, but what if it's Gerald?"

"Why would you think that?" he asked.

I replied, "Well, isn't it strange that he was right there when I first got here, available for work? He and his brothers?"

He shrugged. "A fortunate and convenient coincidence, I'd say."

"It's just that he knows so much about the land. He knows so much about the history of the area. Especially about this estate. He seems to be so handy that I can't believe that he isn't more successful in his field, rather than just doing odd jobs around this tiny village. He's even made some almost eerily random comments in regards to this whole wall/letter situation that makes me think he knows more about it than he's letting on. And maybe I'm being paranoid or reading into things a little much. I can probably even apply it all to you with how fast we've connected and such. And, yes, I know being a writer gives me some license to having an overactive imagination or something. But I can't seem to not start connecting him to it all somehow." I was rambling.

His finger pressed under my chin, lifting my head. "Tight as a guitar string or chill as an ice box; I truly like you either way. You obviously are tight as a brand new string right now, not giving any slack, no matter how hard I try. That doesn't mean I won't work toward helping you to keep calm and relaxed, though. But it does mean that either way, I think you are amazing."

I tried to bring him back to my point. "But what do you think about what I said?"

He brushed a lock of hair out from in front of my eyes that had fallen during my rant. "I think it is something to see if anything comes of it. But it, just as everything else right now, does not lend near enough to come to any sort of conclusion. So, we pocket it with all of the other bits of information." He could see the disappointment in my eyes. "You can ask him if you like. But maybe let it play out a little more before you accuse him of something so strange. That's my suggestion."

I sighed. "Reid, I'm serious."

He took a deep breath. "I know you are, Love. And you have every right to be curious and cautious. This whole thing is strange. I can't explain it. I can't even explain why I can so easily go along for the ride. But my gut says to. My gut says he's not involved. My gut says this will all come to light eventually. And my gut says to follow my heart with you."

"Your gut sure is chatty," I quipped.

He smiled then leaned down, the crook of his finger back under my chin, and kissed me deeply. His other hand, set on my lower back, pulled me into him.

I felt his lips curve as he smiled against my lips. "Come on. The camera is installed. I'll link it to your laptop and show you how it works. Then I want to take you into town for dinner. You need a meal that doesn't involve meeting with people to talk about this and isn't while camping out."

"I don't want to miss something here. What if..."

He put his hands on my shoulders. "That's what the camera system is for, dear. Plus, once it is synced, you'll be able to view it through your smart phone any time you like."

"Really?" I mentally acknowledged the phone in my pocket.

"Technology. Isn't it amazing?" he joked.

The ball of tension had started growing again. The idea of allowing myself some time away just to have fun was something I would struggle to let happen. But he was right. I needed to. Even in my writing, I knew, when I was truly stuck, I had to either step away and just shake it off, relax and do something fun, or to, at the very least, switch projects and focus on something else for a while. And since I was at a loss as to what direction to go with the whole letters in the wall thing, and I couldn't do anything more until I received another one, I might as well shake it off.

Besides, I was feeling crazy enough. Everything over the prior six months had me feeling a bit off kilter. The move. The estate. The work. The writer's block. The letters. The possibility of them coming from a man in the nineteenth century, despite me clinging to the notion that it was still only a remote possibility of being a ghost. You know, since logic still prevailed - and thank goodness for that. I would have had to literally check myself into some mental ward for evaluation for continuing to ignore that the man of my dreams was not only helping me out but also trying very hard to get past my very solid, wrought iron gates I'd fastened around my emotions.

I gathered myself and let a smile slip onto my lips as my hands slid across his back. "You're right. You're right. Please. Get me out of here and force me to distract myself. I need a break from all of this."

He leaned in and kissed me, his lips gliding over my cheek to my ear. He whispered, "I don't think you'll have to look for a suitable distraction if I can help it."

A pleasant chill ran over every inch of me, and I blushed. "So it seems."

It didn't take him long to finish setting things up and connecting them to my phone. He had purchased an external hard drive for the device to record a number of hours of footage onto, as well as everything needed to play the footage on my laptop. I offered to refund him, but he refused, stating that he'd always wanted a reason to play spy. By his enthusiasm for the entire process, I didn't doubt that his boyish dream was real. Plus, no matter how much I tried to give him the money, he remained steadfast in his refusal.

On the way into town, I periodically pulled up the live stream. Each time, he would remind me that I was using a lot of data, to which I would scoff and argue in favor of just taking a peek. Silently, I would close the app, agreeing and knowing I could just watch the footage later.

The Golden Crown was one of two full restaurants in town. Everywhere else that served food was either a pub or one of the three, tiny establishments that seated less than fifty people. In America, we called them mom and pop stops. So, we opted for *The Golden Crown*. It was beginning to be our staple place to go. Something I was not against since it felt good to have someplace there where people were getting to know me by name.

"I hope *The Golden Crown* is fine for tonight. I don't want to shake you out of your comfort zone too much, Price," he teased me as he parked the car.

I opened my mouth to retort, but the smirk on his lips stopped me. Instead, I shoved his shoulder and rolled my eyes. "Ha. Ha."

It was a little earlier than a traditional dinner time, but the place was busy. A birthday party that was scheduled for the back reservation room had spilled out to the main dining area. Festive? Yes. Chaotic? Double yes.

The greeter waved us toward a table in the back. Seeing that she was obviously very busy, Reid took the menus from her and said we would find it on our own to allow her to get back to her other tasks. Gratefully, she handed them over and thanked him.

After several attempts to excuse ourselves through the crowd, we found a clearing as well as spotted our table. My hand was holding his sleeve so as not to get separated in the midst of the waves of people when I saw a second hand shoot out and grab his shoulder.

"Reid Wilkinson? Is that you?" a distinctly feminine voice rang out over the din.

He turned. "Pamela?"

She ignored the woman attached to him as she flung her arms around him. "It is so good to see you! You look just absolutely delicious, as usual."

She was a pretty woman. Beautiful, actually. Poised and glaringly confident. Her long, dark hair looked as if she'd ordered it from the same catalogue as her outfit. And I had to refrain from asking who her makeup artist was ... or if she was one herself, since it was so flawlessly applied.

Instantly, I hated her.

He smiled and, to my relief, pulled back, slipping his hand in mine. "Bubbly as ever I see. This is…"

She cut him off. "I hear you've taken on some interesting projects lately. Digging up some family history?"

"Yes. Nell and I have been learning quite a bit together." His hand tightened down on mine slightly.

I interjected, "Hello. I'm Nell." I held my hand out.

She shook it, appearing slightly annoyed. "Pamela." She turned her attentions back to Reid. "I'm only in town for my uncle's birthday weekend."

"I heard you had moved to Paris. I'm glad you finally took the plunge." He was looking at the menu. I took it as a hint that we were there to eat, not socialize.

She didn't pick up on it. "Yeah, well, you wouldn't. So, you know. I couldn't wait around forever, ignoring my dreams and all."

"True. But look now. You're far better off living where you've always wanted. So it all worked out." He flashed her a half smile.

Pain shot through her eyes for a fleeting second before she regained her composure. "Yes. So it seems. Anything new in your life other than work projects? Not that that would be new."

He straightened his posture. "Actually, yes. As I tried to formerly introduce you earlier, Pamela Webb, this is Nell Price. Nell, this is an old friend, Pamela. Nell and I met on one of my new projects. Her project, actually. And we've hit it off rather nicely."

"Mixing work and personal life for once I see?" Her remark was executed a bit through her teeth. "I suppose that would be the only way you'd make time for love, wouldn't it?"

"I suppose so. Well, we had better get to our table before someone takes it. It was very nice to see you, Pamela. And, again, I'm happy for you on your move.

Hopefully you'll find what you're looking for there." Reid took a step, not waiting for her reply.

He was stopped by an older gentleman in a suit, obviously a bit drunken. "Reid, my boy! It has been far too long. I see my niece has found you."

"It is good to see you, Thomas. Happy birthday." Reid's shoulders slumped.

"Thank you! We miss you around the office. You know you're welcome to come by and take on a few tasks for us. Just because you broke little Pamela's heart doesn't mean we cut you off entirely. Your skills are dearly missed." Despite the man's best efforts to take Reid with him to another spot in the room, he stayed planted, holding my hand just a little tighter.

Pamela's expression was pained. As the two men briefly chatted, she leaned toward me slightly. "I have never seen him like this with any woman before. Not even with me. I don't know what it is about you, but he's more than smitten, love. Don't break his heart. He's a keeper, this one. You're making a number of women jealous around here. That's for sure." She straightened up, dusting off her skirt as if some filth had gotten onto it. "And you're very lucky."

I glanced over at him. "He's been very kind to me so far."

"Well, if you don't appreciate him, I'd be happy to take him off your hands." She crossed her arms.

I quirked an eyebrow. "Sweetie, if that were possible, you wouldn't be standing here talking to me. You'd still be on his arm." I stifled a laugh as a look of shock plastered across her face. "Besides, it isn't that he's not amazing. It's simply that I don't generally dish to strangers about my love life, let alone strange women that used to sleep with the man I'm spending time with. It's more of a principal of etiquette. Traditional values, if you will. Rather than this whole raunchy, drama loving, self depreciating, classless way of today's society." I paused and then covered my mouth with my hand. “Oh! Not that that’s what you are. Just that it’s fairly common practice, and I choose not to be common.”

I turned, a smile from ear to ear on my face as her mouth dropped open. Her arms dropped, and she stormed away. Reid was just shaking Thomas’s hand and wishing him a happy birthday once again as I pulled up closer to him. “Happy Birthday, Thomas,” I repeated.

“Thank you.” He bowed his head to me. “I’ll let you two get on with your meal.”

A little more than relieved to be free of them, Reid pulled my chair out. “I’m a bit impressed with how you handled Pam. A very skilled verbal backhand you have there.”

“You heard that?” I blushed.

He chuckled and took his seat. “I was privy to a bit of it, yes.”

“Yeah, well, I suppose I was a bit harsh.” I took one of the menus and started scanning it.

He did the same. “Harsh? Not at all. She needs more people to stand up to her like that. Especially around here.”

It dawned on me how he introduced us. “Webb. You said her last name is Webb? As in my estate, Webb?”

“Yes. Don’t feel entirely bad for them or anything. After the estate was lost, the family took up a smaller one, but it has been fruitful in the farming business. Her and Thomas’s lineage is from a line of cousins to the ones that owned your estate. The name is still quite revered around here. As you can see, Pamela was raised with a certain amount of entitlement.” He waved down the server.

Iris arrived, greeted us, bringing us a couple sets of silverware with water. She took our orders and whisked off again, busy with trying to keep the birthday party wrangled in so other guests could enjoy their meals.

"She's not very good at the game, though. Pamela." I took a sip of my water.

"What makes you say that?" he asked.

"If she was trying to scare me off, she shouldn't have made the comment about not seeing you as you are with me with anyone else."

He didn't say anything. He just looked down at the table, a corner of his mouth lifting.

I tilted my head. "What did she mean?"

He didn't reply right away. His eyes searched the tablecloth, allowing his thoughts to come together before letting them out. "I tend to put work first. I also wasn't very affectionate with her. She demanded things from me. From everyone. I suppose I would deny her just so I wasn't giving in to everything she wanted. Mature or not, it was a part of me that she brought out. And it was that part of me being out that told me we were not a lasting, happy couple. Seeing me hold your hand probably angered her since I rarely did that with her. It was one of her complaints."

"And your other relationships?"

"Work. It was always work first. And, honestly, I rarely allowed myself to get involved with any woman. I didn't look up from my research long enough to notice them much. So it's not as if I have had many relationships at all. And I'm truly sorry that you had to endure her inappropriate comments." He started to look uncomfortable at my line of questioning.

I reached out and placed my hand on his. "It was good to see a glimpse of you outside of all of this; all of my issues."

"I like your issues." He turned his hand over so our palms faced each other.

I bit my lower lip. "So what happens when the thrill of this mystery wears off? What happens when spending time with me isn't like being at work anymore? Will other projects take precedence?"

He blinked. "No."

"How do you know?" I asked.

He let out a quick breath. "I've met women while working projects before. Sure, nothing with the possibility of being paranormal. But research projects. Some of the historical importance kind. Those fizzled out after, sure. But there's something different with you."

"Because I'm American?" I shrugged.

He shook his head. "No. It's not that."

I went back to my lip. "Is it because of the paranormal aspect to all of this? That makes it more exciting, I'm sure."

"It does, but that's not it." He acknowledged the look of genuine curiosity and concern on my face. "I've always held women at arm's length before. I'm sure they saw it as work first, but I always felt a distance. We didn't have dinners like this. Everything in our relationships would be about work. It isn't like that with you. I want to let you in. Ask me anything, and I'll tell you. Ask anything of me, and I'll probably do it. From the moment I saw you, I felt some strange sense that you were who I've been waiting for, even if I didn't know I was waiting for anyone."

Iris arrived with our meals. "Do you need anything else at this time?"

I looked around the table. "No. Thank you. I'm all set."

"Looks fantastic, Iris. Thank you." Reid started dressing his burger.

We both took a bite of our dinners, silently acknowledging what he'd just admitted to me. I wanted so much to tell him that I was feeling the same way. I wanted to tell him that the first time I'd laid eyes on him, I felt a rush. A sense of something that was pulling me to him. I wanted to tell him how each time I ran to him about what was going on, I was confused as to why I was doing just that.

I didn't run to people with things. And, most of all, I wanted to tell him that I was scared that I was falling for him. Not just falling but falling so fast rather.

I looked up just in time for our eyes to meet. My chest did a combination of jumping and seizing. I opened my mouth, but nothing came out. I closed it again.

He took the lead. "Nell, I meant what I said. I feel drawn to you in a way I can't explain. And I think I'm falling for you."

My eyes grew, and my chest was heaving as I started inhaling and exhaling quickly.

His expression dropped as he went back to his plate, pushing his food around. "I hope I didn't scare you."

"You do," I blurted out.

He looked back up. "I'm sorry. I just..."

"No." I held my hand out to stop him. "You do. But you do because ... because ... I just ... I fee ..." I started coughing.

He started to stand, but I waved my hand, finishing my coughing fit. "I am no good at this."

"Obviously, I'm an old pro," he said, sarcastically.

I took a drink to wash down my fears. "Reid. You scare me because I feel the exact same pull. Well, I assume it's the same pull. But still, I've been so scared of falling for you, but I know I am."

"Good." His face had lit up. "We said it. It's out there. So, now we can just enjoy it and get back on task, right?"

I giggled. "Yeah. That sounds easy to do."

"I just wish we would have done this at my place," he said.

"Why is that?" I asked.

He leaned over the table slightly. "Because I now have this overwhelming desire to hold you."

I tried to play cool. "Well, I suppose it will just help build the desire, won't it?"

He smirked.

"You two are simply adorable, aren't you?" Pamela placed a hand on his shoulder.

He gently lifted it and deposited it back by her side. "Have a wonderful trip back to Paris, Pamela."

She huffed and walked off.

I gave an enthusiastic wave as she stormed across the room. "She's a peach."

"Did you want me to call her back? You seemed to enjoy her company quite a bit." He started to raise his hand.

"No!" I motioned for him to stop. "I think we're good."

The room was starting to thin out a bit as we continued to eat. Conversation flowed between us as it always did. Only then, we not only had our usual fluidity, but we also had a certain amount of comfort on another level. One that was there with the knowledge that we both had such strong feelings, and it was all laid out onto the table.

"As far as the whole letter thing goes, we can check the cameras a little later, but I say we wait until morning. Do a little of that relaxing that I was talking about? Maybe stay in town tonight as well to give you some distance. You're welcome to stay with me if you like. Then, we can go back there tomorrow morning and see if anything is there."

"Are you trying to distract me by enticing me with some alone time with you at your home?" I leaned onto the table, casually.

He mirrored my posture. "I would prefer to say that I am attempting to keep you on a healthy mental path, and if I get the benefit of having some quality time alone with you, then it would be a bonus for me as well."

"You have no idea how hard it has been to not keep looking at that footage." My hand grazed my phone.

He slipped my phone into his pocket. "Then let me help you and help save your sanity."

"That's what I don't get; why are you so calm about all of this?" I set my fork down on my plate.

His eyebrows pulled in. "I don't know. I just am."

"Are you sure that's wise? Shouldn't you be at least a little worked up about it?"

He thought for a moment. "Truthfully? I'm trying not to show that I am nervous. Maybe not as much as you, but I am. I figured that if I stay calm and level headed, it would keep from feeding into your anxiety over it."

"But it isn't," I retorted.

"I see that now." He reached across the table and took my hands. "Listen, I am very puzzled by all of this. And, yes, it is a bit concerning. If it's a paranormal thing that's going on, that's its own level of scary. But if it isn't? Then we must figure out if you're in danger, or if we have a local with a screw a little loose. Either way, we have to work out how to deal with them. There's no easy outcome here."

"Exactly." Relief ran through me, knowing he saw everything just as I did.

"But," he continued, "that's the thing. There's nothing easy about it no matter what direction it goes in. So, I figure there's no reason I should get worked up since it is what it is. And we will deal with it no matter what."

I pulled my hands back, letting them rest on the edge of the table. "But why stick around? Is it the fact that you're so passionate about history? Because it involves your ancestor? I mean, if it ends up dangerous, which you just admitted it could, why put yourself in harm's way?"

There was no hesitation in his reply or even a hint of wavering in his tone. "Yes. All of that. And you."

That night, I went back to his home with him. I quit interrogating him. There really wasn't much more to say. I knew he was right. We had to wait for more information. And as much as I wanted to stay glued to the camera footage, he was also correct in that it would have just drove me insane.

He set our phones down on his desk, clicked them to vibrate and took me upstairs. That night, we played a couple board games, watched a movie while eating popcorn and chatted. He told me more of his family and his past, and I even divulged a few things about myself. He explained why he was so well behaved when it came to not jumping into anything physical with me, stating that he grew up clinging to a more respectful line of thinking. It wasn't a no-sex-before-marriage thing. He simply wanted to get to know a woman mentally and emotionally before physically. Which, he told me, had cost him several potential relationships. He didn't disagree when I said it must not have been a good fit if that was the case.

We turned off the lights about eleven and went into bed. The moonlight drifting in through the window, I laid there with his arm around me, listening to what little noise the tiny village offered. Occasionally, a car would pass by. But what I loved most was to hear the owl that was perched somewhere nearby.

A few years prior, I had written a book that was steeped in superstition. Owls were one of the focuses in that work. Lying there that night, I thought of so many different folklores and myths that surrounded the gorgeous bird, including how the Kwakiutl people believed that they were the carriers of souls, and if you killed them, it would kill the soul it carried. Of course, that thought carried my mind off to various places that connected to my situation as my imagination took hold.

Restless, I finally gave up and went into the living room. About two in the morning, he came out and found me curled up on one end of the couch, writing. My mind had been reeling. No matter how much I was enjoying being curled up with him, I needed to let some of my thoughts out. And working on my manuscript seemed a much better option than thinking myself into an anxiety attack.

I went to set my laptop down on the coffee table, but he stopped me. Picking up a blanket, he draped it over my legs. "Thirsty?"

"Yes. I could use something. Thank you."

He returned after a few minutes with two mugs in hand. "Will hot chocolate do?"

I took one of the mugs. "Perfect. Thank you."

He sat down next to me, picked up a book and settled in, pulling my legs over his lap. And for the next hour, we sat there, quiet. I wrote as he read. I had never felt so at ease as I had in that moment. Writing was always something I did that was work, but it was also therapy for me. And it was an escape. But with him there, with him reading, I was immensely happy.

A bit over an hour later, I felt him lift the laptop off my legs. My eyes fluttered open as he hit save and shut it down, setting it on the table. "Let's get you to bed, love."

"Mmm ... love. I like the sound of that," I mumbled.

He pulled me up, catching me as I stumbled, still half asleep. His lips grazed my earlobe as he whispered, "My love."

With his hand on my arm, we made our way to the bedroom. The night air drifted in through the windows. It was just cool enough to send a chill across my bare arms after being warm on the couch, under the blanket. He felt the goosebumps form and ran his hands over my arms.

The view from his bedroom was breathtaking, the night air rousing me from my grogginess as we entered the room. The row of homes sat at the top of a hill just outside of the center of the village. The roads wound their way down into the downtown area. His window allowed the viewer to see across the rooftops and even into the vast set of fields that sprawled out beyond the village limits.

The moon was full and bright. As he went to the kitchen to rinse out our mugs, I wandered over to the window and took a deep breath. A few wisps of clouds moved across the skyscape quickly, and stars shone across every inch of outer space I could take in. "You don't get to see the stars like this in Manhattan. It was one of the things I have loved about this area," I said as he came back in.

"It's probably even better from the windows at the estate." He came up behind me, wrapping his arms around my waist.

"This is breathtaking here. You're lucky that you get this every night," I said.

He took my hips and turned me to face him. "I could spout a thousand cheesy lines like you're even more breathtaking. Or that I'm more lucky to have you here even for one night. But..." His hands were gripping firmly as he stopped speaking. I was pressed against him, the heat of his body seeping into mine. The fight of words versus action playing out just behind his gathered expression.

I slipped my fingers up under his shirt, playing just under the elastic waistband of his sweats for a moment. I grinned as he closed his eyes briefly, losing the inner battle to behave obvious in his eyes as they opened again.

Lifting his shirt, I moved my hands up across his abdomen, over his chest and to his shoulders. I placed soft, careful kisses on his torso as his fingers flexed against my hips until, slowly, I withdrew my hands. As much as I wanted to push, I knew he had a moral code he lived within, and I didn't want to compromise that. The last thing I wanted was to come off as loose or pushy. With his shirt back in place, I laid my hands back on his chest and looked up.

His breath was deep, but it was steady as he looked down at me. He hadn't moved from the same stance he'd been in since before I started my move. The only change was that his muscles were a bit more taught.

"Nell." He cleared his throat.

I pursed my lips. "I know. I'm sorry. I get that you maybe don't want to or just don't want to rush anything."

He looked shocked by my statement. "After everything I said about how I feel, you doubt that I would want to make love to you?"

"Being drawn to me could mean different things. It could just mean that you feel very close and protective, but not in a sexual way." I bit my lip.

He groaned and let go of my hip with one hand, moving a lock of hair from in front of my eyes. "So easily you dismiss how I've kissed you on a couple occasions. I doubt you kiss friends like that. And if you do, we might need to talk about some ground rules here."

"Ground rules, huh?" I fought a smile.

"Yeah, well." He put his hand back on my hip. "If we're going to be together, I don't exactly like to share. And kissing friends how we've kissed is a little too intimate for me."

I swallowed. "Together? Like a couple?"

"Yes." With that, he reached up and pulled me into passionate kiss.

Our lips collided and searched each other eagerly. Freeing his hands of me, he pulled his shirt off before taking a little more time with mine. Then, we were pressed against each other without barriers.

No more holding back.

No more walls.

We embraced each other with an intensity I'd never experienced. And as the sun started to peak over the horizon, we collapsed, sweaty, out of breath, and in the middle of what must have looked like a location where both a tornado and an earthquake paid a visit.

He was sitting up on the floor, leaned against the side of the bed. I was sprawled out next to him with my head resting on his chest, his sheet draped over us both as he ran his fingers through my hair. "So, I figured out how to compromise with you on the whole work/relax thing," he said.

"Oh?" I quirked an eyebrow. "How is that?"

"Let you work. But let you write. Not anything else," he said.

"I thought you were going to say sex." I giggled. "But you're still letting me work. And according to you, that's not relaxing."

"Sex? Well, that, too. But the writing? That is for you. Sitting there on the couch last night, your legs over mine, me reading and you writing, you were completely content. Even though it is work, technically, there's something about it that soothes you," he explained.

I smiled. "Well, if your goal was to get to know me before taking the step we just took, you achieved it. Nobody has ever figured that out about me."

"They just weren't paying enough attention." He kissed my head and got up.

My smile grew, and I watched as he strode across the room, still unclothed. I stood and wrapped the sheet around me, tucking it in like a long dress, and followed him. "What's on the agenda for today?"

He stopped in the kitchen. "Coffee, and then back to the estate."

"Don't you need sleep?" I handed him the can of grounds.

He filled the filter and pressed start, the sound of the first few drops of water sizzling as it hit the heated glass. "You relaxed last night with me on the couch, then we ... we made love. I am sure that I can run today on the high of that."

I chuckled. "Yes. That's a very polite way of putting it. But aren't you exhausted?"

He turned red. "I'm not going to torture you as I sleep. There's a good chance that you'll just pace my house until I wake. I'm fine with taking you out there to check the footage and the wall now."

I bounded up to him like a teenager and planted a kiss on his cheek. "Thank you."

I practically ran back to the living room and shoved my laptop into its bag with my notes. Then, I whizzed through the floor, getting dressed, brushing my teeth and gathering my things, only stopping to take the coffee he offered me. Of course, it was perfectly mixed just as I liked it. It didn't take him long to get ready, so we were on the road rather quickly.

I had stopped by the door, waiting for him to turn off the lights and the coffeepot. My smile grew as he approached, his bag already over his shoulder. "Thank you," I said.

"For what?" He picked up my bag.

I followed him to the door. "For seeing me."

He kissed me before walking me out to the car.

"The kitchen, your bedroom, one of the living room spaces, the den, as well as a couple of the bathrooms have all been completed, including the paint and wall paper selections you requested," Gerald announced proudly.

He took us around as I fell completely in awe of their work and how quickly it was coming together. "How many people are working on this? I can hardly believe that this much is done already!"

He flashed a toothy grin. "As you saw, the electrical and plumbing crews were pretty sizeable. Each had called in extra workers from local people that weren't scheduled on jobs just to move things along faster. I called in the painters yesterday as you said to do when we were at the point we were ready for them. They also have a few extra bodies."

"Budget. How are we looking on that?" I was concerned that more workers would send it through the roof.
I had gotten a fair amount of money from my latest book, and my releases were selling well. Plus, I had purchased the estate for such a small amount that it almost felt like I was stealing it. But I was putting a lot of money into it. Gerald and I had sat and mapped it all out, purchasing materials ourselves in order to have our fingers on the calculator the whole time. But I also didn't want to go broke and have to stall the project until more royalty checks came in.

I hadn't made concrete plans for what I was going to do with such a huge house in another country. I hadn't decided what I was going to do with my home in New York. I hadn't even worked out how to go about my idea of renting out the out buildings to writers or any sort of program associated with that. The last thing I wanted was to sink every last penny I had in the estate and not have anything to make that a possibility.

The more I had rolled around the concept of a writer's retreat and program, the more I had grown to like it. I had started working out some of the details, including jotting a few notes down. England was a culture that was rich in literature from the past to the present. To bring my own touch to that culture as well as aid others in bringing out their own voices was something that called to me.

Gerald interrupted my mental calculations. "We are still on track, Nell. Remember, we purchased the materials. The extra labor is mostly included in what we already were quoted. Don't worry about the rest. It will not be of much importance to you. I have it all sorted out."

"Are you sure?" I asked.

He patted my shoulder. "Absolutely. Now, I should get back to work. I believe you and Reid have something to check on."

"Can I ask you something?"

I fidgeted with my keys. When left to my racing mind, I second guessed everything and everyone. But when standing in front of him, I knew Gerald wasn't who I was looking for in all of this. I knew he was someone to trust, even if he did spout out with eerily predictive comments. But, frankly, that wasn't any more strange than the letters themselves.

"Yes; we can start moving in the furniture today. Would you like to start staying here after today?" He smiled.

"No, no. Take your time on that. But, Reid." I motioned toward him, standing in the next room, starting up the computer for the camera view playback. "I know that you know pretty much everyone around here. Am I getting myself into something good or bad?"

His eyes shone proud. "If I were your father or your brother, I would give you my blessing whole heartedly."

"Thank you." I gave him a quick hug before rejoining Reid in the Kitchen.

He put an arm around me. "Are you ready to go out and see if there is anything there?"

"You sure you don't want to spend countless hours watching the recordings first?" I asked, sarcastically.

He chuckled. "Oh. Yes. Can we? And then, can there not be a letter in the wall, too? So we did it all for nothing?"

"Sounds perfect!" I started for the door.

The morning was cooler than the ones we'd been experiencing. Summer was starting to give way a little, which was nice. It wasn't as if England's summers were anywhere as hot as the ones we had in the States. But part of the basis of the appeal every time I'd spent time in England for vacations was the more temperate weather conditions. I was looking forward to coming out of the heat wave we'd been having.

It was second nature by then to make a straight line from the kitchen door to the loose rock in the wall without having to do much navigating at that point. "Do you want to do the honors, or me?"

He motioned toward the wall. "Go right ahead."

I paused. Looking at it, it looked just like any other rock wall. The stone, itself, felt just like any other of its kind. The old, crumbling mortar was the same as every other patch of old, crumbling mortar in that structure. Yet, if it turned out that things were of a paranormal nature, I couldn't help but wonder what about that spot made it so special. Was it the wall? Or was it something else? Maybe it was the fact that it was the place they felt their love for one another the most each time one of them would leave a letter for the other. That moment, crouched down, looking to be sure nobody was watching for just a second before placing the document that professed their most passionate feelings about the other. Papers they used to transcribe their plans to flee the judgements of those around them to be able to have a life together.

They would pause, just as I had, to look around and check their surroundings before tucking their secret correspondence into the wall. That thought came back to me, and I straightened back up. Doing just that, I scanned the area, my focus being drawn to the back of the property, along the tree line.

There, just as I'd seen before, was a figure. Only, this time, the features were more in focus than I'd seen in days prior. He didn't disappear right away. He stayed there, looking back at me. I could see enough of him then to know that it must have been Joshua.

He was about Reid's height, and what I could make out of his features, there was no doubt there was a family resemblance. His hair, full lips and chiseled jaw line were almost mirrored from the man standing behind me. However, his clothing was authentically styled from the mid to late eighteen hundreds.

Reid had followed my gaze and had gone completely rigid. "That's him, isn't it?"

"I think so." I sucked in a breath.

Just then, the figure raised his hand in a slight wave just before turning and disappearing into the tree line again.

"Reid?"

"Yes, Nell?"

Neither of us had pulled our sights away from where he'd been standing.

I reached back and grabbed his hand. "I don't think it's a neighbor trying to mess with me."

"Nope." He gripped my hand. "Has he ever come back after you saw him disappear?"

"No. But he's also never waved, either."

"Good point."

I shook out of my awe. "Okay. Let's see if there's another letter."

"Right." Reid let go of my hand and took a step back.

I knelt back down and pulled the rock out of the wall. There, just like each of the others, sat a letter. The aged paper with the red, wax seal on one side and scrawled, old, black ink on the other.

To Nell

I took a deep breath as I looked it over. "Are we sure we want to know what it says? I mean, it's a ghost. This could be some evil energy thing messing with us."

He helped me up. "I don't get that impression at all."

"But we don't know, do we?"

He chuckled. "Are all writers this imaginative?"

I looked him in the eye. "We're writers. We create worlds, people and lives. Of course we're full of imagination. How else could we do what we do?"

"I suppose you're right." He started for the house, quietly laughing. "But we are still going in and opening that letter."

I caught up with him. "Fine. But you're reading it."

"Can do."

At the table, he set it down flat and lifted the seal just as he had with the others, unfolding the page the same as well. Once it was flat, without hesitation, he started to read.

June 1867
Dear Nell,

Greetings.

I am completely unsure what to say about your last letter. You have quite the story to weave there. But if what you say is true, then we need to find some proof. That is, if you are like me, you are wondering who is pulling a prank on you.

Granted, your time difference would explain a fair bit. Things have started to look a bit different. I am also curious if the woman I keep seeing out by the wall is you. She wears pants that are tighter than men's under garments. And her tongue is not any sort of speak that I have heard before. And I've met people that have spent time in the United States of America before. So, this has taken me aback quite a bit as far as her character goes.

She also has a gentleman with her during some of her trips to the wall. He looks very familiar, but I can not place who he could possibly be. He does, however, wear a unique style of clothing. My only guess is that it is possible they both have recently visited another country like Italy, bringing home with them their latest fashions.

So, what do you propose we do to clear this up? I will admit that I am reluctant to believe anything more than you both are visitors of the Webb family and find it to your amusement to play this game with me. But, for now, I will play along.

Please just do me one favor. Please tell my Cora that I miss her ... with all my heart.

Sincerely,
Joshua Wilkinson

"I don't think that he knows he's dead." I was standing by the back door, hoping he would reappear by the trees, thinking maybe I could try to communicate with him.

"So you believe now?" Reid asked.

Finally, I looked away from the landscape. "I don't know what I believe. I just know that I can't make sense out of any of this or pin logic on it. So why not? I mean, you saw what I saw. How could I deny it after that?"

"Fair enough," he replied. "Now I feel less along in this insanity."

"Reid?" I glanced down at the letter and back to him. "What happened to him?"

"As in after he died?"

"No. As in how did he die?" I sat. "We've been trying to piece together the bits of information we have, but there's things missing. What if we're meant to find those missing pieces, not wait for them to come to us? What if we have access to what is missing? After all, he doesn't seem to have any clue. Maybe we're supposed to help him know."

"I hadn't thought of that." He joined me.

I put my head in my hands. "This is crazy. I can't believe we're entertaining the thought that this truly is a ghost."

He held the letter up. "I can't imagine how he is feeling."

"You're brilliant!" I went straight to the table and pulled out my paper tablet. "How *does* he feel?"

Immediately, I started writing. I knew exactly what to say to Joshua in the next letter. A few words in, I broke my focus and placed a hand on Reid's forearm. "We need to go into town."

"What for?" he asked.

"We need to find out how he died and when. Maybe then we can piece something together for him? With as many historical archives you and Elijah have, I can't imagine at least one of you wouldn't have access to or even the documents themselves that will answer this question," I explained.

He scratched his chin. "I know that I don't have anything on my end, but I hadn't really looked into how any of my ancestors have died before now. But you're right. I would imagine that we could find it somewhere. It is early enough. We can make a few stops if necessary while places are open."

I tucked the started letter into my laptop bag and went for the car. I was determined to find out that day, and I didn't want to waste any time. Something was driving me.

As I stood in the open door of the car, just about to climb in, I saw Joshua standing at the trees again. The distance was too much to actually make out his expression, but he was there, looking in my direction.

I waved.

He waved back.

I wanted to find out what happened more than ever.

Reid called Elijah on our way back into town. He couldn't think of anything he would have that would solve the puzzle of Joshua's death, and he asked why we were wondering. Reid told him we simply needed to find out what happened to one of his ancestors just to know. He wasn't ready to explain everything over the phone, unsure how crazy it would make us look.

"I'll meet you at the library," Elijah replied and hung up abruptly.

He pulled in next to us almost simultaneously. We got out and went inside. The women at the counter gestured hello at the two men they were familiar with. I, on the other hand, was greeted with peculiar looks and much weaker welcomes.

The two of them sat down at a couple of computers in a back, research room. I settled in next to Reid. Internet search after internet search, they came up empty. Reid even tried tracing his lineage back on ancestry sites just to see if something could be found there. But, still, they came up empty handed.

Elijah closed his browser and started rifling through a box of old papers. "What is so important about this person? You've never really cared much about your own lineage before. Historical events? Sure. Your own family history? No. Why the sudden change?"

With a sigh, Reid explained everything. By the end of it, Elijah's mouth was slightly agape, and he sat, wide eyed, pupils bouncing back and forth between the two of us. A roadblock of words was building just behind his eyes, threatening to come pouring out.

"Are you sure?" Elijah tried to pretend he wasn't as taken aback by what he'd just heard and started flipping through archives of old newspaper headlines.

Reid pulled out a book of carefully cataloged obituaries. "There's little I've ever been this sure of, Elijah. As crazy as it sounds, I cannot think of any other explanation other than some elaborate hoax. And, honestly, around here? I'm more inclined to believe a lost spirit than that. I think my great grandfather is the one writing to Nell and doesn't quite understand that he died. I think he is still looking for the woman he loves."

Elijah set aside the box he had just gone through. "I have known you pretty much all our lives. If you tell me that this is your great grandfather several generations back, and he is haunting your girlfriend and sending her letters? Then, as crazy as it sounds, I believe you."

Reid patted his shoulder. "Thank you, Elijah. Your belief and support mean a lot to me."

The two men exchanged looks of gratification and respect. Being in the same field of work yet in a small area, one would think that they would be rivals. But not Reid and Elijah. These two men had an obvious bond. One you would typically find between cousins. Not colleagues. And *that* I attributed to them both having grown up in the same small village.

"So we are looking to see how your great grandfather from the eighteen hundreds died so you can tell him and show some proof to make him understand that he's not alive any longer?" Elijah didn't lift his eyes from the new box of documents he was searching through.

A corner of Reid's mouth lifted into a smirk. "Yup. Pretty much."

Elijah nodded casually. "Brilliant."

The village library was a little behind the times. Not much of their archives had been uploaded into digital. And what had been didn't really follow any pattern. More or less, it was whatever the person that had time to work on it wanted to upload that day. With that, both Elijah and Reid had become accustomed to sorting through storage boxes and large books full of documents, magazines and newspapers to track down their information.

I read over every subject that had been uploaded. After going through each, I determined that nothing in there went that far back, let alone anything on any Joshua Wilkinson. I signed out of the computer and started pacing.

Reid held out an arm as I went by for my tenth trip across the room. "Come. Sit. You're starting to make me nervous."

"I'm sorry." I took the seat next to him. "I just really want to find out what happened today so I can include it in the letter."

"I know. It's only mid-day. We have time." He kissed my cheek and went back to scanning the book in front of him.

About an hour later, I'd gone through three more cups of coffee and realized that I probably needed to use the restroom. Excusing myself, I left them to their search and took a couple extra minutes for some time alone to try to let some of my thoughts settle into something less chaotic inside my head.

As I returned to the research room, I saw them both pouring over a stack of newspapers and loose papers. "What did I miss?"

Reid looked up. "Elijah found an obituary and a folder with some paperwork on the estate."

I bolted across the room to see.

Elijah pointed to a page. "It seems he had an accident on his farm the morning he was, according to his letters from what Reid says, supposed to run away with Cora Webb."

"An accident?" I flipped the page over, half hoping to find an article telling more than the obituary did.

"That's all we can find," Reid said.

"That's it?" My frustration was growing.

"It looks like it," Elijah interjected. "The file folder of documents is about his uncle that took in his son, Clive, having sold off his property, liquidating the entire estate." He passed the file over to Reid. "Here's an itemized list of all that was given to them upon their agreement with the courts to take on Clive."

Reid read the list. His posture drooped the more he read. "He wasn't a poor man. By everything I know of what he did and of the times, he was actually a smart man that knew how to handle his money. Yet it wasn't enough for the snooty Webb family. And, in the end, it all was for nothing but lining yet another set of turned up noses."

"Wow. I don't even know what to say!" I was angry. "An accident? The morning he was supposed to go away with Cora? That's all anyone said? Was it really an accident? What if it wasn't? And where *did* little miss snooty go? Had she changed her mind? Did they have a fight? Was she talking to more than one man? Anything is possible. But, still, for him to die that day? It was either foul play or completely tragic. Either way, it's not fair."

"Here." Elijah slammed a finger down on a page. "It says here in the story in the local paper that covered the sale of the property that Joshua Wilkinson was found dead in his home the morning of June the 16th, 1867. It appears that he took his own life by way of rope."

"Took his own life?" I went around to his side of the table and read it. "I don't think so."

"Does it say something to the contrary?" Reid turned it so he could read it.

"No." I crossed my arms. "It just doesn't add up. I don't buy it."

Elijah shrugged. "That's what it says."

"May I?" I tugged the article from under Reid's fingers.

Taking it and his obituary to the printer, I copied them both, twice. I set them down and pulled out my paper tablet. With the pen in my fingers, I went to work on trying to shed some light on an obviously lost and hurting Joshua.

2017
Dear Joshua,

Reid and I did some research. We also did a little soul searching. The idea that you are not only the real Joshua Wilkinson but also writing us these letters from your time in 1867 is something I, for one, have struggled to accept. But now, having seen you out by the trees on my estate, I cannot deny it any longer.

After enlisting Elijah, Clive Brown's descendent, we went through quite a bit of archived items at the local library. And after a couple hours of searching, we have found your obituary as well as an explanation of your death, according to reports. But, frankly, I don't believe it. I have included it for you to see. Maybe it will jog your memory.

I'm so sorry to bring this news to you, but you seem to be a lost soul of some sort. The fact is, you're writing to us in 2017. That is why our clothing looks so foreign to you. And, yes, that is why I speak so differently. Take a look around the property as well. I'm sure you will see the modern tools and even the motor vehicles.

My question to you is why you're here. How long have you been active in the area? And what is it you want? We want to help bring you peace. But we are at a loss for what you may be seeking. Maybe Cora? However, sadly, she would have died a number of years ago as well. Otherwise, she would be well over 150 years old. That is, unless she's immortal, and we're dealing with more than one folklore here.

Sorry. That was supposed to be a joke.

Please, help us help you. Let us know what we can do. That is, unless simply knowing you've died is enough to help you move on ... to whatever there is to move on to.

Sincerely,
Nell

I folded the letter, along with a copy of both his obituary as well as the explanation of his death circumstances and put them in an envelope. I put Joshua's name on the front of it and handed it to Reid.

"Do you mind if I take a look?" He lifted the flap.

The wooden chair I was sitting in screeched as I slid it back to stand. "Nope. I was hoping you would."

There was a window in the back of the room. As I approached it, I saw that the glass had a layer of dust on it that not only fogged the view but was rivaled only by the thickness of the dust on the sill itself. I squinted to try to see out and wondered if the cloudiness of my view resembled how Joshua was seeing us. Or, at least, how he did see us when he was out of focus to me. I then wondered if his view of us was clearing up as my view of him was.

"I like it."

"Huh?" I spun around.

Reid had walked across the room and joined me by the window. "It is clear, concise and to the point without being rude. I also think it is brilliant that you're including the paperwork that tell about his death."

"You don't think it is too harsh, do you? That is, providing this is actually him and all?" I asked.

He handed me back the letter. "I think that if this is someone else writing these, we are showing that more people are looking into it. Maybe that will scare them off. But if it *is* him, then he needs to know. I can not imagine any easy way to tell someone that they've died."

"You're right." I closed my eyes. "Okay. Let's go deliver this."

He kissed my cheek. "Then we watch the footage?"

I'd completely forgotten about the cameras. "Yes. Elijah, want to join us in seeing if we caught a ghost on tape?"

He perked up. "Absolutely!"

We cleaned up the archives we had dragged out, photocopying a few more items. Elijah followed us back out to the estate, which gave me a little time to sit back and enjoy some quiet. I leaned the seat back and watched out the clean window at the landscape as we drove down the country roads.

The fields had grown over the summer, and the orchards were in full bloom. Along the path we drove back and forth between town, there were several stands that sold various fruits, vegetables and flowers. A couple even had some goods that the farmer's family would make and sell. I had been making a habit of purchasing most of my produce at those stands. In doing so, one woman had put me in touch with her neighbor, who was what she referred to as the area's best and most reasonably priced butcher.

My mind wandered to making a grocery list when we pulled into the drive. As the two of them got the playback ready inside, I jotted down my list for later. I think a part of me wanted to cling to something normal; something that didn't involve creeping neighbors, ghosts or scandals.

Then, I walked out back. With the letter in hand, I made my way to the wall, as had become habit at that point. But I stopped and stood back upright. Turning, I walked to the back of the property and stood close to the spot I'd been seeing who I was all but convinced was Joshua.

Granted, I hadn't seen him more than once a day. But was there any rules to what was happening? No. I couldn't even be sure that I wasn't losing my mind and imagining the whole thing ... Reid and Elijah included. And, for a moment, I wondered if I was actually sitting in some asylum somewhere, drugged up and strapped down to a table or curled up in the corner, hallucinating everything.

But for the sake of playing it all out, I wanted to see. "Joshua? Are you here, Joshua?"

I didn't hear anything other than the wind in the trees and a few animals making their way through the inner wooded area, probably scared by the sound of my voice. An owl fluffed its wings in the tree above me. He hooted and settled back onto his branch, closing his eyes.

"They say you all can carry the spirits of the dead, buddy. Is that true? Are you Joshua's guide?" I looked up at the bird, half waiting for it to reply like the *Tootsie-Pop* cartoon owl.

"How many licks does it take?"

I scoffed at myself.

Feeling completely ridiculous, I ran my hand through my hair and turned around. "Just put it in the wall, Nell. Just put the letter where the others have gone and go inside. The cameras will tell you. *Not* an owl."

"Are you the woman that signs her name as Nell Price?" a man spoke from behind me.

I whipped around. Seeing a man standing in the tree line, dressed in clothes indicative of the eighteen hundreds and slightly transparent, I screamed and stumbled backward. He reached out to try to catch me, but his hand went right through my arm.

We both looked at each other with wide eyes as I landed on the ground.

I scrambled to my feet as he started to back away. "Wait! Please don't go."

He looked like he was slipping into a panic. "How? I do not understand."

"I don't know," I stammered.

He looked me over, stopping briefly on my hand. His eyes grew wide, and he started to back away.

I gathered myself and thrust the letter out in front of me. "Here. My next letter. I was going to leave it in the wall, but I was curious if you would be here."

"Impossible," he gasped.

I shook the envelope. "Here. Read it."

He held his hand out to take it, but, again, it went right through solid material. His expression deepened in fear, and he began to fade.

"I don't understand." I lowered my hand.

"How can this be?" He disappeared.

I was shaking, unable to move. "I'll put it in the wall. Please read it." My voice was low.

My mind shorted out briefly, and I froze. I was pretty sure my feet wouldn't have taken me anywhere if I had tried, but I couldn't even think to tell myself to move them. I just stood. It felt like all of the blood had drained out of me, and I was equally as ghost-like as the presence I had just been interacting with ... as Joshua Wilkinson.

"Nell!" Reid was sprinting across the gardens with Elijah right on his heels. Reid took me by my shoulders and stood in front of me. "What happened? We heard you scream. I hadn't even realized that you had left the house."

My brain was refusing to function more than replaying the scenario over in my head.

"I had to look on the cameras to find you." He tilted his head to be in my line of sight. "You were talking to someone, but I only saw a glimpse of someone or something in front of you. I couldn't make out what it was. What happened? Are you alright?"

"Joshua." That was all I could get out.

"Was he here? Did he say anything?" Reid slid his hands down my arms and took my hands in his, directing his next comment to Elijah. "I think she's gone into shock. We need to get her inside."

Elijah stepped up next to us. "Nell? Can you walk with us?"

My breaths were coming quick. "I ... I ..."

"I'll carry you. Put your arm around my neck." Reid pulled my arm around him and lifted me. "Elijah, can you get a glass of water and a cool towel ready?"

"Absolutely." He ran off ahead of us.

Several paces away from the house, I snapped out of it. "Wait!"

He set me down onto my feet. "What is it? Is he back?" He looked all around us.

"No." I lifted my hand, the letter still in it. "He couldn't take it from me. His hand went right through it. I need to put it in the wall."

"He tried? As in you two communicated?" A look of awe covered his features.

"Yes." I started for the wall. "I told him I would put it in there. I need to do it in case he is waiting."

He caught up to me, clearly stunned. "What did he say?"

My pace picked up. "He was scared. Of course he would be scared with his hand going through mine and then through the letter. But there was something else. There was something about *me* that startled him."

I quickly rolled the rock onto the ground and tucked the letter into place, feeling the ground around me until I gripped the stone and placed it back in its place in the wall. I stood and faced Reid. "Something about me scared him, I think."

"Well, you said his hand went through yours. Like you said, of course he was scared. That confirms he doesn't know he is dead," he reasoned.

I blinked. "No. I think it was more than that."

"Maybe he will write back. I can't imagine he won't. That is, unless the knowledge of being dead is all he needed. I suppose we just wait and see." Reid put a hand on my back as we started walking.

I stared back at the rear of the property. "Yes. I suppose so."

Elijah was anxiously waiting in the kitchen with Reid's requested items. "You're looking a little less catatonic."

I sheepishly grinned. "Yes. I think I'm back to the land of the functional."

He held out the glass of water. "Thirsty?"

"Thank you." I took a long drink.

Reid took the wet rag and motioned toward a chair. "Sit. I still think you need another moment." He pulled another chair up to face mine and pulled my hair aside as he placed the cloth on the back of my neck. "She had an encounter with Joshua's spirit."

Elijah leaned on the table. "You what? As in you spoke with him?"

"Not much. He tried to catch me when I stumbled. That was the scream you heard. He also tried to take the envelope from me, but both times, his hand went right through me," I retold the story.

His jaw went slack. "Wow. Brilliant! That proves it then. We're dealing with a ghost."

"Apparently." Reid turned over the towel, allowing the cool side to rest against my neck.

"I told Reid that I think he was scared of me," I said.

"Scared of you? Was he scared of you, or was it that his hand went through yours served as proof that he is, in fact, dead? I know that would scare the daylights out of me." Elijah tried to reason.

"I don't know." My breaths were finally back to a normal rate. "But I got the feeling it was me. Or maybe both?"

"Regardless, I think the focus should be that you just had an interaction with an actual ghost, face to face." Elijah sounded excited.

I giggled. "Check you out. A historian with an interest with the paranormal."

"Hey. Not all of us are stiffs." He snorted.

"Elijah?" Gerald came into the room. "Is everything alright here?"

"Gerald!" Elijah stood and went to the man, giving him a hug.

"Do you two know each other?" I asked.

Gerald put his arm around Elijah. "Yes. He is my cousin."

"Cousin?" Reid repeated. "Oh, yes. That's right."

Elijah patted Gerald on the back. "Yes. We don't get to see each other as much as I would like with us both working so much and all, though." The two of them went into the other room, busily chatting on their way.

"How are you, truly?" Reid leaned toward me.

I sat up in the chair. "I'm better. Although, I do feel a bit foolish."

"Foolish?" He blinked.

I looked down at my hands in my lap. "Yes. I just freaked out. And not in a silly, fast talking, stammering over my words kind of freak out. You had to carry me. Maybe foolish is too soft of a word? I feel ... ridiculous."

"So you have a wild imagination, *and* you're hard on yourself. Duly noted." He smirked.

"Yup," I replied, attempting to feign a sense of pride for it.

I loved how he made me at ease so easily. I hadn't liked how almost uptight I had gotten over the years. Yet, somehow, he could make a single comment, and my fragile walls would all crumble, even if for only a little while. It only served to make me crave him that much more.

"Then, before you hide yourself away physically *or* mentally, we will keep on the move." He stood and held his hand out.

I took his hand, but didn't stand. "On the move? Doing what?"

He tugged me up. "Anything. We can go into town and research ghosts, stay here and help with the remodel, get out of here and do something completely unrelated. I'm not going to let you sit here and stew on what just happened. If you want to productively research? Fine. If you want to feel of use here? Fine. But if you want to step away and wait for a reply? That's the choice that has my vote."

Each of the options had a certain level of appeal to them.

"While you decide, I'm going to get the camera going again," he said, getting up and walking over to the counter where the laptop was sitting.

"Should we go over the recordings?" I asked.

He glanced back. "After what you saw? You sure you'll see anything more convincing?"

I shrugged. "Then is it important to keep recording?"

“You know? That’s a good question.” He pursed his lips. “But I think so. Just in case. We can review footage at any time.”

I nodded. “You’re probably right.”

He finished typing in some commands and closed the screen. “Okay. So what are we going to do?”

“What about Elijah?” I motioned toward the two men just over the threshold into the foyer.

Reid grinned. “I don’t think he will mind. After all, he not only was part of a ghost story, but he’s found Gerald to entertain him.”

I stood up, my shoulders back and a mildly forced confidence in my stance. “Okay then. Get me out of here.”

He smiled from ear to ear. “Your wish is my command.”

***

The drive was gorgeous that day. It was mild out, temperature wise. Enough that I rolled the window down and leaned on it for quite a while. The wind whipping my hair back, I ignored the fact that it was probably going to look like an ancient, decrepit bird nest by the time we got anywhere. But with the large, puffy clouds occasionally blotting out the sky and then bursts of the warmth the sun’s rays sent down … I was loving every minute of it.

After a while, I reluctantly pulled myself back into the car fully. Leaning back, I curled up in the seat, facing him. He turned to look at me briefly, smiling, and put a hand on my knee. Happily, I entwined my fingers with his and watched him as he stayed focused on the road aside from the occasional glance over at me.

I loved how he looked at me. There was a sense of protection, admiration, gentleness and passion in how he saw me. In the beginning, there were only fleeting moments of him giving in to his interest in me. Then, he would not only pull back, but he would yank his feelings back.

However, as things progressed, he never tried to hide it anymore, which made me feel bad for the fact that I was still struggling with letting him in. But his unrelenting patience allowed everything else to stay in place while he waited for me to catch up to him. And with how quick everything was going, I was happy he wasn't trying to force me to keep up.

He didn't need any time to accept his feelings. They were what they were, and he was more than happy to enjoy every second of them for as long as he could. I could feel that. And it made me want to do the same for him.

I leaned up and switched on the radio. Connecting my phone to it, I hit play on one of my playlists. It was full of olde jazz tunes and modern songs remade into the olde jazz style. It was perfect for the drive.

He started singing along to one of the songs.

"You have a really nice voice," I commented.

He grinned and kept singing.

I dozed off listening.

When I woke, we were parked. He was gently rubbing my shoulder. "Nell. Wake up. We are here."

"Mmmmm..." I forced my eyes to open.

My window was still down, and a slight breeze was coming in. I stretched and moaned.

"Oh. No. Don't start that," he said.

I yawned. "Start what?"

"Those noises. Just get out of the car before I can't help myself right here." He abruptly got out and shoved the keys in his pocket.

Giggling to myself, I got out and joined him on the other side of the car. "So..." I dragged out the word. "Where are we?"

His fingers entwined with mine. "This is my family's vacation home. My father keeps it in his name, and I do a lot of making sure it is upkept."

Family vacation home.

Father.

I hadn't even thought about his family being a tangible thing. Nor had I even considered a parent being a factor. Up until that very moment, Reid was a solitary element in my new life. But there we were, about to enter a house that belonged to his whole family. One that had memories and history and was about to introduce me to an element of his inner personal side that I was both scared of and thrilled to enter.

Nonetheless, it was beautiful. White brick columns on the front holding up a balcony over the front porch and black shutters hung, flanking the sides of each window. The landscaping was detailed, and the back yard a decent size from what I could see. It wasn't near as large as Webb Manor, but it certainly rivaled it in beauty and charm.

"You alright over there?" He took a step forward, looking back at me.

I took in a sharp breath. "Yep."

He shook my arm gently. "You coming?"

"Is anyone else here?" My eyes were fixed on the front door.

"No." He started walking again. This time, taking me in tow.

He set his bag down on the side table in the foyer before taking my purse and laying it down as well. The interior was equally as well styled and clean. "You take care of this place?"

He led me into the kitchen and took two bottles of lemonade out, handing one to me. "Yes. All of my aunts, uncles, cousins and siblings have access. But hardly any of them take advantage of it. And those that do, it is rare. Plus, my father is usually too deep into his work to allow himself to break away, let alone come out here. I am sure it is the fact that it holds so many memories of my mother. But he uses the work excuse mostly."

"Well, that explains why you push so hard for me to slow down. Slow down. Stop escaping my issues. Pull myself out of my work."

He snaked an arm around my waist and pulled me into him. "That, and I'm a little selfish."

I almost spit out my drink, stifling a laugh. "Did you just say you're selfish?"

He set his bottle onto the counter, followed by mine. "Yes. I want as much of you as I can get."

He swept me up into his arm and carried me upstairs. Turning the corner into the second bedroom down the hall, we bumped into the doorway. He stumbled briefly, letting my legs down, and we clamored across the room and onto the bed, laughing.

I felt his hand as it made its way down my side, over my hip, and to my thigh. His fingers pushed into my leg, lifting it and hooking it up over his own hip.

My hands grappled at the back of his shirt, yanking it up and over his head. He threw it across the room, lowering back down to continue kissing me.

It was that level of passion that continued for the next couple hours until, once again, we were collapsed in a sweaty, heaving mess of tangled arms and legs. His head was on my stomach, hands on both of my sides. The sheets and pillows were all on the floor, and I was dying of thirst. "We should have brought the lemonades up with us."

"Mmmhmmm," he moaned.

I looked down and smiled.

His eyes were closed, and his breath was slowed to a relaxed pace. He was quickly falling asleep. I didn't want to disturb him, so I let him fall completely away, a soft snore and all, before I slowly made my way out from under him.

After tossing on his shirt, I picked up one of the sheets and laid it over him. I kissed his head and whispered, "I'm going downstairs."

"Okay." He rolled over onto his side. "I love you."

I snuck out of the room and leaned against the wall just out in the hallway, still smiling. *With all my heart*. I felt a thick layer of rock wall fall away.

With a renewed sense of elation, I wandered through the house after grabbing my bottle of lemonade. Just off the living room, I found a home office sized library full of books. Everything from education to fiction. *Hemingway* to *Cassandra Clare*. A perfect little hideaway for someone that loved books.

My hand glided across the spines on a couple of shelves. The transition between the various textures brought a smile to my lips. As I crossed the room, I stopped on one section, seeing that it was full of several authors I knew, including *Mary Ting*. Her book, *Crossroads,* the first book in the series, one that I loved to indulge in, was ever so slightly pushed in further than the rest. I pulled it back out and aligned it with the others.

I had heard that she also wrote in other genres than YA under the name *M. Clarke*. So, I was more than elated to see a few books under that name next in line. I pulled *My Clarity* off the shelf, took my lemonade and went out the back door to the deck off the rear of the house and sat down to read.

There was a patio set that overlooked the manicured back lawn, surrounded by miles of fields. I took a seat and opened the book, the wind gentle across my bare legs. The ottoman was the perfect height to kick my feet up and lean back. I took a long, refreshing gulp of the lemonade, set it down on the side table and went back to my book, feeling right at home.

I love you.

Those words crept into my mind from time to time, interrupting my reading. Each time, bringing a smile to my face.

Ten

Reid slept for a few hours, waking mid-afternoon. I had stayed out on the deck the whole time, aside from going into the kitchen for a small snack and another beverage. After a while, I leaned my head back and let my book rest on my chest. It was nice to sit outside in the quiet, and I allowed myself to imagine doing the same thing at Webb Manor once the remodel was completed.

I worried that I wouldn't ever have that there. I wasn't sure if Joshua would ever move on, or what - or whom - else could possibly be floating around on the property. Another concern was, even if he did move on, could I? Could I let go of the anxiety and fears that had plagued me ever since it all started?

Reid had been right. I *did* need to relax. I needed to get away from it all. And our little jaunt to his calm and serene family home showed me that. It reminded me why I had started to distance myself from everyone back in New York. I was never able to slow down. Someone demanded something from me at all times. And that feeling of go-go-go had become habit.

Maybe that was why I took on the estate. To have something that seemed to need me in order to progress. But why? Reid's repeated attempts to get me to cut myself some slack made me see that I allowed too many other things to not only rule my days but to keep me from enjoying the little things some days.

Feeling myself grow more tense again from just thinking about being wound up, I let myself drift off into a fictional scenario where he and I were together, happily. A life where I never got writer's block, and his projects were safe and fun. We lived in that house in the country where no lost ancestral spirits hung out, let alone wrote us. And I would spend my free time out on that deck, reading happily.

He came outside and slowly lifted the book off me, thinking I was asleep.

"Did you have a good nap?"

I kept my eyes closed, still clinging to the serenity of the afternoon.

"Yes. I did. Thank you." He looked over the book before handing it back to me. "Good choice. She's one of my aunt's favorites."

"Thanks." I squinted at him as the sun peeked out from behind a cloud.

The legs of the chair scraped across the wooden deck as he turned it to sit. "I can't believe I slept so long. Actually, I can't believe I slept so sound. It has been a while."

I flipped my hair. "You're welcome."

He laughed. "Can I get you to put me to sleep like that every night?"

I leaned over and kissed him. "You got it."

The sun ducked behind a cloud as he settled into his chair. "Should I let you get back to sleep?"

"I wasn't asleep," I replied.

He rested his arms on his knees and leaned on them. "Then what is on your mind? You seem a bit distant."

My sigh was a little louder than I'd intended. "I was just off in another world."

"Working on your manuscript in your head?" He took a sip of my lemonade and passed it to me.

It had gone warm from sitting in the sun. "No. I am just really enjoying this trip, and not looking forward to going back."

"You're not looking forward to going back to a giant estate that's been painstakingly remodeled in your own taste just for yourself?" he teased.

"Well, when you put it that way, I sound spoiled." The breeze picked up momentarily, sending goosebumps over my skin. I curled up slightly. "If it were just that, I probably wouldn't leave the place. But with everything else, I'm just feeling overwhelmed. I'm starting to feel like I'm losing control over my life."

"We will make it through his." His touch was gentle as he touched my arm.

"I don't know if I can do this, Reid." I put my face in my hands, fighting back tears.

His eyes were set as he spoke. "Yes. You can. You're the strongest woman I've ever met, Nell. I know I haven't known you for long, but I've gotten to know you pretty well in the short time we've been seeing each other. And I am positive that you have more than enough in you to get through this."

"Me? Strong?" I huffed. "I'm falling apart here. And I don't want to take on all of this alone."

"You're not alone." His voice lowered, revealing what I said had hurt him.

My arms dropped, taking my shoulders with them. "I know, but haven't I been enough of a burden? I don't want to keep dragging you through this. You have some family history involved, sure. But taking all of this on with me is probably effecting your work. Besides, what do I need with such a huge house? I should just finish the renovations, sell it and go back to my house in New York."

"Please don't." His expression tightened. "I don't want to lose you."

"Aren't you sick of me yet? I've been a wreck since we met!" I threw my hands in the air.

He took my flailing hands and pulled them to his chest. "You have been dealing with extraordinary circumstances. But I see you. I see who you are. And I have fallen completely in love with *you*."

"But ..." I started.

"But nothing, Nell." His voice was stern. "I love you, and I don't want you to go anywhere. You belong here. I know it. Not just with me, but you belong *here*, in this area. I can't explain it. And, honestly, I don't want to. I've spent my whole life avoiding attachment. But nobody has ever grabbed me like you have, and I'll be damned if I just let you slip through my fingers when I can help you get through it."

"And if we don't make it as a couple?" I asked.

He quirked an eyebrow. "Do you doubt how strongly I feel for you, or do you not feel something strong for me?"

I closed my eyes. "I'm scared of how strongly we feel for each other. It's only been days. And I'm scared that you will change your mind. What if your pull to me is linked to this chaos? What if it feels so big to you because of the excitement? We don't know, and we can't know. And I guess it is my turn to be the one to question it."

"Do you think the way you feel for me has anything to do with all of that?" His eyes searched mine.

I swallowed. "No. But what if it does?"

"Then we deal with it then." He ran his hand through his hair. "But I can feel it in every inch of me that we're not just some silly couple more wrapped up in outside influences or lust. What we have is different, and we both know it."

We *did* both know that, but it was just as hard to allow myself to accept it than it was for me to accept that the letters were coming from a ghost through some time-warped spot in a rock wall. "I'm not the type of woman that just easily goes along with the type of things I write about. Those are fantasies. This is the real world."

"Sometimes, the real world comes from fantasies. Otherwise, where do you think they come from? Purely wishful thinking? I don't believe that. I believe that some people get their fantasy." Reid knelt on the floor in front of me, keeping my hands against his chest. "Nell Price, I ask this not only to show you just how serious I am about how I feel and how sure I am of my feelings, but I also ask this because I feel it is right." He paused. "Nell, will you marry me?"

My jaw dropped. I hadn't entertained the idea of remarrying. I especially hadn't thought I'd do it so soon, let alone to someone I had met so recently. But, in that moment, only one word ran through my mind in reply to his proposal. "Yes."

He looked surprised. "Yes?"

"Did you want another response?" I laughed, half crying.

"No!" He stood, almost too quickly. His chair toppled slightly from the force of the back of his legs hitting it. "I just didn't expect such a sure response. I might not have even expected a yes. But ... wow. Yes." He swept me up into his arms and kissed me passionately.

I bent down and picked up my book that I dropped when he pulled me up off of the chair, setting it down on the seat behind me. "I have never seen anything rattle your confidence."

"Oh?" He was shaking slightly. "And yet, you're as calm as can be. Is that all it takes to get you to relax? To propose to you?"

"Did you need to take it back?" I giggled.

"No!" He took a deep breath. "Not in the least."

With his hands steady, he drew me to him again. This time, there was no stumbling. We made our way back upstairs without a single comedic moment, and without disconnecting from one another.

***

"What are you in the mood for?" he asked.

"More?" I gasped.

"Food, silly." He rolled onto his side and brushed my hair away from my face. "I'm starving. There's not much for food here. We can either scrape something up, or we can make the drive back to town."

I traced swirling lines around on his bare chest. "Oh! Food. Okay. Uhhh... There really isn't anything here to eat. I saw that when I was looking for a snack earlier."

"We do not keep the kitchen stocked since none of us take holiday here regularly. We bring our food when we come normally, even if it is just a couple of days. Something I probably should have taken time to stop for on our way out," he explained.

"Do we *have* to go back?" I whined.

He chuckled. "There is a grocery store not too far, in a nearby town. I could jaunt in there and get something for dinner if you like."

"That's a decent drive. Do you want me to come with you?" I asked.

He thought for a moment. "No. I think I can handle it. Plus, I would enjoy cooking tonight. If you don't mind, that is."

"I could just suck it up and go back to town with you. Then we wouldn't have to make such a fuss," I offered.

He quirked an eyebrow. "That scared of me cooking?"

I hadn't connected our two comments. "It's not that. I just don't want to put you out. You sure you don't want my help?"

He kissed my cheek before getting out of bed. "Nope. Unless you are opposed to it, I was thinking I could go grab some food, and we could stay the night here."

It was probably obvious how much I approved in my expression. "Not an inch of me is opposed to that."

Quickly, he cleaned up and headed out. I, on the other hand, flopped back onto the bed and gave myself a few minutes of smiling time before getting up.

I tried to find something to do around the house to feel useful. But, aside from the bed, everything was clean and in its place. There were a few candles in the den. I found a book of matches in one of the drawers in the kitchen, picked up the candles, tucked my book under my arm and headed for the master bathroom. There, I filled the large bath tub, arranged the candles around it, lit them, sorted through the basket of soaps, shampoos and conditioners on the sink counter and turned off the overhead light.

"Ahhh ..." I sank into the steaming water. "I could totally get used to this."

The candles provided plenty of soft light for me to read, and I took full advantage of it, whipping through the pages, my mind completely absorbed by the story, occasionally refilling the tub with warm water. And, with my toes pruning, I laid the book over the side of the tub and leaned my head back.

I had just drifted off when he came back. "Nell." His words were soft, as were his lips as he kissed my forehead.

"Mmmhmmm?" The corners of my mouth turned up in response.

"You look absolutely tranquil." He sat on the edge of the tub, lifting the book and placing it on the sink counter.

I tugged on his arm. "Join me."

He held his hand up. "Dinner. I need to make some dinner."

My stomach growled. "Oh yes. That would probably be a good idea."

His steps were slow as he went for the door. But before he exited, he turned back and paused, a peculiar look on his face. "I was going to do this later, but you have such a romantic scene set up here."

"Do what?" I sat up.

He returned to his seat on the side of the tub and pulled out a tiny box from his pocket. Looking down at it, he spoke, "This was my great grandmother's."

I looked at the small, red, velvet box sitting in his hand. "Did you just go get that? How did you have time?"

He shook his head, finally looking up at me. "No. I made a call while I was out getting groceries. My father has kept it here since this was their house."

I pulled the towel off the bar next to the tub and got out. He got up and gave me room. As I toweled off, he stood there, running a finger over the box and looking completely nervous.

Having finished drying, I wrapped the towel around myself. "You made a call, though? To..."

"My father," he answered.

"And is it key to something here? A piece you need for work? What's in there? I mean, for you to have called your father ... Is it something for work, or something you've forgotten?"

He held it out, sitting upright in his palm. "It's for you."

"Me?" My voice was a whisper.

"Yes."

I took it and looked up at him.

He nodded for me to go ahead.

With a slow, deep breath, I opened it.

Inside was a ring. But not just any ring. It was quite possibly the most gorgeous piece of jewelry that I had ever seen. You wouldn't think anyone had ever worn it with how unmarred the gold was. And the diamond, set in a filigree nest of gold was easily well over a carat.

His hand touched mine. "To make it official."

I blinked. "So, your father knows?"

"Yes," he replied, simply.

"And you want me to wear this?" I couldn't take my eyes off it.

He looked startled. "Do you not like it?"

I almost dropped the box. "I do! I didn't mean to imply that I didn't. Sorry. I just ... it's just so gorgeous. And, as you said, a family heirloom. Are you sure you..."

"Want it on your hand?" He took the ring from its placeholder and held his hand out for mine. "I am no less sure than when I asked you to marry me earlier."

My eyes filled with tears as he slid the ring onto my finger. And, of course, it fit, perfectly.

He grinned. "Perfect."

"Exactly what I was thinking," I said.

I placed a hand on his cheek and looked at him. I was no less sure about us than he was said he was. And, in that moment, I knew it. I was scared of it, but I knew.

"You get dressed, beautiful. I'll go start dinner." He kissed my hand and left the bathroom.

There was no wiping the grin off my face as I drained the tub and cleaned up the candles, stopping occasionally to admire my new accessory. I went into the bedroom and found, laid out on the bed, a set of the softest and most comfortable pajamas I had ever seen, complete with slippers.

Instantly, I pulled them on and hugged myself.

I held my hand out and looked at the ring on my finger one more time before I marched downstairs to the kitchen. "You had better not change."

Startled by my outburst, he whipped around, wooden spoon in hand. "What?"

"This!" I waved my arms. "You're helpful, sensitive, generous, romantic, *great* in bed and pretty much all around amazing. I'm pretty sure a woman, or five, will put a price on my head for this. But don't be putting on some show to get me and then turn into someone else later."

"I don't gather your meaning." His expression turned to confusion.

I glanced at the ring again. "I am in love with you. But what I don't want is a version of you that isn't *this*. So many people put on a big song and dance when dating but then become lazy or even cruel once they are settled into a relationship. And I don't need to add another failed attempt at love to my roster."

He set the spoon down and put his hands on my shoulders. "Love, I wouldn't even know how to begin to put on a show, as you say. I am not terribly versed in the whole thing as it is, as I explained to you. You are getting the real me. That is something I can promise you."

I put my hands on his arms. "I know that I know that. I just needed to be sure I said it, too."

The pot started to boil over. "Oh crap."

We both laughed as he got it under control.

"What are you making?" I peeked around him.

His lips grazed my shoulder. "You will see. It will be another forty-five minutes probably."

"Anything I can do?"

"Nope."

I looked around, trying to find some way to be helpful, but he shooed me out of the kitchen. Pouting on my way out, I went about returning the candles to their homes and settling on the couch to read, occasionally glancing at the ring on my finger once again.

Eleven

The next morning, I slipped out of bed and went to the bathroom to freshen up. Reid had bought some toiletries while he was out the prior evening as well. Thankful for his thoughtfulness, I brushed my teeth and my hair then returned to bed a little more presentable.

I propped myself up on an elbow, leaning toward him a bit and took a moment to admire his tone physique under the sheet and messy hair, realizing I was going to be able to wake up to that the rest of my life.

The rest of my life. My heart leaped.

I whispered in his ear, "I love you."

"With all my heart," he replied, his morning voice deep and tinged with a growl.

"Do you want to sleep longer?" I placed a series of kisses on his shoulder.

"Mmmm ..." he moaned. "No. We should probably get into the estate and check on things.

A mix of disappointment and anxiety flooded me. "Oh yes. *That*."

He opened his eyes and propped himself up. "Aren't you curious?"

I knew I was. But at the same time, the whole situation had brought with it so much stress. "I guess I'm still a bit lost and afraid."

I could see him organize his next statement. "Nell, no matter how different or crazy that whole thing is, I wouldn't want to give it up. If it wasn't for Joshua's letters, you and I wouldn't have what we have. It was because of him that we met. And it is because of his continued contact that we have spent so much time together. For that, I am more than grateful. And for that, I am more than happy to see this through to find out what he needs to finally get some peace."

"Wow." I rubbed my forehead. "I feel completely selfish right now. You're right. You're so, so right."

He sat up the rest of the way and touched my arm. "I didn't say it to make you feel that way. I only meant to explain why I am so eager to keep working on it."

I tucked my pride into the back of my mind. "Alright. Let's get out there. I feel bad I didn't see it that way before. But, like I said, you're right. I want to help him find peace, too."

He cupped my cheek and kissed me. "Alright. I'll get dressed."

We both got around and loaded up the car. The day was cloudy, and as we got closer to the manor, it started to rain. The crews had moved everything inside. But, despite the weather, as I had been each day, I was surprised at how much they had gotten done.

Gerald met us in the foyer. "Good morning."

"Good morning, Gerald." I shook off my wet hair.

He offered us each a hand towel. "The status report is that the main house should be finished within the week for plumbing and electrical. It shouldn't take longer than that for the paint and fixtures. Then we will move onto each of the out buildings. Maybe a month total."

Reid's eyebrows rose. "Wow! That is impressive."

"Yes. Thank you." I hugged him.

"You here to check on your wall?" He followed as we went into the finished kitchen.

I nodded. "Yes."

"Well, I haven't seen any activity. But you never know. Things like this aren't very predictable, are they?" He stood in the doorway.

"That's very true." I put my hand on the doorknob.

"I will let you get to it." He took his leave.

"You want me to go with you?" Reid asked me.

I stepped out the door. "No. I'll be right back."

He held up the empty pot of coffee. "I'll get on this then."

It wasn't raining hard, but I wiped several drops from my eyelashes as I got to the wall. Before leaning down, I looked out by the trees. It looked too calm. Too dark. Too void of activity. But the sky was extremely overcast, and I chalked it up to the weather. But when I removed the rock to find the spot empty, part of my heart sunk.

I realized that I'd grown attached to Joshua in a way. Yes. Reid was correct. We owed a major part of why we were together to him. That was without a doubt. But, on top of that, Joshua seemed like a genuinely nice man. I enjoyed the intrigue of our correspondences. I also had wanted to help him, but thinking that my help had just sent him away, even if it was for the better, was still a bit heartbreaking.

When I walked back through the back door, Reid was there with a dry towel, looking anxious. "Is it soaked?"

It took a minute to register what he was referring to. "There was nothing there."

His eyes grew wide for a second and then quickly went back to normal. "It is probably the rain."

"There was nothing there. I don't know why. Do you think rain would stop a ghost?" I puzzled.

He shrugged. “I don’t know anything about ghosts to know. But it’s possible, I suppose.”

“I guess that’s true.” My fingers ran through my soaked hair.

“Tomorrow,” he exclaimed.

“Tomorrow,” I agreed.

But the next day didn’t bring a letter either. Reid and I had spent the day working with the crews and then stayed at his house in town that night and returned to Webb Manor early the next morning. It was still very overcast, but it wasn’t raining. I didn’t even go inside before making my way to check the wall.

Reid was waiting inside with a pot brewing again. “So?”

“Nothing,” I replied, unable to hide the disappointment in my tone.

“Tomorrow,” he stated.

I closed my eyes. “What if we were right? What if just knowing he was dead was all he needed, and it’s over?”

“Wouldn’t that be a good thing?” he asked.

“I thought so, but it doesn’t feel like that's it. Or at least that it should be it.” I kept glancing out the window. “I’m going back by the trees.”

“I’ll check on the crews.”

“Thank you,” I replied, absentmindedly.

There was a chill in the air, and I was glad I wore a sweater that day. I pulled it around me and wrapped my arms around myself as I crossed the property. The same emptiness plagued my nerves as had the day before.

Again, there was no new letter.

Having walked to the tree line, I stood in the same place I had stood the day I interacted with Joshua and looked around. The only thing I could feel was something that resembled an invisible wall. I placed my hands in front of me, palms facing out, until I could feel a slight tingling on them.

"I'm so sorry," I spoke, hoping that if he was there, he could hear me.

A couple minutes ticked by as I stayed there. The only thing I heard was the wind blowing through the trees. The only thing I saw was the woods before me. After several minutes, Joshua still hadn't made an appearance. I finally turned and went back to the house.

That day, I went into town and loaded up some boxes and stayed working in my new bedroom, unpacking and arranging. It was the only thing I could think of that would allow me to stay tucked away from others *and* stay productive ... other than writing. And I wasn't in the mood for that.

Reid made a couple trips in for more boxes and a few pieces of furniture for me, taking Gerald's work truck each time throughout the day. Other than that, he helped the crews with various jobs.

He peeked his head in through my bedroom door. "I am amazed how quickly they have done all of this."

"Yeah." I was distracted, sitting on the floor and looking through a box of photos.

He came in, closing the door behind him. "Are you alright?"

"Huh? What?" A few photos dropped from the stack in my hand.

They fluttered haphazardly as he crossed the room to help pick them up. "I didn't mean to interrupt. What did you find?"

I held up the photo I had been looking at. "Those are my kids. It had been a sunny day, and the four of us had gone for a walk in the park before my eldest left for college four years ago." I pointed at each person. "That is my eldest, Emma. She is going to school to be a lawyer. Murphy, my son. He is a firefighter, inspired by the 9-11 attacks. And my youngest, Lucinda. We call her Lula. She is in her second year at college for art history. But her ultimate goal is to be a museum curator."

Gently, he took the photo and looked at it. "You look so happy with them."

I sighed. "Yeah. They were my everything for so long."

"How did they react when you told them about your move here?" he asked.

"Emma is at *Harvard*, studying. I barely get to see her. Murphy spends long hours at work. So neither of them said much about it. I think they're still adjusting to the divorce. Lula, on the other hand, is excited. She wants to come stay with me next summer if she can get an internship at one of the museums here."

"We will have to see if we can make that happen. I might have an in or two." He smiled.

I'd never actually thought of him having any kind of pull in that kind of direction. In New York, it was all about who you knew and who they knew. That was how you got anywhere in any business. There were so many people in such a small area, all vying for their part of the top in whatever field they were in. You *had* to know people to get a boost. That, or have dumb luck. Part of me left that mentality behind when I left the city. It was that moment that I realized I was still secluding myself in some ways.

I took the photo as he handed it back, looking at it again before returning it and the others back to the box and shoving it aside. "Okay. I'd better get back to work." I stood and dusted myself off.

"Anything I can help you with? Or are you ready for another load of things?" His eyes scanned the room.

Most of the boxes had been gone through. "I'm starting to get anxious to have everything brought over. I know I don't have near enough to fill even a third of the house. I'd like to see what I have that will go where and what more I'll need."

"Maybe a walk through will do you some good? Could be therapeutic, even. Make some notes in regards to what you *do* have and what you already know you want to get." He'd picked up a pen and pad of paper from my dresser and handed it to me.

I took it. "That's probably a good idea. Could also help me avoid emotional pitfalls like boxes of old photos."

"Would you like me to go get some more in the meanwhile?" he asked.

"You sure you don't want me to come and help if you do?" He had refused each of his other trips, saying I was of more use there, unpacking the boxes he was bringing.

He kissed my head. "No, my dear. I've got it."

We spent the remainder of the day like that. Him getting more loads and helping the crews as I planned and unpacked. Occasionally, I would pause and look at the ring, still in complete awe. And on some of those occasions, he would be nearby and see me ... and would smile.

***

Again, we spent the night in town, at his place. And again, we got up early and headed out to the estate. That morning, however, I hesitated going straight to the wall. I didn't want it to be another day without a new letter. But, also, I didn't want to find that he'd returned and worry about why he'd been gone. Either way, neither of the options were one hundred percent good.

I wanted a sign if he had moved on. Something to tell me that he was at peace. But my trips out there had left me unsettled. Not feeling the sense of happiness and closure. My walk out to the trees the previous day especially wasn't one that left me feeling that all was well. I felt blocked out.

It was early, and the sun was just coming up. For the most part, the clouds had cleared away. The weather was similar to the day that Reid and I had spent out at his family's vacation home. I leaned on the kitchen counter and looked out through the window. Gerald had already given me the update for the morning, along with that day's plans. But what was going on inside the house was much further away from the front of my mind than what was possibly going on outside.

"You going to go check?" Reid walked up behind me and wrapped his arms around my waist.

"Do I have a choice?" I knew there wasn't.

He pointed out the window. "You see that wall? It is *just* a wall. And no matter what you find in there, it will remain. But as far as the whole Joshua and Cora thing goes? If there's no letter there today, then we should see it as he's found peace. And that is exactly what you wanted. Even if we do not get some sort of sign, we just have to believe. But if there is a letter, then we have more work to do. We have to keep it simple like that. If we don't, we will drive ourselves mad."

My shoulders heaved with my breath. "Yes. Simple and logical. Wow. I'm bad at that."

"That's why you have me, love." He kissed my shoulder. "I'm going to go help Gerald and his brothers put up the drywall in the library."

I patted his hand. "Okay. I'll let you know what I find."

He left the room, and I pried myself away from the counter. The warmth had returned to the air outside, and I took my time as I walked through the garden. Several men from the electrical crew were out back, installing some lines to run from the main house to some of the smaller buildings.

Aside from them, the area was pretty calm. Birds fluttered about overhead. Then, I saw a deer peer out from the trees. Admittedly, I was hopeful it was Joshua. Part of me wanted to take off in a sprint and go back there. But when my brain registered what it really was, I forced myself to stay on my path to check the wall.

"Come on, Nell. You're being ridiculous," I scolded myself as I stood there, glaring at the "X" on the rock. "Just look."

I leaned down and pulled on the marked stone. That time, it didn't come out easily. It actually didn't come out at all. I wedged my fingers along the curve that connected with the mortar, but it refused to give.

"Seriously?" I yelled.

Feeling the ground around me, I searched for something to help me pry it out. Finding nothing right around me, I went to try to search further out when I saw him.

"Joshua?" I stumbled back. My elbow raked down the rough edges of the wall, cutting me and shooting pain up my arm. Instead of grabbing the wall to catch myself, I fell onto the grass with a thud.

Again, he reached out, his hand going right through mine. "We both need to stop that."

"Scaring each other?" I brushed bits of dirt and grass off my lap.

He looked worried. "Me scaring you, you falling and me attempting to help you." He nodded toward my wound. "Should you go inside and get that looked at?"

Blood had coated my forearm as well as the side of my shirt and jeans. I pressed my hand to it. "I will. But I came to check for another letter. I've been curious if you had moved on. I needed to know. But the stone won't come out of the wall. Why?"

"It means that I wanted to give you this letter myself," he replied.

I checked the bleeding, thankful it had slowed. "You can do that?"

He laughed. "Sort of. I suppose in the same way I have been. I know I cannot hand it directly to you. But I wanted to say thank you, so I figured delaying you receiving it until I could was just as good."

"Thank you? What for?" I couldn't imagine he would want to thank me for telling him he was dead.

"The letter; it will tell you what for. But I also have a favor. It is written in there as well. I need to go." He started to fade.

I did as he said and turned around. "A favor?"

I felt him go. The pressure in the air seemed to change. To lighten. And, with a blink, he was gone. My hands went directly to the marked stone. It pulled away easily, and there was another letter. With it in hand, I practically ran into the house.

"Reid!" I yelled as I busted through the door. "Reid! Are you on this side of the house?"

"Coming!" he hollered from down the hall.

I yanked a seat out and sat down, getting right to work breaking the seal and unfolding the paper. As Reid entered, I started reading aloud.

1867
Dearest Nell,

Thank you for your kind approach at bringing me such delicate news. I only regret that I have been so rude as to have taken so much time to respond to your letter.

I did as you said, Nell. And as I spent some time processing the information you gave me, I took in my surroundings. To my surprise, I did see some contraptions that people seemed to get in and out of that moved with them inside. I even saw you and your friend, my ancestor, Reid Wilkinson, getting out of one. I can only assume that those are the "vehicles" you spoke of in your previous letter.

Furthermore, I observed the tools and lights and strange hardware that the workers were using. And, yes, I noticed that Webb Manor was going through some construction I do not recall it needing.

With all of this and more, in short, I cannot find a way to argue with your explanation of the goings on. It would also explain why I do not recall going home over the time that we have been corresponding, eating or anything that would otherwise fill my days. I only recall my time on your property. Which, I believe, brings me to one of your questions. I do not recall anything between leaving to meet Cora and leaving that second letter in the wall aside from a brief memory of writing the first letter and leaving it in the wall. It is possible that your removal of the first woke me in some way.

As to your other question, I do not know what it is that I am looking for. I believe you may be correct in your guess, however. Cora is my focus. I simply want to know what happened to her and if she is alright ... was alright after my death. I would never have killed myself, though. Take that to heart. So that worries me as to her wellbeing; if she was caught up in such treachery or not. Maybe we can start there. Please help me find out what happened to Cora.

Other than that, my only hope is that you and Reid get the chance at happiness and love that Cora and I missed out on. Our - my and Cora's - two families have a connection that cannot be broken. I only hope he is as good to you as I wanted to be to my Cora.

Sincerely,
Joshua

We both looked at each other.

I breathed, "Cora. Of course."

"You looked rattled when I came in, Nell." Reid's hand was on my arm.

"He was there," I replied.

"At the trees again?"

Realizing I was being vague, I explained, "No. I went to the wall, but the rock wouldn't move. He was standing right there. He wanted to thank me." I turned to face him.

He noticed the blood on me. "Nell! What happened?"

The wound had more or less stopped bleeding, but I probably looked like someone had tried to kill me. I'd nicked a vein pretty badly, and with my arms moving, I'd wiped a lot across my side.

"Oh! That." I went over to the sink and started washing it off. "I wasn't expecting to see him, and it startled me. I fell back, raking my arm down the stones."

"You have got to stop doing that." He ran a towel under the faucet and helped.

I scoffed. "That's what he said."

"He's not wrong." Reid sounded irritated. "What did he want?"

"He just said he wanted to thank me and tell me he had a favor, but everything would be in the letter. He just wanted to deliver it himself."

Reid's eyes grew wide. "He was able to hand it directly to you?"

I shook my head. "No. I think he just wanted to do as close to that as he could, though. I hadn't been able to remove the rock before he spoke, but when he disappeared, the rock moved, and the letter was there."

Reid ran his fingers over his creased forehead. "But he didn't hurt you?"

"No," I replied. "He was very polite and even was concerned about my wounding myself. He wanted me to come inside and get it looked at."

"Okay. Well, it doesn't look like it needs stitches or anything." He let out his breath. "What do you want to do? Do you want to attempt to find out what happened to her? Or are you done?"

"I need to see this through," I exclaimed.

He grinned. "Good. We can go into town and start straight away. Do you want to leave him a letter and tell him?"

I bit my lip, already running through what to say. "Yes."

"I'll go tell Gerald we're going to leave for a few hours."

"Thank you."

2017
Dear Joshua,

You're welcome. I feel bad that you're thanking me for delivering such sad news. But, to answer your question, I'd be happy to see if I can find out what you are asking. I make no promises, but I will look, as will Reid.

Reid and I will go into town today and start. I will stay in touch and let you know of any progress we may make.

Sincerely,
Nell

I tucked the letter in the wall and met Reid by the front of the house. Gerald was standing there with him. I looked back and forth between the two men. "Hey guys. What's up?"

Reid spoke, "Gerald asked if he could join us. He has something he needs to show us."

"Yes. I can meet you at *The Golden Crown* if that is alright. I need to make a stop by my house first." Gerald slid his keys out of his pocket.

"Okay? Is something wrong with the renovations? Would you like to ride with us?" I asked.

He shook his head. "No. But if it's all the same to you, I'll meet you there."

He took off for his truck, leaving Reid and I standing there, confused. Reid put a hand on my back. "We will find out soon enough."

"True." I followed his lead.

The restaurant was fairly empty as Imogen greeted us. "Reid! Nell! It is so good to see you both! Elijah told me that the two of you were getting on very well."

Reid held my hand out. "Yes. Very well, indeed."

Her jaw dropped. "Wow! This is all very fast. Must be love at first sight."

"You can say that." We hugged.

She hugged Reid next. "I'm very happy for you both. Come. Let me get you sat."

"Your cousin, Gerald, is on his way to meet us," I informed her.

"Table for three then. It will be nice to see him. I do not get to enough these days." She smiled and showed us to a table.

Gerald arrived, hugging his cousin before ordering his beverage. "Coffee, please."

"I'll return momentarily with that." She flitted off.

"Sorry for the secrecy," he started.

"Don't worry about it. But you do have us a little more than intrigued." Reid leaned back in his chair.

"And worried," I added.

Gerald laced his fingers together. "Then I will not delay any further. You see, when Joshua Wilkinson died, my great grandfather, Clive Brown, was with him. He held his best friend in his arms until he took his last breath. But, in the conversation that ensued prior to his death, Joshua informed Clive that he had been saving. That there was a sizable amount of money that he'd intended on using in whatever way Cora wanted once they were married."

Reid held his hands up. "Wait a moment. The papers said he'd hung himself. Clive was there?"

"No. I mean, yes. Well, according to what I know, Clive found him hanging, but he didn't believe that is was of his own doing," Gerald explained.

"But he had been saving? For their life together?" I asked.

"Yes. Joshua had buried the fortune along with some jewelry and other gifts on his property for safe keeping. He requested that Clive retrieve it and to make sure that his son was taken care of. He'd known that Cora would be fine financially, so the only thing he requested go to her was a ruby ring. It had been his mother's. I guess it actually had been handed down through a few generations on Joshua's side before he left it to Cora."

Reid shot up. "I heard about that ring. My grandfather used to talk about a ring that many generations back had been given to a great grandmother of mine by the King of England. Something about a love affair. Some speculated an illegitimate child. I tried to see if I could find anything in the history books about it or even the ring among our heirlooms, but I came up empty."

Gerald nodded. "That day, he went straight to the meeting spot to tell Cora what happened. Later that afternoon, once he was sure she would recover and was safely back home, Clive found the ring, along with the money and several other items, just where Joshua said it would be. He rode back to Webb Manor and gave the ring to her."

I looked down on my hand. "A ruby ring? In gold? With diamonds on either side of it?"

"Yes." Gerald looked at me, puzzled.

Reid's expression was the same. "Why do you ask? Did you find something in the house?"

I held up my hand. "My mother gave me this ring. She said it had been passed down through generations but wasn't sure where it had originated. Just said it was very old, came from England and was riddled with heartbreak. Something about a gift from a lover that had died. I'm not sure she knew much more than that. I never used to wear it. I only put it on just after my divorce was finalized."

"Right before you stumbled upon Webb Manor?" Reid examined the piece of jewelry.

"Yes." My eyes grew wide.

"That explains a lot." Gerald didn't look surprised at all.

Reid looked torn. "I want to come back to this, but what happened to the rest of his assets? Did Clive Brown keep it all?"

Gerald continued, "What I've been told is that Joshua's son, your great grandfather, Clive Wilkinson, was taken in by an uncle. According to what was said, the relatives that took him in didn't handle everything well. They sold off the Wilkinson estate since theirs was larger, including all of Joshua's belongings, livestock, what they didn't keep that is but kept all of the proceeds. Young Clive got nothing more than a semi-comfortable living arrangement."

"What did your great grandfather, Clive, do with it all?" Reid asked.

"He buried it," Gerald replied.

"Buried it?" we asked in unison.

Gerald chuckled. "Yes. He buried it in hopes of giving it to your Clive once he was of age when it wouldn't be taken from him. But he died before that could happen. And for the next several generations, it stayed there."

Reid sat back. "Then how do you know of all of this?"

Gerald took a box out of the bag he'd carried in. He set it on the table, turning it to face us. "My family has stayed on the same land for four hundred years. We may not be a wealthy family, but we are a long-standing one in this area, as you know. We've taken pride in our land and have made sure we stayed in our family home through the generations. Then, last year, my grandfather was redesigning one of the side gardens and found this. His health had been failing, but we didn't argue with him when he demanded he be allowed one last landscaping project since it had always been a passion of his."

Gerald teared up as he explained further. "That summer, my grandfather died. As the family gathered to say their goodbyes, he waved everyone off to share some things with me. Among a few family secrets and a thing or two he'd picked up along the way that he thought I may want to know, he told me of the box he'd found. In it, there was a letter that would tell me everything as to its origins. But he was a true believer of fate and various superstitions and spiritual things. And he told me that day not to just seek out the kin. He said to hang on to it and not do anything. Not until the time came that it would finally go toward what it was initially intended for. Admittedly, I was puzzled at first."

"Why didn't you tell me?" Reid sounded hurt. "You knew that was family. Didn't you think I would want to know all of this?"

"I do. And I wanted to." Gerald pushed the box forward. "But I did as my grandfather instructed me to do. I kept it safe. Aside from reading the letter and taking a look at the contents, it has not been disturbed. One thing I learned while he was alive was to believe him when my grandfather spoke. He seemed to know things others didn't."

Reid relaxed a little. "I heard that about him. Some said he was psychic. Honestly, I simply chalked it up to village gossip."

“When I was younger, so did I,” Gerald agreed. “But as I grew older, I saw enough to know better.”

“Are you going to open it?” I put a hand on Reid’s leg.

He put his hand on mine. His forehead creased. “That ring…”

Gerald caught his look. “I think it is.”

“But how did you know?” He searched my eyes.

“I don’t know. When you guys we're talking about it, something tugged at me. And you have to admit, the timing fits.” My thumb ran over the ruby.

“So this, whatever is in there … it initially was to go from Joshua to his and Cora’s life together. For Cora to do as she wanted in order to start their life together?”

Gerald nodded.

Reid turned toward me. “I think we need to look into your heritage.”

“The box, Reid.” I pointed. “What’s in the box?”

“Yes, yes.” He pulled it toward him. “But until we find out if there’s a connection here, no matter what is in there, we won’t be doing anything with its contents until we sort that out.”

“Why not?” I couldn’t imagine what any possible connection I might have with Cora would have to do with his possible new found inheritance.

Gerald put a hand on my shoulder. “One thing at a time, my dear. Let him process this.”

He was right. “Sorry. It’s just that the more we find out about what is going on, the more there is to look into.”

Gerald squeezed my shoulder. “It will all work out. You’ll find out what it’s all about soon.”

Reid flashed me a smile. So much was circling around in his head, and I could see it in his eyes as he took the small key from Gerald’s outstretched hand. Slowly, he opened the lid and revealed the contents.

I leaned in. “Wow.”

We sifted through the items. A few pieces of jewelry, some trinkets and a couple stacks of rather old paper money. Reid held one up. "They don't even make these bills any longer. Haven't for a very long time."

Gerald replied, "No. And from what I found on various collector's sites, they are worth more now than if they were still in circulation - especially with how they are in such good condition."

"Seriously?" I gently flipped through, roughly calculating about two thousand pounds. "This would be close to hundred thousand pounds in today's currency! Relatively that is."

"Or more," Reid added. "He wasn't as poor as I thought he was."

"No. He wasn't," Gerald agreed. "Apparently, his estate brought his uncle quite a comfortable living on top of the one they already had. But I haven't delved into that much."

"It is now on my list of things to take a look at," Reid announced. "But first, I want to know about this ring business. How can we find out if it is the same one?"

"My grandmother is still alive. She's in a nursing home in Virginia. Maybe she will know something. Between what we can dredge up here and what she might possibly know, maybe we can get some answers."

Reid set the money back inside the box and closed the lid. "Maybe this is what Joshua was talking about in his letter. Remember? He mentioned a connection that hasn't been broken? I couldn't think of who he might be talking about since I really rather deplore Pamela. But if you're a Webb descendant, that would make sense on so many levels."

"Yes; it would." Gerald stood. "It is good to know that my grandfather was right once again, as spooky as it all is. But time is ticking away. I am going to get back to work. Thank you for meeting me." He patted my hand. "I will see you back at Webb Manor tomorrow, Nell. Reid, I will wager a guess you will be there as well?"

Reid nodded. "Yes. I most certainly will be there."

"Good, good." He grinned. "So many finishing touches going up! I'm excited to see that beauty back to its former glory."

I knew his statement was about more than just the trim, paint and light fixtures. Seeing Reid and I together, the Wilkinson and Webb family united, was something his ancestor was trying to make happen. Looking at the possibility that I was part of the Webb lineage, it made sense that he would pick up where Clive Brown had left off. After our chat that day, I actually was wondering if he knew all along. But I was sure that he, at least, suspected it. And with all the hard work he'd been doing for me on the estate, it obviously was something he wanted to see finally fulfilled. With how he had reacted to everything at that table, I could see he was convinced, more than he was prior to seeing me with that ring, that I was Cora's descendant.

We ate a light lunch and headed back to Reid's house. With the box in front of us as we sat at the dining table, I nudged him. "Maybe we should read the letter. I'm curious what Clive Brown had to say."

"Yes. I agree." Reid's hands were on the lid, half anxious to open it and half holding it closed.

The lid creaked in the quiet room as he finally lifted it. Without the distractions and noise of the busy restaurant, it was easy to see and smell the age of the box and its contents. He laid out each piece onto the flat table. The metal and gems of the jewelry were coated in dirt and dust, yet somehow still glistened when hit with the light from the overhead fixture.

"Here it is," he announced, lifting it from the bottom.

Both of us sat and looked at the letter. It appeared to be aged similarly to Joshua's letters. The wax seal had been broken already, and it showed a little more wear from having been read a couple of times.

Neither of us knew what information it was going to give us, but we were both a little more than curious. So when I nudged Reid, he didn't say a word. Instead, he reached out and unfolded it.

2 September, 1867
Dear Clive Wilkinson,

I wanted to write this letter before hiding this box of your father's away. As I am sure you know, your great uncle that took you in took everything from you that was your father's; that was your mother's as well. That is, aside from what is in this container.

Your father and I were the best of friends. That is why he named you after me, as well as entrusted me with the knowledge of the contents of this box in order to get it to you. But when I saw how your great uncle was taking everything, I kept it held back in hopes of being able to give it to you as an adult and to tell you everything in person.

The most important thing that I want you to know is that Joshua Wilkinson did not take his own life. On the 16th of June, 1867, I went to your home to join him on his trip. You had been staying with family in London as he planned to leave that day with who was supposed to be your new mother, Cora Webb. They were going to marry and then return for you. I was going to be their witness of marriage.

But when I arrived at your estate, I witnessed two men who were running from the rear of the house. I do not know who they were. Instead of pursuing them, I went into the house to see why they were running, concerned more with the safety of your father. Sadly, the two men got away.

Inside, I found your father, hung by a rope from the rafters. As quickly as I could, I lowered him, but it was too late. His struggling to free himself after what appeared to be quite a fight with the intruders had caused too much damage. He was alive, but he was mortally wounded. I held him and comforted him until he drew his last breath.

He spoke of his concern for you, as well as Cora, requesting for you to receive the contents herein. But, as I said, I did not want you to lose this to your great uncle as well.

Please know that he loved you very much. It would have broken his heart to find out that you were treated as such a burden, especially by family. I can only hope that they treated you better than it appeared from an onlooker's stance. But, above all, I pray that you find a good path in this world and make a good life for yourself.

If you ever need anything, please know that my family will always welcome you.

Sincerely,
Your uncle through friendship,
Clive Brown

Reid's eyes were filled with tears. "He was murdered."

I wrapped my arm around him. "Yes. That's what it sounds like."

"And we will never know why. We won't know if it was over Cora or over money or just a random robbery."

"Probably not," I replied.

His jaw set. "Then we owe it to him to give him what we *can* find out at least. We will search for Cora and figure out what happened to her. Plus," he took my hand, "we will tell him if you're her descendant."

"Just point me in a direction. This is your field. I'll follow your lead."

"Right. We need to get to the library."

On our way, Reid called Elijah and told him what we had found out. Elijah was all too happy to join us on our search for information. Luckily, the librarians gave us the research room one again as we poured over boxes upon boxes.

I sent myself on the task of looking through the limited digital references once again. But by five in the evening, the library was closing up, and we hadn't found anything more than the paper trail that told of her birth.

"Damn it." Reid slammed his notebook closed and shoved it in his bag.

It was my turn to ease his stress. "There's more to go through. We aren't done, Reid. Just done for today."

"Yes, yes. I know. I was simply hoping we would find something already." He held the door open for me.

I bowed my head as I went through. "Me, too."

"Tomorrow?" Elijah asked as we exited the building.

"First thing in the morning," Reid confirmed.

I added, "I just want to check the wall before we start. If he left a letter, I want to respond. Well, I want to leave him an update regardless."

"I will just plan on coming here at nine then, when they open. You two come once you accomplish that. Maybe he will have something more we can use to help us," Elijah suggested.

"I didn't even think about that," I said. "I'll make sure to ask a few questions tomorrow. We just won't get a response until the day after."

"Which will come in handy if we come up empty handed again," he replied, his usual casual demeanor in his stance.

"True," Reid agreed, solemnly.

We parted ways for the night.

Later, sitting at dinner, I got to thinking about something Joshua was saying. About how we didn't know the rules. He was right. And we had proven that.

"I want to check the wall this evening, if you don't mind," I announced, breaking the silence we'd been sitting in..

Reid finished chewing his bite. "Sure. Is everything alright? That was sort of out of nowhere."

"Just curious, I suppose." I went back to my plate.

I spent the rest of the meal trying to figure out what to ask. What I wanted to avoid was coming off as an interrogation letter. The poor man had just had to come to grips with being dead. I didn't want to put him through such a humiliating and traumatic situation.

Reid stayed in the car as I went to the wall. His headlights shining on my route there, making it easier to check. I was disappointed to find my original letter still in place. And, for a moment, I second guessed my plan.

Instead of turning and walking away with it, I pulled a letter out of my pocket. Unfolding the page, I reread it just to be sure I'd said what I wanted.

2017
Dear Joshua,

Today, Reid, Elijah and I spent the day searching through the library's archives to find something about Cora and her life – when it ended, if she moved on, etc. But, sadly, we came up empty. We haven't exhausted our resources by any means. We plan to return tomorrow and keep looking. Honestly, we are all very interested in finding out as well.

However, in the meanwhile, tell me more about Cora, please. Who she was. Why you fell in love with her. Her dreams. Her goals. I gather that you are not the type of man to have loved a woman and not have known these things about her. I would assume that they would have been the reason you would have fallen so hard for her.

Maybe with some details, we may be able to find something more on her.

I will watch for your letter.

Sincerely,
Nell

I chose to leave out our questions about my biological connection to Cora's family. It was an element that we had no leads on yet and could very well be painful for Joshua to hope for and us be wrong. I know it was something that I, myself, was trying not to wish too much on.

Satisfied I'd said enough, I folded the letter and stuffed it behind the first one. Adjusting the hem of my shirt, I stood, looked around and went back to the car.

I stopped a couple steps short of the vehicle and looked at the large, brick house. It loomed over the land, even in the dark. A couple of lights shone through the windows. Ones I'd said to leave on throughout the night, in case I decided to return for any reason.

It was a magnificent home. With the remodel coming together nicely, I was becoming more and more in awe of the fact that it was mine. And any thoughts I'd been having that I wasn't going to be happy there were quickly dismissed with the feeling that I belonged there filling me.

I pulled my phone out of my pocket and sent an email to the nursing home where my grandmother resided, asking for them to have her call me when she was awake and capable. I wanted to know what she knew about our lineage ... and that ring ... if anything.

Twelve

Back at Reid's that night, he busied himself with menial tasks, unable to relax. Finally settling down at his computer, checking the previous couple days' worth of emails. After a few minutes, he went for the door. "I'll be right back."

He left before I could even think of a response. I heard him descend the staircase down to his office, rustle around down there and then ascend the stairs even faster. He carried a box as he came back into the room and set it onto the table.

I joined him as he lifted the flaps. "Find something?"

"I certainly hope so." He had the look of apprehension in his eyes. "This is my family lineage. It is everything I have on my ancestors and everything some of my other family members have found."

"It looks like quite a lot," I said, seeing the box was full.

He pulled out a stack. "Yes. It covers a lot of different parts. But there's a folder on my direct lineage. I figured that even if we couldn't find out anything on Cora today, I may be able to see more about what Clive Wilkinson did with his life."

I put a hand on his arm. "That would probably make him very happy to know. I know it would me."

He laid out all of the folders, flipping through each to be sure nothing had been misplaced that he might need. Once he was finished, he tucked the folders of extended family members back into the box.

“Okay. These are where we start.” He handed me a brown, weathered folder and took one himself. “They are from that branch of ancestry.”

I yawned and opened the file he gave me. “Alright.”

His look of determination faltered. “You should just go to bed. I can take care of this.”

“No. I can help,” I protested. “You’ve done so much for me.”

He closed his file. “It’s after midnight. Go get some sleep. I’ll look through for a little while and join you. What I don’t get through tonight, we can go through tomorrow.”

A yawn escaped me again. “Are you sure?”

He chuckled. “Yes.”

“Goodnight.”

I gave him a kiss before heading to the bedroom.

“Goodnight.”

He was already pouring over the file before him.

It was a welcome sensation. Falling into bed. The down comforter wrapped around me, cocooning me in like I was protected in a cloud. As usual, I kicked one foot out, rolled over onto my side and curled up into a ball. The window was cracked slightly, allowing a gentle breeze to come in. The sounds of an owl filtered in.

I whispered, “We will find out. I promise.”

***

I woke as the sun came up over the horizon, filling the room with a gentle light like an autumn bonfire. I kicked off the comforter and stretched, realizing that Reid wasn’t in the bed with me when my arm hit the pillow next to mine instead of him.

I'd packed a bag at the request of Reid and had left it at his place so I would have clothes and other things when staying over without having to make a stop at my flat every night. From it, I pulled out a pair of sweats and a t-shirt. Then, I slipped on his pair of slippers, half smirking because they were his and so much bigger than my own feet.

With the slippers making a dragging sound, I shuffled out into the living area. Reid, gently snoring, was sound asleep. His head resting on his arms, he was propped up on the dining table where I'd left him, an open folder under him.

I glanced at the clock. Seeing it was only half past six, I took the seat next to him, placing a hand on his arm. "Reid." I kept my voice gentle. "Reid. You should go into bed for an hour or so. Get stretched out. This can't be comfortable."

His eyes opened slightly as his head rose from his arms a little less than slowly. "I didn't mean to fall asleep out here." He rubbed his eyes. "Although, I have to admit, it happens sometimes when I'm really into my work."

"I can almost visualize that. You, pouring over your work until all hours. Your coffee wearing off and you slowly losing the ability to hold your head up." I giggled.

Humored, he laughed with me. "Yes. That sounds about right."

I motioned toward the bedroom. "Go. Get some sleep actually lying down. I'll run into Webb Manor and check the wall and grab some breakfast on my way back. Then we can go in and meet Elijah."

"You sure you want to go out there alone?" he asked.

I shrugged. "Sure. I think I've got a grip on myself this morning."

Approvingly, he bobbed his head as he stood. Looking down, he burst out into laughter. "Are those my slippers?"

“Yes.” I flashed him a toothy grin.

He kissed my cheek and left for the bedroom. “With all my heart.”

I glanced at the paperwork spread out over the table. It was obvious that he had found what he was looking for when I read the top two headlines about a Dr. Clive Wilkinson being the founder of a state of the art medical center for the needy in one and a Dr. Clive Wilkinson being the inventor of what would later become a very important and regularly used piece of medical equipment. My heart warmed, knowing not only would Joshua be gladdened by this news, but I knew that it would help Reid after having found out that his great grandfather had been murdered.

Staying in my sweats, only changing into my shoes, I closed the door quietly on my way out. It was strange getting into my own vehicle after a few days of riding with Reid everywhere. But considering how close I’d allowed myself to break down from the stress of everything, it was even nicer to feel independent and sure footed once again.

Gerald met me at my car, inquiring as to Reid’s whereabouts. I filled him in on what I’d seen in Reid’s findings, as well as what we didn’t find at the library.

“Is he angry with me for not telling him about the case before now?” Gerald asked.

I wasn’t sure how to answer that. “I am not for sure. I know he is very vested in this whole thing.”

“No less for your sake as well as his own ancestry.” Gerald’s remark was truth.

I agreed, “Yes. I believe so.”

“I never got the chance to say it yesterday, but congratulations on your engagement.” He tipped his hat.

Shocked, I glanced down at the ring and back up to him. “I didn’t say anything. We haven’t told anyone. It’s not that we’re actively not telling people. We just haven’t.” The words were just tumbling out of my mouth.

He chuckled, holding his hands up. "I merely observed the new, delicate piece of jewelry on an important finger of yours. Who and when you tell people is your business. But bear in mind, the longer you wait for some, the more people might actually take offense."

My thumb ran over the diamond. "Yes. You're probably right. I think I'm more nervous about how they'll react, knowing how fast this has happened. Imogen is the only one that knows so far. Honestly, I don't think it has quite sunk in yet."

"Better now than after you two decide to actually tie the knot." Again, he tipped his hat. This time, he left for the house.

His words made me pause. Neither Reid nor I had even brought up a *when*. We just simply expressed the longing to do so. It made me think of Joshua and Cora and their whirlwind love. Granted, they had told others. But their relationship developed fast as well.

I lifted my chin and narrowed my eyes toward the tree line. "Why couldn't I have just vacationed in Transylvania? That's probably less freaky than all of this."

Huffing at myself, I went to the wall. Both of my letters were gone, and, as I expected, one from Joshua was in its place.

I went into the kitchen and read it.

1867
Dear Nell,

Where do I begin about Cora Louise Webb? She is the sun and the moon. Her light penetrates every corner of darkness in the world. After seeing you, I can say that the two of you have similarities in appearance. The same hair and figures. For a moment, I am sure I have mentioned, I thought you were she when I first saw you, just to give you an image in your mind.

With Cora, there is something in her very essence that had me captivated from the very moment I saw her. I was, by no means, the only man of whom she caught the eye. But I was certainly the only man that seemed to catch hers. That was something I am eternally grateful for.

As far as her dreams and interests go, Cora is an avid dreamer. But her favorite hobby is to read. Her dream, though, is to be a writer. Her love of books helps her already veracious mind extend out into such an imaginative vessel. I am truly entertained every time she shares one of her stories with me, verbal or written.

Is ... was. I suppose, for you, it would be was.

Cora was a beautiful woman, inside and out. I understand why her parents wanted her to marry well. She deserved all the riches in the world. But what they could not understand is that of all the riches she only truly wanted love. I was simply the lucky man whose love she wanted.

I look forward to hearing more from you, my dear.

Sincerely,
Joshua

Tears fell from my chin. He spoke so lovingly of her. My ex-husband had always been kind to me. But that was it. He was kind. Supportive and generous, yes. But there was nothing more than that between us. He never showed that deep, passionate, above-all kind of love. The kind that you fiercely protect ... or wait beyond death and across time for.

Reid's face flashed through my mind.

Setting my pen to the page, I scribbled a quick note to Joshua, informing him of our continued search for information on Cora as well as Reid's research on his son, Clive. I tucked it into the wall and drove back to town.

My phone rang. "Hello?"

"Nell?" an elderly woman replied. "Is this my little Nell?"

"Grandma? It's so good to hear your voice!" I hadn't spoken to her in over a year.

She let out a cough. "Yes. Time certainly does pass us by when we're busy, now doesn't it?"

"That's quite the cough," I observed. "How is your health?"

"Well, I'm stuck in this damned wheelchair," she scoffed. "Otherwise? I'm ninety. But I'm still kickin'. My grim reaper hasn't come calling yet."

I couldn't help but smile at her dark humor. "I miss you."

"I miss you, too," she repeated the sentiment. "But I am sure that isn't why you called. What do you need, dear? I heard you got a divorce. Do you need money?"

"No, Grandma. I'm very comfortable financially. My books are doing very well," I said.

"Your books." I could hear that she'd forgotten by her tone. "And who says hobbies can't end up careers?"

She was one of the few people that didn't scoff at me when I would talk about wanting to be an author when asked what I wanted to be when I grew up. She actually encouraged it in some ways, asking me to share my writing projects from school with her.

"I was actually calling about that ruby ring that was handed down to me. Do you remember it?" I was hoping. But at the same time, I wasn't holding my breath.

She gasped. "The one that's been passed down for many generations? Oh yes. Do you still have it?"

"Yes. I'm wearing it now." I looked at it, that hand being on the steering wheel. "When it was given to me, I wasn't told much more than it had been in our family for several generations, and it was riddled with heartache. Is that all we know? Or do you know where it came from?"

She didn't respond.

"Grandma?"

Nothing.

"Are you still there?"

I heard her clear her throat. "I'm still here. I was just making sure I recalled correctly. And, if I do, I believe that ring was given to your great grandmother a couple of times removed. I believe her name was Cora Price. But it wasn't from her husband. I believe my grandmother told me that it was a present from her first love. I do not know what his name was. But I do remember that her husband's name was Jack. Jackson Price."

"Joshua," it came out in a breath.

"What's that, Nell?"

"Joshua," I repeated. "Joshua Wilkinson."

"You know? That name rings a bell. Is he a friend of yours?" she inquired.

I ignored her question. "Do you know why they didn't marry if they were in love?"

Again, she cleared her throat. "I'm sorry, dear. I don't know anything more than that. We once did a lot with our genealogy, but I fear I've forgotten most of it. Elderly brain and all. Are you sure everything is alright?"

"I've got to go, Grandma. I promise I'll call soon."

"Oh. Okay." She sounded disappointed. "Have a good day. And thank you for calling."

"Grandma?" I stopped before rushing off the phone.

"Yes, dear?"

"I love you."

I could practically hear her smile in her response. "I love you, too."

I pulled the car into a parking space in front of Reid's just as I clicked off the call. Yanking the keys from the ignition, I practically ran in through his front door, banging my shoulder on the door when I went to push it open before the key was fully turned.

He was awake and fixing a mug of coffee. "Nell? Are you alright? What's wrong?"

I was out of breath. And rubbing my shoulder. Unable to speak, I held my hand up.

"Five?" he replied to me, holding up all my fingers.

"No." I whipped my head back and forth. "The ring."

He took my hand. "The ruby one? Did you find out something?" His concern for me took over as he put an arm around me. "Come; sit and catch your breath. What? Did you run all the way back here? You sure do like to spook me."

I snatched his coffee and took a drink. "She called her by name. Cora. My grandmother was telling me what she knew about the ring, and she said she believed it was given to my great grandmother, Cora Price. And she said it had been given to her by someone she was in love with before her husband. But she didn't know anything more than that."

"Cora Price? As in Nell Price?" he asked.

I nodded, taking another sip. "Yes. It seems so."

He stood upright, purpose settling into his features. "That's going to be a rather helpful lead, love. Providing she's correct."

"Exactly." I leaned back, his paperwork from the night before that was still strewn across the table catching my eyes. "Did you find out anything about Clive?"

A sense of pride lifted his expression. "Yes, actually."

He filled me in on our way to the library, where Elijah was busily filing through old newspapers in the research room. I'd asked Reid to make a stop, and we grabbed a round of coffees and a box of bakery goods, half to keep us going, and half to celebrate the progress we'd made.

"You two look like cats in a birdcage." He smirked.

I handed him one of the steaming cups. "We had a couple breakthroughs."

"Oh?" Slowly, he lifted the lid to one of the cups and stirred in some cream and sugar.

"Yes." Reid set down the file he'd brought from home, containing Clive Wilkinson's history.

After looking it over, Elijah nodded in approval. "So, he was successful and turned out pretty well, despite his circumstances."

"He did." Reid looked proud.

Elijah crossed his arms. "And Cora? Anything on her?"

It was my turn. "I spoke with my grandmother." I held out the hand with the ruby ring on it. "She mentioned that she was told that this was a gift to our ancestor, Cora Price, before her marriage to Jackson Price."

"Cora Price, huh?" Elijah grinned.

"Cora Price," I repeated.

Reid peeked into the box Elijah had been sorting. "It's all a pretty good amount of information to work from."

"We've worked with less," Elijah said.

"We certainly have," Reid agreed.

Together, the three of us riffled through more boxes. However, with my lineage and Cora's married last name in our arsenal, it was easier to find what we were looking for.

Thirteen

After a rewarding day of research, Reid and I had opted to stay in and make dinner. We'd been going from place to place so much, now that we had what we had been looking for, he wanted to stay in and hide away.

"Don't you think we should get a letter to Joshua? Tell him what we've found out?" I asked, chopping tomatoes.

He stirred the ground chicken, adding a spice mix he'd made to make it taco meat. "I do not think we should rush off and just blurt it out. We can take our time, eat a home cooked meal and write it. What if this is your last letter to him? Don't you want to make sure it says all you want it to say?"

"Of course. I didn't think about it that way." He had become my voice of reason and calm in my chaotic and keep-moving brain. "I love you."

He turned away from his pan for a moment. "With all my heart."

I washed my hands after I was finished, allowing the warm water to run over them an extra minute. "Should I get started writing?"

"Actually," his eyes ran over me, "I wanted to talk to you about planning."

"Planning?" I drew out the word like a question.

He turned down the burner. "Our wedding. I was hoping to get some details planned maybe."

"Oooff." I touched my lips, thinking. "Details. Plans. Wedding. Yes."

He laughed, coming up to me and putting his hands on my hips. "Would it be too soon to consider the end of next month? It would be the end of August, which is a gorgeous time on the land as well as temperature wise."

My palms got sweaty. "Next month?"

"Too soon?" His hands dropped.

I chewed on my lip. "No. Next month sounds fine. But can we do it here? On the last Saturday? The renovations should be completed by then."

"Here sounds brilliant." He pulled me in for a kiss.

I pushed back. "My kids."

"Of course. They should be here. I'm looking forward to meeting them." He went in for another kiss.

I stopped him. "Do you think they will be okay with this?"

"Were they angry about the divorce?" he asked.

"No. They each said they weren't surprised."

"Were they angry about your move?"

"Nope. They each said they were busy enough with their own things. As I said, they were more excited about the opportunity of visiting."

He wrapped around me again. "Then I am sure they will support you in this, too."

"You're probably right." I ran my fingers through my hair. "Now, do I call them first or write the letter first?"

He picked my phone up and handed it to me. "I would say contact your kids. If I know you, you're going to spend a lot of time writing that letter. They're going to want to hear from you *before* the wedding."

"Very funny." I slapped his shoulder. Looking at the blank screen of my phone, I pulled up Emma's number and dialed as he went back to cooking.

"Hello?"

"Emma?"

"Mom! How are you?" It was nice to hear her excited to hear my voice. "How is England?"

"About that..."

Over the next two hours, I called each of them. Emma was hesitant, but after telling her how Reid and I had teamed up on a couple projects, leaving out the paranormal aspect of it all, she was happy for me. I gave her the details on when and where, and she booked the airline ticket while on the phone, telling me about her new boyfriend and asking if it would be okay to bring him along. Of course, I said yes.

Murphy was a little busy to hear everything, but he wished me well and asked about the date, stating he would do everything he could to join us if possible. He was very much like his father in that aspect, always quiet and supportive, not giving too much of himself in anything.

The bell rang in the background, signaling that he needed to suit up and head out. "Love ya, Mom. Chat soon."

Lula was heading into class. "Mom? Hey! I can't talk. Can I call you later?"

"Sure, honey. I just had some news to tell you."

"I have thirty seconds before the prof comes in." I heard papers rustling in the background.

Quickly, I said it before I couldn't. "I'm getting married next month, and I want you to come if possible."

She hung up the phone.

I hoped that her professor had walked in, and that was the reason for her abruptly ending the call. She was my firecracker of a child. So I couldn't be sure if it was that or something else.

Before I could let myself dwell on it, I made one more call. "Hello, Mom." I put the call on speaker.

"Well, hello, Janelle. How is your little vacation?" She hadn't lost her usual condescending tone.

"Oh, you know, productive." I rolled my eyes.

Ice clinked around in her glass loud enough for me to hear. "Productive? How so?"

"Remodeling an estate I bought, conversing with ghosts and getting engaged. You know, nothing special." Sarcasm was thick in my words.

"You and your imagination." She refilled her drink. "Well, if the engagement is real, feel free to pass on an invitation. It's not every day your daughter gets married ... again."

"It's almost as if I'm actually following in *your* steps, Mother." I hinted at her being on her fifth marriage.

She let out an annoyed breath. "Yes, yes. Me and my mistakes. Let's not skip an opportunity to rub my nose in my many mistakes."

"I'll put your invitation in the mail. The PO BOX in Chicago, I assume?" I was anxious to end the call.

"Correct. We will chat later. It's time for my massage." The call ended.

"Massage?" Reid sounded astonished. "Yes; that would be far more important than catching up with your daughter."

"Mistake," I corrected him.

"Mistake?"

I unclenched my jaw. "Yes. I am one of those *mistakes* she was referencing."

"Does she have to come to the wedding?" Sizzling called him back to the pan on the stove.

I muttered, almost under my breath, "She probably won't anyway."

"What was that?" The smells from dinner wafted toward me.

"Nothing. I'm going to get started on the letter." My phone went dark as I set it back on the table and adjusted the paper tablet in front of me.

It took him another forty-five minutes to finish dinner. In that time, I wrote three drafts to Joshua. The third, though, said everything I wanted to tell him and everything he needed to know.

Reid sat a full plate in front of me. "Did you finish it?"

I glanced at it one more time, reading through it for a last time. "Sure."

He took the page and started to read it aloud.

2017

Dear Joshua,

Today was a rather productive day. We managed to find out quite a bit of information. I would ask if you're sitting, but, honestly, I'm not sure if ghosts can faint. So that saying is kind of useless here.

To get on with it, the first thing I would like to tell you about is what Reid found on your son, Clive Wilkinson.

After you passed away, Clive was taken in by your uncle. He was a rich man, made even more rich by the proceeds of your home, land, livestock and belongings. Apparently, he callously sold everything off that he could, denying your son any rights or even the chance to hang on to anything for sentimentality. However, he never was given access to the box you had filled with the things you intended for you and Cora.

I cannot say he mistreated your son. But I gather he never welcomed him as his own. Yet, Clive did grow up to be very successful in his own way as a doctor and even an inventor. He was a well-celebrated man in his field and seemed to live a happy life once out on his own. From the papers on him and the articles talking about him, you should be proud. It appears that he did a lot of good in his life.

As for the box that contained the money and items you had saved, Clive Brown wanted so badly to make sure your son was able to receive its contents and keep them that he buried it in order to keep it hidden until your son was eighteen. Unfortunately, Clive Brown passed away before that could happen. The box remained buried until not long ago, in my time. Your great grandson, Reid, is in possession of it now. He is deciding what to do with the contents. Personally, I think he is leaning toward simply hanging on to it as a memento of his ancestry.

As far as Cora goes, that is a very interesting line of information we have figured out.

Cora lived a full life, including ... well, I might as well just come out and say it. She did marry, about three years after your death. It was to a man by the last name of Price. He was from another town but knew her family by connection of business. Together, they had four children, and she even had a few of her stories published. They lived in Webb Manor for the duration of her life, but most of her children moved away.

Her youngest son, Murphy Price, moved to the States and started the lineage there. A lineage that would continue to this day. His name being repeated in his great grandson, unknowingly, a few generations down the line ... in my son.

In other words, I am a direct descendant of Cora Webb. It is something that is a shock for us all, I'm sure. Yet, it makes a lot of sense to the situation.

Oh, and the ring you'd asked Clive Brown to give to Cora? She received it. She also passed it down to her daughter. And it's been passed down each generation up to me thus far. It sits on my finger today, as I write this.

That was actually our biggest lead in things that tipped us off that I was related to her. I called my grandmother and asked if she knew anything about it. She told me all the history she knew, which was more than enough to prove to us that it was true as well as giving us the lead we needed to find out more about Cora herself.

I don't know if you're supposed to move on or stay or what. To be honest, this whole speaking with a ghost thing is very new to me. Either way, I hope this information brings you peace and maybe even a little bit of happiness, just as it has Reid and I.

Funny, isn't it? But fitting. And, yes, Reid treats me very well. We are actually engaged. Fast? Very much so. But you and Cora would understand, in more ways than one.

Thank You,
Nell Price (Soon to be Wilkinson)

Once I was finished with dinner, I had wrapped up the letter. I didn't reread it a million more times. Instead, I slid the envelope back on the table and went to bed early that night. I was at a level of exhaustion I'd rarely experienced in my life, and curling up against Reid as he watched a movie in bed sounded as close to heaven as I could get.

When morning came, we were in the same positions as when I'd fallen asleep. My head was on his lap. Him, sitting up, an arm draped over me. The intro to the *Blu Ray* menu playing on repeat.

It was normal.

And I loved it.

"Good morning, love." His voice was sleepy.

The sun was coming in through the blinds, casting lines of light across the bed like a cage of sunbeams. Their warmth making getting up that much less enticing. "Good morning. How did you sleep?"

He stretched, his abs flexing under me. "After catching up on my show, I slept pretty well. You?"

"Yeah. Good," I replied, my eyes still adjusting to the light.

His lips were soft as he folded over and kissed my head. He gently lifted me as he got out of bed. "I'm going to go shower. Did you want to head over to Webb Manor soon?"

The picture of the finished letter, lying on the dining table, flashed through my mind. "Yeah. Probably should."

"I'll be quick then." He left for the bathroom.

As he turned the water on, I pulled on his t-shirt and made my way to his office. He'd set files of documents in regards to both Clive Wilkinson and Cora Webb-Price on his desk. Opening each, I made copies of a few of the pages that I thought Joshua might like to see. Some, I stayed on a moment, reading through them once again to be sure that I'd recalled the details correctly.

With the files back on his desk and a thin stack of copies in hand, I went back upstairs. Reid was in the kitchen, a pot of coffee brewing and eggs cooking on the stovetop. "Feel refreshed?" I asked.

"Very much so." He was standing in just a towel, spatula in hand.

I giggled and awkwardly pointed toward the bathroom. "My turn. I'll be back."

"Sounds good. I'll save you some eggs. But I make no promises about the bacon." He handed me a mug as I left the room.

I called from the bathroom, water running. "I got an email from the moving company. They should be dropping my furniture and the rest of the boxes off this afternoon. Sometime just after lunch."

"Does this mean that I'm going to lose my new roommate?" He peeked his head in through the door.

"No." I smiled, peeling the last of my clothing off. "It just means we will have to split our nights between here and there for now."

His eyes roamed over me, the look of a prowling cat on his face. "I can live with that ... for now." He smirked and closed the door.

With a warm shower and a delicious breakfast, we set out. I was getting used to him driving everywhere. Tilting the passenger seat back slightly, I would roll the window down and watch as the scenery passed us by. He would talk sometimes, but most of our trips back and forth were spent comfortably without conversation with only the radio playing.

He had started making it a habit to reach over and take my hand. After getting over my first initial reaction of feeling awkward, seeing that my ex hadn't behaved that affectionate to me, I had grown to love seeing our fingers entwined together. I think he picked up on it since he had also started making it a habit to hold my hand outside the car as well.

He pulled into the parking area and got out. "I hope this is what he needs to finally rest peacefully."

I looked down at the letter, unsealed in my lap. Part of me was still torn. Sure, it was interesting having someone from the eighteen hundreds to talk to. But that was it; I had barely gotten to actually talk to him. There was so much that I wanted to learn. Not from a history book but from someone from that time. And him moving on would mean I would never get the chance to ask about the way of life back then.

But I knew that was selfish. I didn't know if he was scared or angry. I also didn't know if there was somewhere to move on to. But if there was, and it was a good place, he deserved to be able to go there. Not to have to stay and answer all my trivial inquiries about a time that, quite possibly, history books would have plenty to teach me of their own.

"Will you walk out there with me?" I pried my eyes from the pages that were firmly pressed between my fingers.

He leaned down and peered into the car. "Of course."

On the way, I slipped my hand in his. I felt silly and selfish and torn between my turmoil over the thing with Joshua and my excitement for my new wedding plans. But as we approached the wall, I felt as if Joshua was looking, and he was happy.

My head jerked up, and I searched the trees for him, but I didn't see any figure there.

"Is he here?" Reid put a hand on my shoulder.

Disappointed, I turned back. "No. I felt him, but I don't see him anywhere."

"That doesn't mean he's not here." He tried to be encouraging. "He could be watching."

"I know." My attention returned to the wall. "Let's just see if he's left anything."

I moved the rock out of its place and looked inside. There, sat yet another wax sealed letter. I sat down on the grass, crossing my legs and carefully opening it, not wanting to wait until inside.

1867
Dearest Nell,

I know that you and my kin, Reid, are working diligently on your research. I hope that what I had to tell you about Cora was of some help. Obviously, I am anxious to know what became of my beloved. But, alas, I will leave you to your task without too much of a distraction. I just wanted to express my deep gratitude and to tell you both how much I have cherished meeting you. You are truly a wonderful woman. I can only imagine how happy you must make my great grandson. Thank you very much for that.

Sincerely,
Joshua

Tears threatened to spill out over my lashes at the thought of him reading the letter I'd prepared. I'd waited to seal it, wanting to make sure that he hadn't included something I might need to address. Satisfied that was not the case, I held mine out in front of me, taking a couple slow breaths.

I felt Reid's hand on my shoulder. "Nell, you did great. Even if he does move on, you must know that he will appreciate what you've done for him."

I sniffed. "That's the thing. Part of me is scared he won't move on. That this won't be what he needs to do so, or maybe he can't. But part of me is hoping he doesn't. I don't know why, but I guess I'll miss him."

Reid knelt down next to me and tilted my chin up to look me in the eye. "You, of all people, know that there's situations that we want to go both ways for very different reasons. Valid reasons. Heart wrenching reasons. But, when all is said and done, we simply cannot have it both ways. We have to choose what is best." His thumb wiped away a single tear that made its way down my cheek.

I choked back more as they threatened to turn into sobs. "I know. And if he has the chance to get out of this limbo, I'm sure that it is for the best."

"And if he doesn't, or can't even, he still deserves the opportunity to have done so. We have to know that we tried to allow him to," he added.

My words came out stifled by restrained sobs. "There's just so much that has happened so quickly in my life. My kids all being moved out. My divorce. This move. You. A *ghost*. Nothing is routine or normal or calm anymore. It's almost like..."

He laughed. "You feel like you're in one of your books?"

"Yes!" I shouted. "That's exactly it. Wow."

Those simple words put it all in perspective somehow. Suddenly, I knew what I needed to do to shake it all off and gather myself. I needed to become one of my main characters. I needed to pull myself up by my bootstraps and take it all on like a pro. No more wallowing in confusion and self-created inner turmoil. It was time to be the heroine of my own story.

"Crap." I let my hands drop.

He looked puzzled. "Crap? What?"

I looked up at him through my eyelashes, still coated in lingering tears. "I'm acting like a secondary character. Not the lead. And this is my own story. I should be the lead."

Humor came back into his expression. "Well, isn't that a peculiar way of putting it."

"Am I wrong?" I asked.

He kissed me. "I could never see you as a secondary character. Yet, I see what you are saying."

I nodded. "Okay then. Time to get on with it."

The letter and extra pages made the envelop stick out from behind the rock as I set it into the wall. I almost had to wedge it back in to hold it all in place. Happy that it was going to stay for as long as needed, I got up off the ground and faced Reid. "What do we have planned for today?"

He shrugged. "That's up to you. I may wrap up the project I've been working on from before all of this. What would you like to do?"

I started for the house. "I would like to get some writing done."

"Here, or back in town?"

The kitchen was empty as each of the workers were busy in other parts of the house. "You know? Here would be good. Why don't you head back into town and get your work done. I'll be fine out here. Maybe you can bring out some lunch?"

"Lunch. Can do." His fingers were warm on my cheek. "I'll be back in time for the movers. Early afternoon, right?"

"Yes."

"Are you sure?" he asked, half turned toward the front of the house.

I nodded, my mouth pulled tight against my teeth as I rolled it around in my head again. "Yes. This whole situation is crazy enough. It doesn't need me making it more so. And like I said: I need to be the leading character in my own story. I'm going to write, center myself and be less ridiculous when you get back."

He looked me over, assessing if I was putting on a front or not, I assumed. After a moment, he took a quick breath. "Alright then. If you're sure. I won't be long. Call if you need me."

After getting my laptop bag from his car and saying goodbye a little more intimately, I went into the kitchen and set up on the breakfast bar. With my furniture and things having yet to arrive, my desire to write in my newly finished den wouldn't have been enjoyable since I would have felt rather old, my body not enjoying sitting and leaning over my laptop on the floor. So, I figured the kitchen space would do just fine.

With music on in the background, it wasn't difficult to get myself sucked into my storyline where I left off. Occasionally, I would look up and glance out the rear window, trying to channel how Joshua would respond to a situation I'd put him in. Each time, I would silently giggle at myself the same way I did when I would find myself trying on a facial expression to be sure I was wording it correctly for a character.

After doing so much research on the couple, I knew I wasn't writing Joshua and Cora's story the way it had happened exactly. I knew I was taking some artistic license, especially with my goal of changing the ending where he actually lives so they could be together. But it was my way of honoring them.

It dawned on me that if they had ended up together, married, happy, Reid and I wouldn't have what we did. *I* wouldn't exist.

That sudden realization paused me for a moment. I certainly had grown an admiration for the man that was the spirit I was conversing with. But knowing that his death meant my life? That was an entirely new level of respect for his situation ... for him. For what he went through.

Not that I was grateful that he had died. Honestly, it was yet another thing that tore me in more than one direction, emotionally. But I couldn't deny that my admiration for him and his situation grew immensely after realizing the delicate association.

Writing his fictionalized story became something different. A small part of me mourned myself in a way, feeling like I was sacrificing myself somehow to give him what he wanted. Even if it was in a completely fictional world.

A few hours rolled by as I filled a number of pages with my developing manuscript. I stretched and opted for a walk through the house. Taking a fresh mug of coffee with me, I meandered down the hall way toward some of the back rooms.

Simply put, it was breathtaking. I could hardly believe that they were so close to being finished in such a short amount of time. But knowing how many workers Gerald had roped in for the job, I guessed it wasn't so unbelievable.

Just as if on cue, Gerald came out from one of the rooms. "Nell. It is good to see you. Is Reid on the grounds?"

"No. He is back at home, getting some work done." I mock cleared my throat. "You know, that thing he's been putting off to help me on all of this craziness."

Gerald chuckled. "That's good. I didn't realize you were here, or I would have come to get you sooner."

"Oh?" I quirked an eyebrow. "Is everything alright?"

He looked as if he was pondering that question for a moment. "Well, come with me."

The old me wanted so badly to start spouting questions. To find out as much as possible as quickly as possible. To be braced for whatever it was. But everything with the estate, with Joshua, with Reid, had changed me. Working with Gerald had changed me.

I managed to tie my anxiety down to the floor of my thinking and just follow the man into one of the rooms. The last room on the top floor.

He stopped in front of the door. "If I'm not mistaken, this room was Cora's sitting room, her bedroom having been the one you've chosen for yourself. But up here, she was granted time to herself to read, sew and do as she pleased, away from having to be social with the others in the household."

I peeked in around him. It was not quite complete with the trim in a pile in the center of the room, carpet not yet installed and walls not refinished. "It is cute. Thank you."

"That's not all." He stepped out of the way, motioning for me to go inside. "Please. Take a look."

Inside, I saw more of the room. There was a section of one of the walls that was built-in library bookshelves. One of them had been removed, assumedly to install the new electrical since there was updated wiring run between the wall studs.

A certain sense of comfort washed over me as I walked through the room. It was smaller than the bedroom, for sure, but not too small to make you feel closed in. There was a single window off the back of the room. It was recessed slightly to make room for a ledge wide enough to sit on, overlooking the back gardens.

I sat on the window bench and saw that it was perfectly aligned to see the place in the wall where the two exchanged their love letters. My heart swooned as I could almost envision Cora sitting there to watch for Joshua to come. And I could see him looking up to see if he could catch a glimpse of her sitting there as he slipped his letter into the wall, hopefully unseen by anyone else.

I swung my legs off the ledge, turning toward Gerald, who was still standing in the doorway. My fingers wrapped around the rounded edge of the wooden seat.

He nodded at me, not saying anything.

At first, I wasn't sure what he was trying to tell me. But when I went to move my hand, I felt something peculiar under my right index finger.

I furrowed my eyebrows and bent down onto the floor, facing the window. I had to crane my neck pretty far to see up under it, but I was sure I could see something there. I braced the palms of my hands against the under part of the ledge and pushed up. After a little resistance, the ledge seat lifted, revealing a hidden space.

I spun around. "Gerald! Did you see what was in here?"

"I saw that there is a time capsule of things that belonged to your great grandmother. I did not disturb it in any way, though," he said.

Wondering where to start, I picked up the letter that was sitting on top. There was nothing written on its folded exterior, nor held a wax seal. That made it easy to open. Which I did as Gerald quietly took his leave.

Joshua, My Love,

Tomorrow, I am to marry. Not to you, as I had planned, but a man that is good and kind and generous. This has caused me great strife since he is not you. Lord knows, I would give it all up even for one more day together.

In all my turmoil and sadness, I have closed myself off to others, agreeing to this marriage simply because it is what one is supposed to do, to marry well. I suppose my options could be worse. He could be selfish and cruel. So, I am thankful for that.

Your name has not been spoken, nor have I written it since your death. It has been too much to bear. But tonight, I am writing to tell you that I love you still, despite knowing you will never know.

You will never hear me speak it. You will never feel the touch of my hand on your cheek. And you will not be standing opposite me tomorrow in front of the priest and altar. And, for that, I cannot forgive nor will I ever get past. I am angry. No. I am furious. And I wish you were here to help soothe me and calm me. But, alas, if you were here to do that, you would be alive and I would not have such rage inside me.

I miss you.

Please wait for me in the next life.

Yours Always & Forever,
Cora Webb Price (Wilkinson)

Instantly, I ran for my office. The room was empty except for a couple boxes that I had brought over. Knowing exactly what I was looking for, I set Cora's letter on top of another and tore through the tape of one of the boxes.

After dumping the contents out onto the floor, I found what I was looking for. A page scanner. I whipped it up, along with her letter and ran for my laptop. Plugging it in, I scanned the letter, making sure it came through alright.

Then, I ran for the rock wall.

Relieved that my book of a letter was still in the wall, I almost ripped the envelope from yanking it out so fast. I tucked Cora's letter inside mine and put it back inside the envelope, stopping to write on the outside before replacing it.

Also, I have included something I found that is yours.

Before returning to the house, I looked for Joshua again, hoping for the chance to say hi or maybe even get to tell him some of what we found out in person. But, again, I didn't see him.

I emailed the scan of the letter to Reid and went back up to the sitting room. As I went through the doorway, I froze. There, sitting on the floor, holding a handkerchief to her face, was a woman, dressed in a blue gown. It was adorned with gold and green floral patterns along the skirt, sleeve hems and the collar. She was young. Early twenties. Her lips were full while her eyes were round, and she was poised.

I instantly knew exactly who she was.

At first, my brain wanted to rationalize who I was seeing. But with everything, I couldn't deny it. It was her.

"Cora?" I gasped.

She looked up, blinking through tears. She blinked several times. "Nell?"

"Yes?"

"Why do I know your name?" She looked around frantically. "Why does my sitting room look so different?"

I hadn't seen Joshua when he first came back. But he said it must have been connected with me finding his letter. It dawned on me that finding Cora's letter in her window seat must have done the same for her. Only Joshua had to come into what was going on, on his own, slowly. He had to wait until I accepted everything and could show him. Something I felt bad he had to go though. Looking at the petite woman in front of me, I wanted to find the words to gently explain to her what was going on. I hadn't prepared for that to happen, let alone considered it. But there she was, and I needed to help her understand.

"I don't know where to start. Quite a lot of it is going to come as a shock to you." I made my way across the room.

She closed the bench and sat up on it, brushing off her skirt. Slowly, I took a seat next to her and started. "As you can see by the room, my clothing and possibly what is outside of that window, this is not the time you remember."

She sat and listened as I explained everything. Joshua's letter in the wall. His spirit being on the property. Reid and his connection to Joshua. My connection to the estate, and to her. My connection to Reid.

Once I was finished, she sat in silence, fidgeting with her handkerchief, looking at me. Knowing that she quite possibly was a lot like myself, I gave her a few minutes to process all of the information, giving her some space.

Finally, she spoke. "Surely, this is some silly prank. Did one of my children put you up to this?"

Initially, I was unsure what to say that would make it believable. I rubbed my hands over the tops of my thighs, worry coating them in sweat. Then, it dawned on me. I reached into my pocket and pulled out my cell phone, holding it up for her to see.

She looked even more confused. "What is this?"

"It is what we call a cell phone. Well, a smart phone. It's a portable telephone and computer all in one," I explained.

"I know what a telephone is, but what is a computer? And where is its cords? We had a telephone installed in the main drawing room in eighteen eighty-nine. Expensive contraptions but so interesting." She looked it over. "This looks nothing like that."

I hit the power button to illuminate the screen. "A computer is something that does a million things like take and hold pictures, process and save documents, allow you access to the internet, which is a digital place where you can look up just about anything, or talk to people all around the world." I laughed. "Honestly, I can't even begin to tell you all it does. But I can show you a thing or two."

I proceeded to click on a series of things, including a game, messenger, *Facebook*, *Twitter*, searched up images for a couple historical events and more. Then, I sent a text to my eldest, saying I hoped she was having a wonderful day, to which, she responded in kind.

"Do you want me to make a call?" I asked.

Her eyes were as wide as saucers, her jaw slack. "No. No thank you. I think that is plenty enough to grasp as is."

"I don't mean to overwhelm you." I put my phone back into my pocket.

She reached out to place her hand on my shoulder, but it went right through. Just when I didn't think she could appear any more shell shocked, she reeled back, unsure what to make of what had just happened.

"Joshua had a tough time remembering he couldn't touch people either," I said.

"Joshua? So you've seen him? That's right." She leaned toward me again. "And you are my great grandchild a few times removed? And Reid, your fiancé, he is a direct descendant of Joshua's? Is this correct?"

I nodded. "Yes. He and I met while trying to figure out where the letters were coming from. He accepted that Joshua was a wandering spirit well before I could."

"His emotional dispensation is probably just like my Joshua's then. And you're like me." She let out a gentle laugh. "And yet, you so easily accepted me."

I mirrored her laugh. "Well, I suppose that once you accept one ghost on your property, it's easier with a second one."

"I suppose so." She crossed her hands in her lap. "I suppose my things are now yours?"

"That's not how I see it," I replied.

She looked to the window, reaching out and going to touch the lock, but she stopped and lowered her hand. "Whether or not you do, and whether or not I want it this way, it is how it is."

She was right. That *was* how things were.

"What did you hide away in there?" I asked, curious.

She smiled. "Shall we take a look?"

We both stood, and I lifted the bench lid. Inside was quite the varied accumulation of items. I picked them out one by one as she told me where each one came from and why she had chosen to keep them there.

Among the items were the first edition of her favorite book, *The Woman in White* by *Wilkie Collins*, a first edition *Leaves of Grass* by *Walt Whitman*, the necklace that Joshua had given her in place of an engagement ring when her parents refused to allow the ring to be displayed, a small jewelry box with the pieces her parents had given her, a few random keepsakes and a white gown. The gown she was going to wear on her wedding day to Joshua Wilkinson.

I held the dress in my hands. "All of this appears to be from before your marriage."

"You are very observant, my dear." She slowly bowed her head. "Yes. When I married my husband, I knew I had to let go of the past. But I couldn't entirely. So, I tucked these items, along with parts of myself, in here. I wrote that letter you read, and I went forward with life the best I could."

"But you never did fully, did you?" My words were to the point but spoken gently.

The corners of her mouth turned up. "I am here. So, no. I suppose not."

"Why aren't you running to see him? Why sit here with me?"

Her gaze turned toward the window again. "I will, dear. I will. I'm just not sure he will recognize me."

"Why not?" I couldn't imagine he wouldn't. Especially since he had only recently accepted he wasn't back in his own time. Something I had explained to her. It wasn't as if he had years upon years to cloud his memories. He was still back in that time in a way.

She looked down. "I died at an advanced age. I can only imagine how I look."

I stifled a laugh. "If you consider somewhere around twenty an advanced age, then you're right. Otherwise, you've come back about the same he would remember you as."

Her hands flew to her face. "Really? Oh, really?"

Once again, I pulled out my phone. This time, I put it on forward facing camera and held it out toward her, unsure it would work. But, by the shocked and happy look on her face, it had.

She sucked in a breath. "That is me. A little transparent but me. I remember that face. Yes. This is just as I appeared when we last saw one another."

I snapped a picture, hoping that I would be able to see her in it later. Slipping the device back into my pocket, I smiled and motioned toward the door. "Shall we see if he's around?"

"Is he usually?" She looked apprehensive.

"Is who what?" Reid stepped into the room.

"Reid!" I jumped.

He looked around the room. "Who were you talking to? And what is all this?"

"Cora! I'd like you to meet Reid." I waved my arm out, but she was gone. "She was *just* here!"

"She was?" He looked around. I could tell by his expression that he believed me and was eager to meet her. "I got your email with the letter and came straight away." He looked around at the items strewn about the floor. "Where did all of this come from? Was she tied to it?"

I picked up the wedding dress. "I'm not for sure what happened. All I know is that Gerald had noticed something was under the window sill. I came up to take a look, and he explained that this used to be Cora's personal reading room. When I took a closer look, I found that it wasn't just a sill bench. It was her place to pack away certain keepsakes. On the top was that letter I scanned and sent to you. It was for Joshua, telling him about her wedding and her continued love for him. Of course, I wanted to get it to him if possible, so I put it in the wall. When I came back, Cora was in here."

"Did she speak to you?" He knelt down and inspected the books.

I pressed the dress to my heart. "Yes."

He looked up. "Yes?"

I closed my eyes. "We talked quite a bit. I helped her understand what time she's in and told her about Joshua, you, and even who I am to her. I told her about the internet and even showed her a few things on my phone. We even went through all of these things she had tucked away, and she told me where each one is from and why they meant something special to her."

He motioned toward the gown I was holding to my heart. "Was that the dress she had planned to wear?"

I nodded.

"It is beautiful," he exclaimed.

"Yes; it is," I said, almost under my breath.

"You need to eat." He held his hand out to me, standing in the middle of Cora's things. "This is all very exciting, but you're rambling, and I don't think it is just from that. Let's take all of this to your bedroom while they finish this room this week. But then, let's get food in you. I brought lunch with me as you requested."

"You're right. I'm famished. Can we eat first? I am not quite ready to move her things out of here yet. I'd like to see if she comes back," I requested.

"Of course." He set the dress down on the bench gently.

I took his hand. "I love you."

"With all my heart."

Fourteen

Reid got a clean box from Gerald after we finished eating. Together, we loaded up the things from the storage bench in Cora's sitting room and set it in my bedroom, just as he had suggested. She hadn't reappeared, but I knew leaving them in there was risky with the crews working.

Of course, I worried about her ability to return with them all moved, but I knew that she would rather I keep them safe with the remodeling still going on. Even more so, I knew that was why Gerald had asked me to see if anything was there. I felt like he didn't find it his place, and he wanted me to keep them safe as well.

I set the box down just outside of the newly installed closet. Gently shaking out the gown, I hung it to allow the wrinkles to let out, even if only a little considering it had been folded for well over a hundred years. The white of the lace and satins had yellowed slightly, but the pearl buttons remained bright, which I could only assume were real pearls.

Reid had gone down to the main level to help with the painting of one of the rooms. Once I was done marveling the wedding dress, I went downstairs to find him and see how the progress was coming along. With him working with Gerald, I figured the two of them were chatting away while working.

I stepped off the bottom step into the foyer and heard a voice come from the sitting room, just to my right. "Have you lost your mind?"

"Mother?" I mocked.

It was my youngest.

Her arms were folded, and she wore a stern and serious look about her that reminded me exactly of how my mother spent most of my life looking at me. "What are you doing here? I mean, I'm very happy to see you. But why the abrupt trip, and why not tell me you were coming?"

"Excuse me?" She huffed and took a couple steps toward me, her arms firmly locked in front of her. "You jump into some sham marriage, and you wonder why I would take the first flight out here? And what is this? You're a single woman. Why in the hell do you need a place like this? You can't blame it on boredom. I know you better than that."

"My engagement and upcoming marriage to Reid is *not* a sham. And why I bought this estate ended up being for a very good reason. I can explain everything, but just as you wonder if I've lost mine, I am starting to wonder what is going on in your mind." I was astonished at her audacity. "This isn't like you. You don't lash out like this. What makes you think this is acceptable?"

She didn't stop there. "Listen, we all get that you're scared or feeling insecure or whatever. But this is ludicrous, Mother. You're too old to be making such big mistakes. I think we should get you to a therapist or something. I want to help you. Maybe the right meds will help you see that you're acting like some ... I don't know. Maybe you need attention or something? Or is that it? Are you just pulling this stunt for attention? Don't you know that this guy is probably just using you for your money ... or for this place?"

I wanted to slap her. "Listen, child. You may disapprove, but I am still your mother. I would think that you could find a far more respectful way to express your concern. Not that I am required to answer to you, but if you could get your attitude in check, maybe we could talk. But, until then, I'm afraid that your trip here will remain fruitless."

"Hello, ladies." Reid came into the room. "It seems I have immaculate timing today. Who is this?"

I was scared that she was going to be just as cruel to him or maybe even accuse him of being a con artist to his face. That wasn't the Lula I raised and knew. Sure, she was full of spunk and had a bold personality. But rude and disrespectful? Not in the least. I could only chalk it up to her being extremely concerned. But I couldn't just let her behave that way and accept it.

I spoke before she could. "Reid, this is my youngest, Lula. Lula, this is my fiancé, Reid Wilkinson."

They both reached out to shake hands. She corrected me. "Lucinda."

"I am very happy to meet you, Lucinda." He greeted her with a warm smile.

"I take it you're the man looking to marry my mother so quickly?" Her eyes were like darts.

I nervously chuckled. "We were just talking about our quick engagement, Reid. I figured I may take her out for tea and coffee and tell her all about how we met and how special this house is."

He looked at me, trying to hide his concern. "I'll give you two a ride into town if you like."

"Thank you," she snapped, "but I have a rental car. I'm pretty sure we will manage."

"Lucinda." It was my turn to sound curt. "Go out and wait in the car. And while you're there, see if you packed your manners or just completely forgot them. If so, I will help you relearn them when I join you."

She turned on her heels and stormed out the front door, snorting in disapproval. I was so embarrassed. Did I expect everyone to approve? No. But I certainly didn't think one of my children would fly all the way there to scold me like our roles were reversed.

"I'm so sorry." I didn't know what to say beyond that.

He crossed his arms and glared at me, not saying a word.

Emotionally, I shrunk as words started falling out of my mouth. "I don't know what's gotten into her. I hadn't even gotten to tell her. I told her that I was getting married, but we didn't have time to talk. Her class was starting. But I hadn't gotten to tell her anything about the circumstances or you. She must have called one of her siblings ... or maybe my mother? Or maybe my mother made her own round of calls? That's entirely possible. And if she spoke to my mother, lord only knows what they had to say."

He held his hands up to stop me. And, finally, his lips cracked into a smile. "I'm just playing with you, Nell. Your daughter being protective, even if it is done in the wrong way, is a good thing. Go. Talk to her. Hopefully, you can quell her furry quickly. If not, I am sure she will get over it at some point."

I hugged him and ran off, calling back on my way out the door. "I love you!"

"With all my heart!" he called out after me.

I opened the passenger door and climbed in. "Are you hungry?"

"Coffee would be fine, Mother," she snapped.

"Listen," I turned in my seat to face her, "I get it. You're angry. For what exactly, I don't even know yet. And, yes, I want to know. But if you're going to act like a petulant child, just as I said earlier, I won't do this. I don't deserve it."

She let out an exasperated breath. "Fine."

After a couple of attempts to make conversation, I stopped. From that point, aside from me giving her directions, we didn't speak for the drive into town. Both of us getting out and going inside in silence. I knew her. Once she was upset at something, it was difficult to pull her out of it. So, I waited for her to speak first. Part of me wondered if we were going to spend the entire visit only glancing at one another.

The barista brought us our coffees. Lula wrapped her hands around the mug as if it was cold out and breathed in the steam. Taking a sip, she sighed. "Okay. Please tell me what is going on."

"Where do you want me to start?" I asked.

She looked up, anger returning to her expression.

I held my hands up. "I am not trying to be difficult. But, knowing you, you are talking about more than Reid."

She nodded, her eyes closed. "I just don't understand. My entire life, you have been you. But with us moved out, and Dad left you ... you seem to have lost your mind."

I laughed.

"It's not funny! I'm being serious," she snapped.

I cleared my throat. "No. I know you are. And I'm not laughing at you. It's just that I've asked myself that a few times recently."

She reached out and put her hands on mine. "Do we need to get you some help? I know of a great psychologist back in New York."

I turned my hand to hold hers. "I'm not going crazy, baby. But, yes, a lot in my life has changed ... and fast."

"*You* have changed, Mom." She looked concerned.

I ran my hand over my mouth, trying to form the right way to tell her everything. "The night your father moved the rest of his things out, I felt something I hadn't in a long time. I felt alone. Now, don't get me wrong. Your father and I parted amicably. Our marriage had dissolved into nothing more than a friendship. And I hope to remain friends with him. But being alone wasn't something I was used to. And, honestly, I had only planned to take a vacation. But when I saw the listing for Webb Manor, I jumped on it. It was as if I was being pulled to it."

"Oh, come on. You have scoffed at me for years for what you've called foolish whims." She sat across the table, defensively, her arms crossed, pulled in tight, head tilted, eyebrow quirked and lips pursed. It reminded me of her early teenage years when she pushed buttons to try to test her boundaries.

I bowed my head. "I have. And I'm very sorry. I get it now. Granted, as your mother, I will always want you to be more boring or less adventurous. Basically, I want to keep you safe. But I understand. And just as you probably would have, I bought it and moved right here, digging my hands into the work and immersing myself into it. Now, I know that it was partly me hiding or escaping or whatever. But I don't regret it."

"And the guy? What is that? Replacing Dad?"

I blinked, completely not braced for that. "No. Not at all. Reid is a wonderful man."

"But why are you in such a rush to get married again?" Her eyes were pleading for understanding.

"Okay. Here's where our roles are reversed again. Haven't you ever just felt like something was right? Deep down?" His face flashed through my mind. "That is he and I. It doesn't feel rushed. It is just what we're doing."

Her shouldered slumped. "But how did you meet this guy?"

I swallowed. "Well, that's where things get interesting. I'd rather take you back to the estate and show you some of it rather than just telling you."

She pursed her lips. "What? Does he look good, shirtless, working on the house?"

I laughed. "Well, yeah. But that is just a bonus."

"Mom!" She turned red.

"Yeah, yeah. I know. Gross."

She lifted a shoulder. "Well, I'll admit, he isn't bad to look at."

We both laughed, hard. And it felt good. "Would you mind coming back and being nice? You're probably going to question my sanity again, but I want to be honest with you. Your siblings probably won't understand. But I'm pretty sure you will."

One of her eyebrows quirked up. "Ummm ... okay?"

"You'll see." I grinned.

On our way, I had her stop by Reid's house. I picked up the box of letters and a few files we'd been collecting. No matter how much she asked, I refused to tell her anything. It was going to be unbelievable as it was. And I wanted Reid there to help me.

But that didn't stop her from asking. I had to set the files in the back seat just so she would stop trying to peek, even when I would scold her for not paying enough attention to the road. She was even giving one last ditch effort as we pulled into the drive.

"But, Mom. What is so mysterious and important that we need to wait until we are back there?" she whined.

I pointed. "You mean back here? Just have some patience! It's not like you have to wait days. Just a few minutes."

Reid met us in the drive. He looked us over as we got out of the car, assessing if our chat had gone well or not. Once he saw us in better spirits, he came out to join us. "You two kiss and make up?"

"Well, she's not trying to burn a hole through me with her death stare anymore." I reached in and grabbed the box and files.

She huffed. "Doesn't mean I won't start again if you don't start talking." She half glared at Reid. "Apparently, we need *you*."

"Me?" he questioned as she stalked past him.

I linked my arm in his as he took the things I'd brought. "I think she's starting to accept that I bought this place and we are together. But I want to tell her about the why. And I've refused to even give her a hint." I nodded toward her. "She's not the most patient of my children."

He smirked. "That's why you brought all of this here?"

"Yes. I also wanted you with us. I thought maybe you'd have a thing or two to add that might explain things better," I explained.

We went into the kitchen. Reid set everything on the counter as I went upstairs to get the box of Cora's items, gently folding the wedding dress on top.

Lula reached for the dress. "What is..."

I slapped her hand away. "Patience."

"Ugh." She sighed. "So, now that your props are all laid out, can we get on with it?"

Reid took a seat as I started. I held my hand up and turned the ruby ring back and forth on my finger. "Just before I came upon the listing for Webb Manor, I put on this ring that was passed down to me."

She cut me off. "One ring to rule them all? Really, Mom? Is this going to be some mythical ring that gave you powers or something?"

"Will you give the attitude a rest and just let me tell you what I want to tell you? What you've snapped at me to know?" I threw my hands up. "If you think I'm crazy after this, fine. Go home and tell your therapist what a loon your mother is and how she's lost her mind. But, for the love of all that is holy, will you *please* let me finish telling you something before you let any more sarcastic dribble fall out of your mouth or you shoot me another one of your four year old death glares?"

"Geez. Sorry." She sat back. "Fine. Tell me your fantastical tale."

I looked over to Reid, who appeared mildly amused. "She really wasn't this difficult as a child."

He was leaned back, arms lazily folded in front of him. "I can see the family resemblance."

I wadded up a blank piece of paper and threw it at him. "Don't encourage her."

She shrugged one shoulder. "Maybe you're not so bad, mystery man."

"Anyway. The ring and this place." I waited for them to both stop snickering before I went on. "I didn't know when I put it on. Actually, I didn't know until much later, but it is possible it pulled me here. I'll get to why in a moment."

The first letter was in the top file folder. I opened it and set it on the table. "A few months after getting here, I found this letter in the wall."

I went from there and explained the entire sequence of events. The progression of the letters. The breaking of my writer's block. Meeting Imogen and Elijah. Meeting Reid and how he was related to Joshua, and how he and I quickly connected, something he was more than happy to help divulge. Then I went on to explain my struggles with accepting that Joshua was actually a ghost until my first encounter. Then, how Gerald was connected. How I found out that we were related to Cora. All the way through to when Cora made her appearance that morning.

Throughout the explanation, I pulled out letters, documents, jewelry and even the wedding gown. Reid added in parts here and there, but, mostly, they both just watched as I spoke. Lula with a look of disbelief and awe on her face.

I was lost in remembering. "Like I said, I put Cora's final letter to Joshua into the wall with my letter to him, explaining everything we found out." My breath caught. "The letter! I wonder if he's come and picked it up yet."

Lula rolled her eyes. "Like some paranormal postal service?"

I had made it half way to the back door when she spoke. I stopped and turned back. "So you think I'm crazy?"

She put her face in her hands. "I don't know what to think."

"Your mother is not dreaming this up, Lucinda. I've seen it all unfold," Reid tried to defend me.

Lula opened her mouth to speak, but I beat her to it. "Believe me or not, but I'm going to go see."

"See what?" she asked.

But I had already stepped out the door. My focus was on the letters and making sure that Joshua had not only gotten the one from me but also the one from Cora.

Cora.

Her name hung in my mind like a thick fog as I crossed the garden to the rock wall at the edge of the property.

I placed my hands on the top of it and looked around, feeling like I was in the middle of something. Not at a crossroad. Not in a war. But being watched from all angles. And, as I did a full turn, I saw exactly why.

At the back door to the house stood both Reid and Lula. Reid had taken a few steps from the house, looking a bit more than curious. From there, my eyes traveled up and saw the window to Cora's sitting room. I could see her watching me. Her hands were on the window, but I couldn't make out her features clearly from the distance.

Then, out by the tree line, Joshua stood. Only, his eyes weren't on me. They were cast toward the window where his beloved stood, now looking back to him.

I didn't know what to do. Could they meet? Should I stop them? Could anyone else see what I was seeing?

I turned and looked for Reid. Relief ran through me as his head whipped back and forth between the two spirits. Lula, behind him, looked terrified. She not only was frantically looking between the two ghostly people, dressed in attire reflective of their own time periods and slightly transparent, but she was also gripped to Reid's arm and glancing over to me, eyes begging for some kind of explanation.

I moved fast to check the wall. Both letters were gone. He knew. He knew about how his son turned out. He knew about Cora's moving on and living a full life. He knew about my being related to her. And he knew about her always loving him, even years after his death.

He knew.

"They're gone!" I called out to Reid.

Reid was starting to look as panicked as Lula. "What do we do?"

I ran for Joshua, who was making his way toward the back door. His eyes hadn't diverted from the window, but when I looked up, Cora was gone. My heart sank. But Joshua was still walking toward the house. "Joshua! Wait! Are you sure this is a good idea?"

He didn't respond.

I closed the gap between us. "Joshua!"

"I saw her. She was there." He hadn't slowed his pace, but he pointed toward her window.

I glanced up. She hadn't returned. "But we don't know what will happen."

"That's right. We don't know." He stayed focused on the upstairs window.

He was right. I couldn't argue with that. Seeing Reid come into view as Joshua and I briskly walked to the house, I knew that if I were in his place, I wouldn't hesitate either. My steps would be just as sure as I went for my love. I would want to do everything I could for even just a moment more with them.

But Cora didn't reappear. Not even once Joshua and I were below her window in the garden. His head was tilted up, waiting, hoping. The shape of his eyes going from wide and hopeful to sad, drooping, exhausted. And, in that moment, I wished he wasn't just a ghost. I wanted to be able to reach out and put a hand on his shoulder and comfort him.

Reid stayed back with Lula, standing in the doorway to the kitchen. She had stopped asking questions rapid fire after we passed them, but her grip stayed tight on his arm, which kept him anchored there instead of joining Joshua and I. I stayed with Joshua for what felt like a long time. I'd expected questions. I expected him to ask questions about what was in the letters from both Cora and I. But he didn't speak. He only stood and waited, his face full of longing, pleading for her to return.

A blood curdling scream came from the kitchen doorway. It was Lula, and I whipped around to see what happened.

She shoved Reid, who stumbled a few paces before catching himself. Lula ran out into the garden and stopped, completely out of breath, unable to speak. Her entire body was trembling and she pointed toward the doorway.

Joshua moved through me before my eyes could focus on what had scared Lula so badly. And when I saw her, my heart leapt.

Cora.

She was standing there, just inside, the door wide open, her eyes full of tears as she watched Joshua close the gap between them. Her long skirts blowing in the breeze that was coming through the doorway, making her look even more unearthly than she already did. Despite it not being necessary to breath, she still held her breath.

"Joshua."

Joshua reached the back deck and climbed the steps. I had ran over to Lula, who wrapped her arms around my waist and burrowed into my shoulder just as she did when she was a child and had been frightened by something. Reid joined us and took one of my hands. He and I watched, in awe, as the two reunited, both captivated and, yet, nervous.

"I am so sorry." A tear fell down Cora's cheek.

Joshua stopped. "Sorry?"

She looked pained. "I was not there. I should have been there. Or maybe I should not have agreed to marry you. If I had turned you away when my parents said to, maybe you would have been able to live a full life with your son. But, because of me, you died, and he had to endure a life with your bloody uncle. That monster did not even grant your son a good living and university. I could not allow for that. Not knowing that it was all because of me."

"What do you mean you could not allow for that?" Joshua's forehead lined as she strained to understand.

Cora swallowed hard. "I could not just let him go out into the world with nothing."

"What did you do?" he asked.

She looked down at her hands. "I did not do nearly enough. I simply provided for him. He was the only one that knew anything about my repayment."

"You did not need to do that. It was for his uncle to do," Joshua said.

She shook her head. "But he did not. He was going to toss Clive out on the streets when he turned fifteen. He had spoken with my father about it, who actually had the audacity to encourage him. I was supposed to be his mother. His mother, Joshua. I was not merely marrying you. I was going to be taking on your child, and I was more than happy to do so. But I had not. When you died, I did not do as a mother would. I allowed that little boy to be taken in by a man that wanted nothing more than what your estate could give him. He was not interested in treating Clive as his own. When I had overheard my father talking about the situation, I felt a deep guilt for allowing it to happen. I could not just sit by and let things get worse for him. So, I started using my personal money to pay for his expenses."

"That had to have been difficult, considering that if your father had found out, he would surely have cut you off." Joshua's ran his hand over his mouth, taking in her words.

Her voice was soft. "It is what a mother would do; take risks to keep their children safe. Clive tried to deny my help, saying he would simply get a job and make his own way. But I had none of it. I told him that I would find a way to get the money to him, one way or another, so he might as well take it willingly and put it to good use. And he did. He made something of himself in a very respectful field."

Joshua laughed. "That is my Cora - stubborn and determined."

She smiled. "Joshua, he saved my life and the life of my eldest."

"What?" He coughed out the word.

She bowed her head. "My eldest had an accident one summer. Was thrown from her horse on her way back from town. She had broken bones and was bleeding internally. He came to the house and treated her diligently for six days, getting the infection under control, setting the bones and making sure the bleeding had stopped. He even returned four times over the following weeks to check on us. He never asked for a penny from us, despite me trying to force payment onto him."

"And you?" Joshua asked. "He saved you?"

Her smile grew with pride. "Yes." She paused, gathering herself before speaking. "I had caught ill one year. My fever was the highest I had ever experienced. I could not eat. My vision was blurry. And worse. Many people had died in the area so much so that I sent my husband and children away so they didn't catch fever as well. I was sure I would not make it."

"Your husband left?" he asked.

"Yes, as I told him to do, to keep our children safe," she explained.

"Did you not have someone to care for you then?" He looked furious. "Could he not have left them with family and returned to take care of you? That is what a good husband would do."

"Joshua." She gave him a gentle, understanding smile. "That is what Joshua would do. He was a good husband, even if he was not you."

Joshua's expression dropped with his shoulders. "I did not mean to offend."

She held a hand up. "I understand. I truly do. But Clive came once he had received word that I was here, alone and dying. He stayed for a month, even catching the fever himself. His heart was just as yours has always been, and he cared for me every day despite falling ill and needing to rest. And once I was on the mend, we took care of each other. By the end of that month, we both were well on our way to being fully healthy once again."

I tried to muffle the sounds of my own sobs as Joshua spoke. "He did that for you?"

She nodded. "He said that is what a son does for his mother."

We all stood in silence for a moment.

Cora went on. "That season, the same fever I fell ill with had taken my father. After that, I told my husband that Clive was to be accepted into our family as one of our own. I explained what he had endured after your death, how I had helped him, and what he had done for both my daughter and for myself. He did not hesitate to agree with me that he was more than welcome."

"So, you got to see him more?" he asked.

"I got to see him, be at his wedding, as well as be around for his children," she stated, proudly. "They called me Mammy."

Joshua reached a hand out and walked forward. You could see the gratitude in his eyes and the longing to hold her in his speed. She returned the gesture, mirroring the same desire to be in her love's arms once again. Lula had stopped trembling and had started watching the two as they discussed Clive. She squeezed my hand as he approached the doorway. Their movements slowed as they were close, their hands reaching for each other.

Then, they were gone.

Just gone.

My heart split in two.

Half of it leaped, overjoyed that they had been rejoined. Part of my goal had always been to help Joshua to move on from being stuck here in our world, hoping there was some place for him to move on to. But it all seemed so lonely. But instead of being lonely, he was with his Cora. They had been able to be together.

The other half of my heart dropped all the way down to my feet. They had just reunited, and now they were gone. Where to? Were they still together? Were they happy? Could they both finally rest?

I felt a tug on my sleeve from Reid. "Nell."

I wiped the tears from my cheeks. "Yes?"

He motioned toward the upper floor. "There."

I looked. The half of my heart that had leaped joined the other half when I saw Cora standing in her window again. Her hands were pressed to the glass, and she was sobbing uncontrollably.

I let go of Lula and spun around to the trees. There stood Joshua. He was looking around him and at his own hands, looking completely baffled as to how he had gotten there.

It only took a moment, but he gathered himself and started running for the house again.

I ran to the deck and turned to face him. “Wait! Something is wrong,” I called out.

My words didn’t slow him. I blinked, and he was standing right in front of me. However, his focus was not on me. He was watching Cora cross the floor of the kitchen toward him.

She stopped a few steps from the threshold. “The curse.”

“Curse?” I repeated.

She wrung her hands. “I had only heard talk of it. I had only heard talk of such things in general. But when I was to be married, I had heard rumors that my father had not only had you killed, Joshua, but he had also had a curse placed on our love so that we could not even be together after your death. You see, my father was very much into the occult, and he worried that your spirit would stay and I would be with you in death. He had hired a caster to place a curse that would not allow you to enter the house, nor I to leave it after death.”

“Had he told you of this curse?” Anger returned to his expression.

“Only in a threat, rather than telling me the entire story. He simply said that our love was so forbidden that it would not be allowed. Not by him. He would say that no Webb would ever allow the likes of a Wilkinson to be a part of our heritage, and I was disgusted with and embarrassed by him for it.” Her tone was sullen.

“A curse?” I spat. “After everything you two have been through? I mean, it explains why you both are here … seemingly stuck. But to be stuck here, together but not together? That is cruel!”

Joshua closed his eyes. "So, I cannot embrace you? I can never hold you again, even being stuck here together? That is torture!"

"But what about moving on? Can you two not move on to whatever we are supposed to go to when we die?" I asked.

She looked at me. "Part of the rumors was that the payment of the curse was our souls to be stuck here. We are not to move on. It was punishment for what he saw as my betrayal to him. I know not of any way to break it."

"How could he? He was your father!" I raised my voice.

Joshua gritted his teeth. "Because he was an evil, selfish, cruel man."

"He was." Her eyes were cast down. "And for that, I am sorry as well."

"Clive Brown was right? He did have Joshua killed?" I took hold of Reid's sleeve as he came up next to me with Lula walking behind him.

"It is all rumor, Nell. He, nor anybody that knew for certain, ever said a word to me on the matter directly," she said.

"What now?" Joshua set his shoulders.

"I do not know." Her eyes filled with tears again.

Lula spoke up. "This is so unfair."

"Yes, child. It is." Cora's gaze fell on Joshua. "It is."

The next few weeks were filled with a mix of happiness and sadness. The work continued on Webb Manor and the grounds. The house had been finished, and the workers had started work on the out buildings. Reid started packing his house up and preparing to put it on the market to sell in anticipation of us moving in together after the wedding. We moved everything from my flat into the estate and signed the papers to release it once my contract was up. Then, we shopped and decorated the remaining space that I did not have items for.

Lula opted to stay in England with us. Seeing Cora and Joshua with her own eyes was more than enough for her to change her mind about me having lost mine. She was so captivated by it all that she researched what would be needed to switch to the university nearby. It was Reid's idea to give her one of the rooms in the house so she could stay with us. A gesture she was more than happy to accept.

Cora appeared throughout the house regularly, just as Joshua did on the grounds. Every day, they would meet by the kitchen door and talk. Some days for hours. Some days very briefly. A lot of it depended on where the crews were working and for how long. Except for Gerald, both Cora and Joshua avoided the others, not wanting the extra exposure and possibility of creating a huge scandal over their existence. But Gerald had accepted their existence with ease, and they were welcoming to him.

Every day, Joshua would meet her by the door. Whether it be at the long chat or a brief encounter, she would say, "I love you."

To which he replied, every time, "With all my heart."

It was that part that was the sadness. Yes; it was a good thing that they could see each other again. Cora told him all about the rest of her life, as well as about Clive and his children. Reid would join in on some of those discussions to learn more about his ancestors. Cora was more than happy to tell him, too. And Joshua seemed pleased for him to be there.

But you could sense that they longed to touch each other. To embrace. To kiss. Some days, as they stood, talking, you could see one of them twitch like they wanted to reach forward and grasp the other. But after a few more failed attempts, they had stopped. It was just too much to end up sling shot back to other spots as if being thrown in the corner ... as if they were doing wrong.

In the middle of it all, Reid and I planned a wedding ... our wedding. The guest list grew over the weeks as Reid remembered more and more people he wanted to have there, sometimes prompted by Elijah's suggestions of friends, colleagues and prominent people in the area. But it wasn't all his doing. Once word got out, I had both family and friends that reached out, asking if they, too, could attend, "Even if it is short notice," as many would say.

The spare rooms of the house quickly filled up, as did what of the smaller houses on the outskirts of the property that were going to be finished. Gerald contacted a friend of his that owned a nearby bed and breakfast style establishment once the hotel filled up. She had stopped taking on guests in her advanced age, and he helped keep her home and grounds maintained. But he said she was more than happy to reopen for a couple of weeks to accommodate guests for the wedding.

People had started arriving a few days before the big event, all excited to sightsee, some willing to help ... some of them a little too eager. Thankfully, Reid was great with setting people on menial tasks and arranging groups to go out and explore. He got it off my plate, which was a good thing.

When my mother got there, he had quite a few things set aside for her to keep her busy and out of my hair as much as possible. He knew how she and I drove each other up a wall, and he didn't want me to have to deal with it any more than he wanted to field our little disagreements. It also helped that Lula, Emma and Murphy were all there as an easy distraction tactic for her, even if they didn't want to be.

Everyone asked about the move and my reasons behind it. Of course, there were those that insinuated it was because of a mental breakdown after my divorce while others speculated their own theories. Lula, Reid, and I had decided it best to leave out the part of Joshua and Cora, knowing that few would understand or even believe. But when it came down to it, seeing my happiness was enough for most.

My mother didn't let up, picking away at my aging and how being in a foreign country would make for a difficult situation for those that loved me if something happened. Or how about her concern for why such an abrupt change after my divorce and several speculations behind that. Then there was the conspiracy theories about possibly evading tax evasion with the income from my 'little hobby'. Thankfully, one of the kids would step in and pull her away when they would see her pushing too hard in one direction or another.

As daunting as everything felt with everyone buzzing around and my mother refusing to let up, it was great to see everyone. Emma, Murphy and Lula went with me to get things for the wedding, as well as helped Reid and I pick out the caterer, cake and so much more. Murphy and Reid bonded quickly, both sharing things about their careers which the other was easily fascinated by. Gerald, Elijah and Imogen were all regulars to the estate, coming and going with anything needed as well as helping get people from place to place.

Often, I would sneak off to Cora's sitting room with my laptop and write. It was both a welcome distraction and an escape. Sometimes, I wouldn't see her. Sometimes, she would just sit at the window and look for Joshua. Then, other times, she would join me on the couch that I had put in there along with a desk, some book shelves and a few pieces of antique décor, all designed to help her feel at home in her own time.

Some of the items I picked up for the house, I had been told, were actually from Webb Manor from various time periods. They had been sold off at various points. Some at auction. One piece, a vanity desk and stool, was at a shop about three hours away. I had found it online one afternoon. Lula and I went and picked it up, asking the owner if she knew anything about its history. The woman explained that it had been from Webb Manor and sold off when the house had been taken by the bank in order to help pay off some of the debt. Lula had fallen in love with it, and we took it home.

We were setting it up in her room when Cora appeared. "Where did you get that?"

"Geez, Cora!" Lula jumped.

"I am so sorry, dear." Cora's eyes hadn't left the piece of furniture. "I just had to come. I believe I felt you bring this in the house."

"This?" I put a hand on it. "It's beautiful, isn't it? Lula and I found it online, and we just went to pick it up. The woman said it was from the estate, but she didn't know how far back or anything."

I watched as Cora stood, staring at it. "It was my sister's."

"Your sister's?" I repeated.

"Yes. Lilly." Her eyes glossed over. "She used sit at it and brush her hair, one hundred strokes each time. Sometimes, she would permit me to sit as she did my hair. Especially before a ball." She looked around the room. "Yes. I believe it was just about right here."

Lula's eyes flew wide open. "Here? Like..."

Cora giggled. "Yes, love. This was her room. And I do believe this piece sat very close to this spot when she had it here."

At first, Lula looked uncomfortable. Just as she had reacted in the garden when she first saw Joshua and Cora, she wasn't sure what to make of it and wasn't sure she was okay with it at all. But, more quickly this time, she accepted it and maybe even had started to enjoy the intriguing aspects that their paranormal state brought into our lives. It was just taking her time to process it all ... just as it had me.

Like mother, like daughter, right?

***

Everything had been planned. Reid had hired several people to help decorate, and they were busily working both inside and outside of the house. The caterers, bartenders and priest were all focused on their tasks. And the weather was absolutely gorgeous.

The wedding party was all at the house. Both my girls and my son were to stand with us. With so many people coming, the bridesmaids and groomsmen lines were longer than we had planned as well. On my side, we had Emma, Lula, my cousin, Tabitha, and his cousin, Heddie. On his side, Murphy, my best friend's husband, Brad, and his cousins, Martin and Alexander. For my maid of honor, I chose my best friend, Katherine. And for his best man, Reid chose his best friend, Clive Brown, who was more than happy to accept.

Because my father had passed already, I had asked Gerald to walk me down the aisle. He had been such a support and a help beyond measure that it seemed fitting. Both Imogen and Elijah came and helped with anything they could. And with both of them knowing about Joshua and Cora, they were a welcome and nice addition to the day.

The girls had hung my dress and put my accessories in Lula's room. That way, Reid and the groomsmen could get ready in ours. That, and we wanted to get me ready at Lilly's vanity. The rest of the bridesmaids were using the room that Emma was staying in, along with her, not having been privy to Cora's existence.

Reid and the guys arrived, and I was shuffled off as they were shown to the den for socializing and a place to keep him out of sight for me. He had stayed with the other men in the party in town, at his house. The whole bride and groom cannot see each other tradition being in full effect and all.

Before it was my turn to prep for the big day, I snuck off the Cora's sitting room. I'd left my laptop in there the night before, but I did stop by my garment bag and picked up a paper sack on my way.

She was sitting in the window, watching the people on the grounds. And, I assumed, watching for Joshua. "I don't know if he will make himself visible today."

We had been exchanging letters still, but most of what I had been writing to him was from Cora as she would tell me what to say to him many days. And what he would write in return was usually directed to her. I had taken down a letter that morning in the early hours that was from me alone.

2017
Dear Joshua,

Today, Reid and I will be joined in marriage. It is something that makes me overjoyed yet sad. Sad only because I wish this for you and Cora. But if that had been the case, Reid and I would not be alive today.

I am sure that you are fully aware of this fact. So I want to be sure that you know how grateful I, we, are to have the both of you in our lives and here on this day.

I know that you may not be able to make yourself seen, but I do hope that you both will come to the ceremony in your own ways. It would mean a lot to me.

Sincerely,
Nell

Of course, I had gone back before being shuffled upstairs to check, and it was no longer in the wall. I smiled back to the trees and knew he had gotten it.

"I dare say he will not," Cora replied. "I will watch from up here to stay out of the way as well. Neither of us want to ruin your big day. But we will watch from afar."

"I wish you could come down and be there," I stated.

The light bounced off her dark curls as she turned back, swinging her legs off the bench to face me. "I do, too."

I held out the paper sack in front of me. "I know you can't open it yourself, but I found this and wanted to gift it to you, to this room, for today."

She folded her hands in her lap. "That is very sweet of you, my dear. But it is your wedding day. I regret that I do not have a gift for you."

I waved my hand about the room. "There's so many beautiful treasures that you had stored away in that bench. They are more than enough."

I opened the bag and pulled out a smaller, ornate picture frame. I heard her breath catch. "That frame. It was my mother's."

"It was?" I looked back and forth between it and her and pressed it against my heart. "I was told it might have come from the house, but I wasn't sure from when or anything."

She looked at it longingly. "Yes. It always sat on top of the piano downstairs. There was a picture of my parents in it. Is it still there?"

"No." I lifted it to look at it. "There was no picture in it when I found it."

Her shoulders slumped. "Well, the frame is beautiful. Did you replace the picture?"

"I did." I looked at it once more before turning it around. "There was one in the box of Joshua's things."

Her hand went to her mouth as she saw what was depicted inside the jewel encrusted photo frame.

"That was the only one he and I had taken together. It was the same week that he proposed, before we had gotten a chance to speak to my father, when we were sure our lives would be blessed." Her hands were trembling. "I cannot believe that you have it. I cannot believe that it survived all these years."

"You two were lovely." I swallowed at the words I used. "Are. You two *are* lovely."

"We were, weren't we?" Color filled her cheeks as she looked at it.

A knock came on the door. "Mom? Are you ready to get started?"

I opened the door, checking to be sure it was just Lula. When it wasn't, I waved behind me to signal to Cora. I chanced a glance back to be sure she was not visible before I finished opening the door to exit.

"You look like you've been crying," my mother observed.

"Nope." I walked past her and joined Lula and Emma, leading the way to the bedrooms.

Imogen was waiting outside of Lula's room and ushered us inside, instructing the others to join the rest of the women in the room next door. Cora was sitting on the stool to the vanity when I entered, the picture frame in her hands.

I blinked. "How?"

She grinned from ear to ear. "I believe I can touch things from my time. Like this stool and the bench in my sitting room. It is simply brilliant! Is it not?"

"That is!" I wanted to hug her but knew better than to try.

She was looking down at the frame in her hands. "It is."

A silence washed over the room, allowing her a moment to enjoy it all. But, just as if on cue, Lula broke in. "Well, this is your wedding day, Mom. Let's get you ready for it!"

Lula and Imogen started right in on doing my hair and makeup, slapping my hands away when I would try to help. They even had my stockings and under garments set for me. Once my hair was set and my makeup was sprayed into place, Imogen unzipped the garment bag hanging on the closet door. We had it sent out to be cleaned and a couple of small spots mended.

She turned back to check that I'd been locked into my corset when Cora let out a loud gasp. "Nell!"

We all stopped and watched as the spirited woman took the antique dress off the hanger and held it up in front of herself. Tears fell down her cheeks, disappearing before they hit the solid fabric.

I slowly stood. "Do you mind?"

She didn't turn around. "Mind?"

I waited for her to say something more, but she didn't. I felt as if I had crossed a line. "I didn't think you would. I'm so sorry. I should have asked."

She jerked up like she broke out of her thoughts. "Nell, I think it is perfect."

"You do?" I asked.

"This dress was made for a Webb to marry a Wilkinson. Literally. It was made for me for my wedding to Joshua. It is only fitting that you wear it today." She crossed the room with the gown draped over her arm. She stood in front of me and held it out. "Will you please wear it today?"

I took the dress and felt my fingers brush hers. We both looked up, eyes open wide, mouths slightly agape.

"Was that ..." I started.

She finished. "My fingers? Yes."

"What do you think it means?" I asked.

Lula came up and tried to set her hand on Cora's shoulder, but it went right through. "Not sure, but it didn't stick."

Cora jerked her hands away from the dress as she took a step back. "Well, put it on, love. You don't want to be late for your own wedding."

Imogen came up and helped Lula fasten the layers of under skirts and the dress, fastening the long lines of buttons on the back and the cuffs into the delicate lace. They did a recheck on my makeup and hair and slipped on the antique shoes we had found online that matched perfectly. My necklace, bracelet and the ruby ring were all applied just before the veil. As Imogen was aligning it, Cora approached, holding her hand out.

"What is that?" I held mine out to meet hers.

She opened her fingers. There, in her palm, was a hair comb made of silver, rubies and diamonds. "It was my grandmother's. I had intended to wear it at our wedding as well. I see that you have the ring. They were such a beautiful set, even if they were not made to be."

"It is beautiful, Cora." I held it in my hand, marveling at the brilliance of it.

She picked it back up, her fingertips grazing across my palm almost too soft to feel. Then, she walked around to the back of my stool and placed it in my hair where the veil started.

Lula thrust a tissue in front of me. "Don't you *dare* ruin our hard work."

I used it to dab under my eyes quickly.

Imogen fanned my face with her hands.

Cora retreated over by the wall, giggling.

Once I had regained my composure, I stood and looked in the full mirror on the wall. "Wow."

Cora came up next to me. "You look beautiful."

"Thank you."

"Wow, Mom. I'm speechless." Lula hooked her arm around mine.

I reached back and pulled Imogen up with us. She nervously fixed my hair, which didn't actually need fixing. "Thank you, Nell."

"For what?" She was helping me. I couldn't possibly think of a reason she would be grateful.

She bit her lip. "Reid has been a good friend of our family for as long as I can remember. He's a good man that deserves all the happiness the world can provide. Thank you for being as good and kind as he saw you to be."

Before I could hug her, as I tried to do, Lula stepped up and thrust the tissue into my face again. "Nope. You can cry all you want after the ceremony and pictures. Until then, toughen up, woman. You need to keep this flawless thing you have going."

I laughed. "Okay. Do we go out now?"

Lula finished her last touches on her own makeup, having put on her dress and accessories in between helping me get ready. "I'll go out and get the rest of them down there. Then, I'll text Imogen to bring you down once everyone is in place."

"You certainly have this all set. You should do it for a living," I teased.

"Organize art or organize events. Those are some pretty great choices." She tapped her chin with her finger.

"Alright, young lady. Get the others down there before the groom thinks we've all run off." Imogen ushered her out through the door.

I could hear as everyone, including the men, all filed down the main stairwell. Lula's room was on the back side of the house, so I snuck a peek out the window to see everything in the garden.

It was absolutely breathtaking. There were large tents on one side that were set up for the reception and fully decorated. To the other side, the area for the ceremony was set up with a center aisle that parted two large sections of chairs, each covered in cream colored linens. A bouquet of multicolored lilies crowned the tops of pillar vases that marked the start of the center aisle, which was covered in a royal blue carpet.

The priest stood at the front, under a wooden arch, decorated with more of the colorful lilies and vines. Behind it was the rock wall, the stone marked with an "X" centered behind the arch and candles lining the top of the wall.

All of the seats were filled with far more people than I thought were coming. There was even a few people that were standing in the back. And everyone was dressed up. Many were fidgeting with their attire, which made me laugh to myself. It was a normal detail in the middle of a life that seemed all *but* normal at that point.

I could see the wedding party lining up in the back. One tux broke away from the rest and made his way up to the front. As he turned, I swallowed hard, fighting my heart from leaping out of my chest through my throat, knowing that he was waiting there for me.

Imogen's phone rang. "Hello? Yes. By the back door. Got it, Gerald. Yes. See you in a click."

"That's my cue." I brushed my hands down the full skirt of the gown.

"We are to meet Gerald by the back door. I will go take my seat before they start down the aisle, and he will take you in from there," she instructed.

I nodded. "Sounds good."

After one last check in the mirror, we made our way down to the rear door. Gerald was already there, his usual, kind smile on his face. "You look simply gorgeous, Nell."

"Thank you." I patted his hand. "And thank you for this. It means a lot."

His age showed in the wrinkles around his eyes as he smiled. "It is my pleasure. Us Browns need to finally be able to do what we promised to do all those years ago."

Imogen gave him a hug. "That's right."

She closed the door behind her on her way out. Gerald pulled his phone out and waited for the text to tell us it was our time to come outside. I stood and tried to keep my breathing under control.

"Are you ready, Nell?" he asked.

I renewed my smile. "Yes. I just keep thinking about Joshua and Cora."

He put a hand on my arm. "This is not the time for you to be focused on them, dear. This is the day for you to be focused on you."

I wrung my hands. "I don't do that very well."

"I have gathered." He smiled.

"Isn't there a way to break the curse, Gerald? Isn't there always a way to break the curse?"

He gave me a fatherly look. "I may have known a lot about this whole situation, but that is not something I have been privy to. I would imagine you are correct, but I do not know what the answer is."

Then, I felt a hand in mine. I almost fell as I whipped around. Cora leapt forward, arms outstretched and wrapped them around me, hugging me tightly.

I equaled her enthusiasm. In that moment, she felt as real as hugging any other person.

Her voice was soft. "Gerald is correct. Please, just focus on your wedding day today. I will be upstairs, watching. I'm so happy for you two. I want you both to be happy in the way Joshua and I had intended for ourselves."

"Thank you." I fought back ruining my makeup.

We pulled apart and saw Gerald, his mouth open. "How?"

"I ..." I pointed to the dress.

Cora laughed. "She's wearing a few of my things. It seems I can touch things when I have a direct connection with them."

He closed his mouth and nodded, pursing his lips. "Okay then. Makes sense."

We all had a good laugh just as his phone went off. "It's time, Nell. They're waiting on us."

Cora gave me one more quick hug. "Go. Go marry the man you're meant to be with."

I took Gerald's arm as he guided me out through the door. Every one of the guests stood, blocking my view of the wedding party from where we stood. I searched between heads and shoulders, but there was no seeing anyone at the front from there. So, I eagerly followed as Gerald led us along the path.

He slowed as we reached the actual opening to the aisle. The music went from a light, soft melody to a more traditional wedding march as we positioned ourselves for the final bit of the walk.

And then, I saw him.

Reid stepped out from in front of the front row of guests and looked back to me.

They say that when you connect with your true love, the whole world falls away and you see and hear only them. It was a concept I had always scoffed at, having never had that experience myself. That is, until right then. Granted, not everyone and everything fell away. I was aware of the man that was walking me down the aisle. I could see that there were other people. I could even hear the music. It was just that it was all so much at a distance from my senses compared to my loudly beating heart and the sight of Reid Wilkinson standing there, at the front of the makeshift church, in a tuxedo, waiting to marry me.

Then, when he took my hand and Gerald gave me away, for a moment, I did see and hear only him ... and the sound of my heart.

Sixteen

I kept looking down at the ring, the same private smile turning my lips up each time, despite how tired I was. It was after midnight, and people were still flittering away either to their rooms or off to the hotel or bed and breakfast. Reid came up and took his seat next to me at the head table.

He passed me a full glass of champagne. "Are you hanging in there, Mrs. Wilkinson?"

I took the glass. "I am."

He looked at me curiously. "You look like something is on your mind."

"How quickly you have grown to know me so well." I leaned my head on his shoulder.

He put an arm around my shoulders. "So? Are you going to let me inside that pretty little head of yours?"

You would think I was a teenager with how I let out such a loud huff. "I'm just hung up on this whole curse thing."

"In what way?" He turned his chair to face me.

The champagne should have been cool and fizzy as it went down, but I gulped it without paying attention. "They're stuck here. What kind of person does that to another person? What kind of father does that to their child? And now, because of his hatred and selfish disdain, our great grandparents were stuck in some limbo and now are stuck here, wandering the grounds and this house, unable to leave and still unable to be together." I grabbed his glass and chugged it. "Sure, they're together in a way, but they can never embrace or hold each other or kiss. It's like they have to spend eternity just looking at each other through a window."

"You've done everything you can, Nell. I'm not sure if there is anything we *can* do," he said.

"But why not?" I practically shouted. "I was sure that *something* we've done now would have. Part of me thought that us marrying would be the thing to break it since nothing else has."

His eyes were full of understanding as he watched me rant. But when I finished, it dawned on me that I was hurting him. In the weeks before our wedding, no matter how much I had tried, I couldn't fully get into the planning because of Joshua and Cora. He had been understanding then, too. And he never said anything about it.

But that day was different. It was our wedding day.

One thing I had learned about Reid was that his main focus was to make me happy. An independent man who had never put a relationship as a priority in his life. A man that many women wished for even a second glance from. And there he was, having not only given me that second glance, but he made me his priority. And I was callously making everything else mine.

"You didn't marry me just in the hopes of freeing them, did you?" His eyes were filled with pleading.

"No!" I jumped up, almost knocking over the glasses on the table. I lowered my voice. "No. I married you because I love you. I want to spend the rest of my life with you. And for the first time in my life, I feel like I belong somewhere," I looked right at him. "With some*one*."

"You are sure? I know that you've been determined to find what is needed to free Joshua and Cora." He slowly rose from his chair.

My fingers went to my wedding ring, tilting it back and forth, watching it catch the light from the fixtures above us. "I can tend to focus on difficult things, trying to puzzle them out. Joshua and Cora's situation? That is difficult. But you? You and I? That is easy. It simply is. There's no figuring anything out. Sure, we're a puzzle. But not in the same way. They are a million piece puzzle that's scattered in a tiny box without room to sort all of the pieces out, and I'm not even sure they're all there. But us? Excuse me for sounding cliché, but we are a puzzle that is made up of two pieces that just fit together perfectly. There's no sorting. There's not numerous mis-tries. We just fit."

His arms were crossed over his chest, but as I finished, he dropped his defensive pose and reached out for me. "Cliché?"

"Too much?" I folded up in his arms.

"Not at all. It was probably the best metaphor for all of this," he said. "There's just one more puzzle."

"One more?" I asked.

"Yes. Nell, *you* are a million piece puzzle, just as they are." He smirked.

I chewed on my lip. "Too much?"

He tilted my head up with a finger under my chin. "I just know that you are the most beautiful puzzle I've seen. And even if it takes me the rest of my life to put every piece together to figure you out, I'm happy to do so."

"Ugh!" I groaned and pushed him away.

He dropped his arms. "What?"

"I love you." It sounded more like a blame than anything.

He laughed. "That's quite terrible, isn't it? However will you cope?"

I pulled him back to me by his lapels. "I'll just have to make do."

"Yes. You're kind of stuck with me now."

I smirked. “I love you.”

He did the same. “With all my heart.”

We kissed deeply and passionately. And I knew I wasn’t going to go back to how I had become in New York. I would never be distant, detached and solemn ever again. Not with him. Reid knew what to say to pull me back every time I slipped. And I knew that he would always be working on my puzzle, examining every piece of me, fascinated and content, just as I was with him.

***

The few days following the wedding were a whirlwind. Some of the friends and family from both sides stayed a few days to see more of the area, and to see more of Webb Manor. My mother left two days after, to my relief, stating she wanted to encourage others to let us get on with our honeymoon. Really, I was pretty sure she just got the hint that I wasn’t allowing her critical remarks and judgmental looks to affect me as they once did.

Dropping her off at the airport, I cried. True, we weren’t terribly close. She had seen to that, with us both having our own lives – her not approving of mine, of course. And that instead of embracing me as her child and loving me for who I was, she was constantly trying to ‘better me’ in ways that boiled down to trying to make me who she wished she was. But, still, she was my mother. And under all of that, I could tell she did love me and she was proud of me in her own way. It was just a way I couldn't subject myself to regularly.

Family wasn’t always what we wanted of them, but they were still family. And she was a part of mine, just as Cora was. Even just as Bernard was. I reminded myself that at least my mother wasn't Bernard, and she didn't try to off my fiancé. So, all in all, it was an improvement in my lineage.

Murphy took the flight back to the states with her, needing to return to his station. Emma's flight was the next day. Her classes only allotted so much time away. Her GPA was a 3.8, and, as she explained, she wanted to boost it. Not tank it. But they both promised to call regularly and visit when possible. And I returned the same promise.

As people left and life started returning to normal - well, as normal as it was for us - Cora and Joshua started making regular appearances again. They would meet at the back door for talks still. His letters had become rare since he was able to communicate vocally. But I'd received one here and there, mostly as a reiteration of his gratitude for bringing Cora back to him.

When guests were occupied, Cora and I would spend time in her sitting room. Sometimes, we would chat. Her take on my mother amused me as it seems that she had a very similar relationship with hers. But other times, I would sit in the chair in the corner of the room and write for hours as she sat in the window and looked out over the property.

I couldn't help but wonder if there was something more we should have done. Something I was missing. Yes. They were happy to have each other again. But I knew they wanted more. I could see it in how they would flinch when they pulled back from starting to reach for each other. I could see it in their faces when she would wave to him from her window. My heart would sink for them. And I can't say that I would have felt any different in her shoes.

Reid and I had opted for a unique take on our honeymoon. We were going to wait until all the guests were gone, and we had bought a trip for Lula to go see a few of her favorite European sites that she'd always wanted to see. Then, we were going to move Reid into the estate. It wasn't a secret. We just wanted to do it just the two of us, to spend two weeks alone in *our* home. And Lula was all for it. I'm sure the traveling helped her enthusiasm.

So, a week after the wedding, the last guest left for home and we dropped Lula off at the train station. Her first stop - Paris.

Reid's house had been packed, and the moving truck was scheduled for the next day. He and I spent a few hours making sure everything was all set for them to arrive and then went down to *The Golden Crown* for a bite to eat. Imogen, Elijah, Gerald and Clive all met up with us for dinner. Clive even brought his wife, Beth, who I had only met a couple times. She had been apprised of the Joshua and Cora situation, and, to my surprise, embraced it very easily.

"When you bought Webb Manor, did you know you'd have such a full house?" she asked.

I laughed. "Not at all. My house had just emptied out. But at least it's a large one. There's more than enough room for everyone."

She leaned forward onto her elbows. "How do they get on? Joshua and Cora? Clive says they can't touch? I would think that's its own kind of torture."

"Hence, curse, I suppose."

I felt my smile fade.

She sat up. "I didn't mean to.."

"No." I held a hand up. "I just keep trying to figure out how to release them of it, but I'm at a loss."

She put a hand on mine. "You will. You've got a big heart and a determination about you. Even if you stumble upon it one day, or if it is a result of days of contemplation, you will figure it out. You care deeply. I can see that."

"Thank you." I squeezed her hand. "I just hope you're right.

Dinner turned into a few hours of friendly social banter. It had been so long since I had allowed myself a group of friends like that one. It was nice. Reid had known them all for a number of years, but it didn't seem to stop them from welcoming me into their circle equally. But, I suppose, being his wife helped out on that, even if Imogen insisted that it was simply that I fit … like a puzzle piece. A comment I giggled at but didn't divulge the irony of.

The round of goodbyes and hugs went on for quite some time. You know, that kind of goodbye where you say it probably six times before you actually go? Reid said it was pretty much the norm for them. A group custom I was more than happy to participate in.

Then, he and I retired for the night.

Both of our places in town were emptied. Mine had been for weeks. I was just paying out the remainder of my lease. I insisted the landlord rent it out early since I'd paid for my full term but didn't have a use for it. She refused, saying that she wanted to give me access to it for the months I'd paid for 'Just in case'.

Reid's house had been emptied by the movers that day. His things sitting in a truck to be delivered the next. A fresh realtor's sign had been set up out front, and it was on the market. I had asked him if he was sure about selling since he had owned it for so long. But he was sure. "We are together, married. That means not owning things like other houses that we don't need. I'm sure that Webb Manor is large enough for us. My shop is far more of an office than a storefront since my work comes in the mail and not through the door. But keep the house in New York. It will be nice to not have to stay in hotels when we go to visit."

It was something I agreed to wholeheartedly.

I tossed the keys onto the stand by the door just as he grabbed my waist and whirled me around to face him. His lips were soft on mine as he swept me up into his arms and carried me up the stairs to our room. He laid me down gently onto the bed, the weight of him pressing on me as his hands found their way down my sides and back up, lifting my shirt from me. Quickly, we were undressed.

"I love you," I whispered, my lips brushing his collarbone as I spoke.

His heartbeat was racing against mine as we connected, nothing in between us. His arms snaked up under me and hands came around the backs of my shoulders. My legs hooked around his hips.

His breath hot as his lips barely grazed mine, he whispered back, "With all my heart."

Then, I was completely lost in his embrace.

***

Right on schedule, the movers arrived bright and early the next day. I had wandered down to the kitchen shortly before they pulled in and started a pot of coffee. A routine for our mornings at that point.

They worked quickly, bringing everything in and taking things to the rooms we instructed them toward. It hadn't been but a couple of hours before they were finished and pulling out of the drive.

Reid had gotten right to work as they unloaded, setting up his study and making sure everything was there. I stayed out of the way for the most part, unpacking the boxes of kitchen items - the few boxes that he had, considering, like a typical bachelor, he ate takeaway most nights.

I was placing the last coffee mug from a box into the cupboard when I felt someone enter the room. I turned, expecting to see Reid there, but it wasn't. Cora was standing in the archway to the kitchen.

"Hello, Cora." I set down the mug. "I'm sorry I haven't come up for a chat lately. I have been running around like..." I broke off.

There was something in her expression. I could see she was barely registering that I was even in the room.

I came around the island. "Cora? Is everything alright?"

"Nell?" Confusion pulled at her features.

I wanted to reach out and put a hand on her shoulder, but I knew I couldn't. "What is it?"

"I don't know." She wrapped her arms around herself. "Something is ... different."

I heard a knock on the door.

"Reid!" I yelled up the stairs. "Reid! Can you get that, please?"

Cora took a couple steps toward the back door, her expression showing an obvious oblivion to her surroundings. Usually, she fled any public area when others were around. But she didn't even seem to register that someone had knocked.

"Reid!" I yelled again.

"Door. Got it." His feet descended the main stairwell fast.

"Cora, talk to me. What's going on?" I couldn't tell if she was scared or not.

"Happy move-in day." I heard Gerald from the front of the house.

"Thanks," Reid replied. "Sorry. I..." I heard him coming into the kitchen. "Nell? Cora? What's wrong?"

I shrugged. "I'm not sure if anything is wrong, per se. But Cora says she feels something."

"Cora?" He tried to get her attention.

She didn't reply. She just took a couple more steps toward the door, her arms still tightly affixed around herself.

"Open the door," Gerald instructed.

"What?" I blinked. "What if it's something not good?"

He nodded. "Open the door, Nell."

I walked over to it, placing my hand on the knob and looked back. All three of them stood, watching me, just as unsure what we were going to find. But I did know she was right. I felt it all through me as I stood there. Every hair on my arms stood on end as I turned it. I let out a scream as the door opened a crack and I saw someone standing there.

"Joshua!" I whipped the door open. "You scared me! Cora said she was feeling something, and I was looking out to see if there was something different outside."

"I feel it, too." He wasn't looking at me. His eyes were fixed on her. His Cora.

"The curse," Reid breathed.

Cora's eyes flew wide open. "Joshua."

"Yes." It wasn't a question in response to her saying his name. He was agreeing.

"Wait." I turned to her. "Please don't get your hopes up. We've tried so much, and it hasn't worked. I don't want to see you two devastated again. I don't even know what would have changed things. We haven't tried anything new."

Gerald spoke. "But you have."

"What?" Reid asked.

I looked around, seeing the empty boxes on the floor and the dishes that once were in a Wilkinson home that were now in the Webb home. I looked at Reid, still in his lounge clothes, standing next to the table where I had placed a few of his ancestral keepsakes so I could find safe places for them.

Cora finally saw me, her mouth dropping open. "Nell, my father's curse was that a Wilkinson wouldn't ever be allowed to be a part of the Webb family. Wouldn't, Nell. Not couldn't. But you did. You and Reid."

My heart leapt with hope. "Gerald? Reid?"

They were both standing still, astonishment joining their looks of realization.

"Please tell me she's right." I asked Gerald, walking toward the two men.

He pointed. "We are about to find out."

Joshua was exactly where he had been, just outside the door. But Cora's tiny feet were carrying her across the room swiftly as she rose her arms. I hadn't had time to brace when the room shook. I stumbled back and fell against Reid as the room filled with a blindingly bright light.

His arms went around me as I buried my face in his chest and closed my eyes until the shaking stopped. When I started to open them, I couldn't see the two. My heart sank, thinking that the shaking and light was because she had ran to him. That they were thrown, violently, back to their areas. But then, the light dimmed more and I saw them, standing just inside the doorway, Joshua's arms around Cora just as Reid's were around me. Cora buried in his chest, mirroring how I had been against Reid only a moment before.

She tilted her head up and looked at him, tears streaming down her cheeks, hands gripping his jacket. His hands came up and cupped her face.

"I love you." Her voice cracked.

He smiled the way only a man, completely in love with the woman in his arms, could smile. "With all my heart."

He kissed her passionately. All of the years missed, the tragedy, the hope, the anticipation came crashing in on them.

And then, they were gone.

Seventeen

We had been stunned when they disappeared, blinking away as if they hadn't been standing there a second earlier. I didn't want to believe they were gone. Yes I wanted them to be released of their curse, to be able to be together, to even move on. But the selfish part of me wanted them to stay.

I ran around the property, looking for a sign that they were still there. But when I had exhausted myself, I shut myself in Cora's sitting room. My feet perched up on the window bench with me, arms circling my knees where my chin rested.

Reid opened the door slowly. "Can I come in?"

"Sure." I sighed.

He sat down next to me. "It is a good thing."

"I know." I pouted. "I'm just being selfish."

He kissed my cheek. "You're being sentimental. Nothing more. It was what drove you to see this through."

I took a stammering breath. "I am going to miss them."

"Me, too." He stood. "Gerald is going to stay and help move some of the furniture. Come out when you're ready. I chopped some vegetables for salads for lunch."

His gentleness continued throughout the day. Eventually, I came out and helped with the unpacking. Gerald left mid-afternoon as Reid and I bounced from room to room, pausing for standard honeymoon activity here and there.

Of course, Joshua and Cora crossed my mind periodically. He would see it in my face and would do something to bring my smile back without hesitation.

That night, I didn't sleep much. Firstly, because he kept me up late. Happily so. But once he collapsed, falling asleep almost instantly, I lay there, my eyes open, drowning in the whirlwind of thoughts that refused to slow.

The sun's light was just starting to crest over the horizon. I pulled on a pair of sweats and his t-shirt and made my way through the house. His slippers were too big on my feet, and they scraped as I walked through the kitchen, making me laugh. I warmed up the last cup of coffee that was still sitting in the pot and stood at the window that looked out at the wall, sipping on the bitter drink.

That old owl sat on top of the stone structure. He hooted a couple of times and sat. His wings fluttered slightly as I realized he was directly over the "X" marked rock.

I sighed at myself and went out the back door as the owl flew off. The dew on the grass soaked into the cuffs on my pant legs. I ignored it as I bent down and pulled the rock out of its place. I don't know what I expected to find. They were gone. But there, behind the rock, was a letter. The same aged paper with the red, wax seal on the seam.

I pressed it to my heart and sat on the ground before breaking the seal, less carefully as with all the others, and almost tearing the letter to open it.

2017
Our Beloved Nell & Reid,

We have been granted one last letter to you. As you may have guessed, you broke the curse, and we have been granted passage to move on. Neither of us can thank you enough for what you have done. We will always treasure the opportunity to have gotten to know you both.

I cannot tell you details of the afterlife, but know that we are together, and we are happy. It is a gift you both gave us. We hope that, one day, we will see you both again. On that day, our hugs will be plentiful.

Not that we have any doubts on the matter, but be good to each other. You both are very special people. Not only to us, but in general. The world is a better place with you in it.

We love you both ... with all our hearts.

With all our love,
Joshua & Cora

I expected to find tears staining the front of my shirt. Instead, my smile threatened to crack my cheeks. I raced back to the house, skidding a few inches as I careened to a stop upon seeing Reid at the counter, refilling the coffee pot with a fresh filter.

"I love you," I blurted out.

He smiled. "With all my heart."

With All My Heart...

About the Author

Colleen Nye is a Michigan based author that has gone from poetry to content writing, movie reviewing, press releases, short stories and everything in between.

Settling on the art of a full length novel, she published her first in 2012, a romantic comedy entitled When in Maui, book one in The Unattainable Series. Her second novel, a tech thriller named Immersion was released May 2015. Since then, she's released several books, including The Long Summer, a coming of age drama, as well as written the biography of Alonzo "Chacho" Gomez in his book From Pen To Page and has been featured in a number of anthologies.

She loves writing short stories and, of course, working on her next novel. She also spends some of her time leading, co-leading and participating in a variety of anthology projects. In September 2015, she opened Blue Deco Publishing and now helps other authors find a home for their books.

Follow and Contact Colleen at:

Email:

author.colleennye@gmail.com

Facebook:

https://www.facebook.com/authorcolleennye

Twitter:

www.Twitter.com/colleen_nye

@Colleen_Nye

Instagram:

www.Instagram.com/authorcolleennye

@Authorcolleennye

Web:

www.colleennye.com

Goodreads: Colleen Nye

Amazon:

http://www.amazon.com/Colleen-Nye/e/B007HR06Z8

Other books by Colleen Nye

Romantic Comedy

The Unattainable Series:
When in Maui
When in Doubt
When in Love – Coming April 12, 2017

Dystopian Thriller

Immersion

Coming of Age Drama

The Long Summer

Made in the USA
Lexington, KY
13 April 2017